PART I

THE BOY DAVID

The
Decent
Thing

By the same author

Angel's War
Mirror on the Wall
Mirror Images
To Reason Why
Ties of Blood
All Manner of Things
The Foolish Virgin
A Lesser Peace
A Chained Satan
Season of Sins

The
Decent
Thing

C. W. REED

ROBERT HALE · LONDON

ISBN 0 7090 7839 0

Robert Hale Limited
Clerkenwell House
Clerkenwell Green
London EC1R 0HT

2 4 6 8 10 9 7 5 3 1

Typeset in 11¼/14pt Baskerville
by Derek Doyle & Associates, Shaw Heath.
Printed in Great Britain by
St Edmundsbury Press, Bury St Edmunds, Suffolk.
Bound by Woolnough Bookbinding Limited.

CHAPTER ONE

DAVID Herbert was a weaver of stories from infancy. Long before he learned to join up his letters on his squeaky nursery slate, he inhabited a rich and very private world of fantasy as real almost as the physical one surrounding him. His nursemaid and the other servants remarked on the toddler's pleasing ability to remain perfectly happy with his own company, burbling and singing softly to himself as he made use of whatever bits and pieces lay to hand. 'Good as gold, ma'am,' was the unanimous verdict, and Mrs Herbert would smile languidly, and admire for a brief while his halo of fine spun gold curls, the angelic beauty of his placid features. Indeed, in his play gowns he was every bit as pretty as his sisters, and might well be mistaken for one of their sex.

He grew up, too, among the dolls and their houses and tea sets. His sunny nature was severely tested in his earliest days, for both Gertrude and Clara regarded him as perhaps their chief plaything, and from the first he thought of himself as much their possession as that of Helen, their easygoing nanny, or the distantly lovely, insubstantial figure of his mother. They petted him, and prodded him, pulled and pushed him, and generally ruled him with a despotism that governed him entirely in the small, private world free from the adults. Mr Herbert, seeing his prettily gowned son and heir playing so charmingly with his sisters, expressed some misgiving. 'He needs other boys to play with, a bit of rough and tumble.'

'Oh, John, dear!' protested his elegant wife, exerting all the force of her dark, extravagant eyes. 'The poor lamb's not five yet! Plenty of time for that sort of thing.'

As she gazed up with that winsome, half pleading look she knew she could rely on to achieve her ends, she felt a swift, fierce tide of resentment sweep over her at the thought of her beautiful golden child's transformation to the rough and tumble masculinity so valued by her husband. She stared now with carefully concealed gaze at the grey thickness of cloth over John's loins, picturing with a mental shudder the processes of nature which God in His infinite but undeniably mysterious wisdom had devised to bring forth the sanctified issue of their marriage.

Four times, having yielded up the supreme sacrifice of her femaleness, she had watched with fear and dread the quickening fruit of their union, endured the sickness, the unspeakable, heavy distortion of her body into the disgustingly distended pod, the blue-white, heaving belly that finally erupted into the bloody nightmare of birth. One of them had failed to come to full term. The torment, all for nothing, had nearly driven her mad. She had not seen the stillborn child, a boy – of course! It would be. Despite the closed, wounded look on John's face, she had privately vowed she would go through the ordeal no more. He had two perfect daughters. That would have to suffice.

She used her illness to establish their nightly separation. He accepted the routine of separate bedrooms, spent more and more time away in town, and she wondered shamefully if he had taken a mistress. She did not know if she should be grateful or jealous. Then, during a Christmas holiday, watching him playing with Gerty and Clara, she had felt a wave of sadness and compassion for him. She had given those unmistakable little signs that invited him to come tapping at her door, smelling of cologne and port and, faintly, of cigars. He was hesitant – they had not made love for months – and his awkward diffidence aroused her tenderness, and her guilt. His lovemaking was passionate and, to her, it seemed desperate. Perhaps after all he had been deprived of bodily satisfaction all these months. To her amazement, her own body was far from repelled at his fervour and his uncertainty. She persevered, and so David was conceived.

The confinement was every bit as unpleasant, the birthing pains as excruciating as ever, but at the end of it all she was safely delivered of a son. Her duty nobly done, she rested, like so many gentlewomen, on her laurels. Vague illnesses possessed her, their vapours keeping John once more from the marriage bed. Even her doctor had conspired with her, advising that the delicacy of her constitution made further pregnancy unwise. In the years since David's birth sexual union had grown rarer. And these rare occasions were carefully and secretly monitored by her, for she was determined she would not fall pregnant again. In fact, she shared far more physical intimacies with her doctor than with her husband.

Young David scarcely saw his father, whose absences grew longer. His mother was a 'presence' about the large house and garden. The children were taken before her most days, just before their tea, and brought in to say goodnight before going to bed. The servants were the ones who figured more importantly in their lives, and, because of their nurse's lazy, easygoing character, and their mother's indifference, they were left with a remarkable degree of freedom.

The girls did not spoil him. Rather, he became their loyal house slave and familiar. Gerty was five years older, Clara three. Their attitude was utterly proprietary, their rule tyrannical. Sometimes their cruelty could be stunning, yet the youngster never thought to challenge it, but accepted it without complaint almost.

When the girls acquired a governess, a pretty, dark haired girl, who blushed a lot and seemed to have little success in controlling her charges, David was allowed to attend classes with them. Miss Marshall set him simple tasks, which he performed so quickly and with such ease that he was soon progressing rapidly, showing himself to be much brighter than his wilful sisters.

'Gertrude! Why can't you try a bit more? Look at David. He writes neater than you already.'

'Then I'll employ him to do it for me!' Gerty answered, with a toss of her bronze, flowing hair. At twelve, Gerty was already showing promise of a striking beauty. Her strong will and selfishness resulted in an almost permanent state of conflict with the new governess. For every admonition, Gerty would fire back a stinging or truculent reply, and very often it was the young teacher who experienced a sense of defeat rather than her pupil.

'I shall speak to your mother about you, Miss!' Miss Marshall huffed, cheeks glowing and her bosom heaving.

Again, the long mane of rich hair swung across the pinafored back. 'Mama will soon get tired of you running to her whining all the time! After all, it just means that you can't do your job properly, doesn't it?'

David was sorry for the governess. He liked her, she was always nice to him. Her arms were soft, and she smelt so lovely. One day he heard her weeping to herself in the schoolroom after a particularly acrimonious exchange. His eight year-old heart suffered keen pangs of remorse on her behalf, and he brooded darkly on the disappointing shortcomings of his longstanding idol. He trailed after Gerty as she and Clara headed across the lawn towards the stream that ran through the bottom of the garden. 'Why are you so beastly to Miss Marshall?' he piped up tremulously, fully aware of the enormity of his action.

Gerty whipped round with a ludicrous expression of amazement. Her eyebrows arched, her mouth formed a red o. 'What was that? What did you say, sprog?'

'She's – she's . . .' He faltered at the rising fury he saw in the grey eyes. 'She was crying. You've no right to be so mean! It's not—'

'You'll be blubbing too, you little wart! How dare you speak to me like that? Clara! Grab hold of him. Master Davy needs to be taught his place, I see. I don't think you realize, I shall be thirteen next week, you miserable little worm! You have to show a bit more respect to young ladies. And I'm not talking about jumped up servants like Miss Raggy-drawers Marshall!' She nodded at her sister, who had seized him by both arms. 'Bring him down here, out of the way. It's time he learnt a proper lesson. One he won't forget!' She strode down the uneven little slope to the stream, where the thick shrubbery screened them from view.

Quickly Gerty made a switch from the bundle of thin twigs she plucked from the nearest bushes. She nodded once more and Clara forced her captive down to his knees, then knelt in front of him herself. She pulled the back of his smock up over his bowed head, which she trapped tightly between her stockinged knees. The girls had frequently slapped him but he had never been beaten before. Though he had shown no resistance, he writhed and screamed now at the first stinging blow, which burned through his shirt, and the succeeding vicious cuts, which fell on his back and buttocks, smarting even through the thickness of his britches. Clara's dress and petticoat pulled tautly over his captured head and shoulders helped to smother his cries. When Gerty finally ceased the punishment, panting triumphantly, and Clara released her vicelike hold, he lay squirming and sobbing in the grass while they stood and gazed down at him with malicious pleasure before turning and running off, their cruel, tinkling laughter fading. He remained still, apart from his involuntary tremors, long after they had left him to his blubbering misery.

The sound of other shrill voices roused him from his abstracted grief and, lifting himself from the grass and leaf mould which clung to his dishevelled clothing, he found himself staring at the entranced gaze of three village children. He recognized the tall figure of the girl, whose tangled, pale golden ringlets tumbled in profusion over her shoulders at front and back. Nelly Tovey was the daughter of their gardener. She was about the same age as Gerty, and of similar stature. The other two were younger, boys a year or two older than himself, and their grubby faces were split in grins of mocking delight. 'Why, look, Nelly. He's bawling like a babby. Look at him!'

David tugged hopelessly at the disarranged smock, pulling it down over his britches once more, and struggling unsuccessfully to stem the flow of his grief.

'Pack it in, you two! And shove off ! You shouldn't be in here, any road, so clear off. Now!'

'Fancy 'im, do yer?'

She went after them threateningly, and they ran off when they saw she was in earnest, their mocking voices receding. David remained still, staring at her in hopeless misery. 'Come on!' she grinned encouragingly. 'You're all right now. What's been happening to you, little Master?'

He winced as he moved, biting at his lip to suppress his whimper of agony, and the girl could see plainly both his discomfort and his distress. She repeated her question, and though he was unable to hold back his tears, he stammered out his sorry tale of the beating. Nelly dug under her pinafore and pulled out a small, grimy square of cloth that served as a handkerchief, which she dipped in the flowing stream, then came back up the bank. 'Let me see. Come here, keep still, you poor mite.' She dabbed gently at the dirt and tear stained face, and David stood still, comforted by her tender concern and her soothing ministrations. 'I 'ope you'll tell your mam and dad what them sisters of yours 'ave done. They want thrashin' theirselves, the wicked madams!'

David kept silent. Already he felt ashamedly disloyal at having betrayed the identity of his aggressors. Besides, his whirling brain was too preoccupied with the storm of emotions and sensations aroused by this golden haired beauty, and her gentle touch. She had held his head close while she wiped away the streaks of dirt runnelled by his tears. It felt pleasant, a tingling, shivery, strange sensation, and he felt a sharp regret when she withdrew her hand and released her hold on him. 'There y'are!' She reached out again and tousled his fair hair affectionately, then, on impulse, she pulled him in tightly to her bosom once more and delivered a smacking kiss to the top of his head. Her blue eyes sparkled, even though she pinked with embarrassment. 'Poor little lamb! You look so lost. Don't you let them sisters of yours make so free with yer. Reckon they'll get their backsides skelped when yer folks hear what they've done to yer.'

He said nothing. Already, his brain was working on the problem of how to avoid letting Helen see the marks of the beating when she came to bathe him that evening. Neither Gerty nor Clara must get into trouble on his account, if he could possibly prevent it. He felt no sense of resentment, just as he felt no desire for revenge. He had brought punishment down upon him by speaking out as he had done. But neither could he regret his action when he recalled the sound of Miss Marshall's muffled weeping. Though it hurt him deeply to reflect on his defiance of his eldest sister, he still felt that he had done the right thing. And at least it had brought him to meet with this other beautiful creature, who was smiling down on him and who had blessed him with the gift of her kiss.

He stood shyly in front of her, tongue tied yet not wanting to part from her. 'I'm going up to the vegetable garden to meet Dad. Shall yer walk with me?'

He nodded, and eagerly stretched to take the hand she held out to him.

CHAPTER TWO

DAVID'S silence brought great relief to the girls. Gerty had privately been considerably worried at the knowledge that she had gone too far in her zeal for punishing her brother. 'I got a bit carried away,' she confessed, with a guilty smirk, to Clara, who sniggered in turn. But they were uneasy until they discovered that David was not inclined to betray them, then they showered him with affection and bribes for a while, until the immediacy of the danger had passed. They even conspired with him to distract Helen during his evening bath, offering to help her in the performing of this task, much to her surprise and pleasure.

'Master Davy's getting to be a big boy now,' she giggled, content to let the girls do most of her work for her. ' 'Tisn't really proper for him to be bathed by you girls no more.'

'*You're* a girl,' answered Gerty pertly, her sleeves pushed up above her elbows. 'Anyway, it's not as though we haven't seen him bare before. He's been in to chat while I'm in the bath.'

'Miss Gerty!' Helen squealed in delighted outrage.

The beating, far from rousing any spirit of rebellion in David, made him even more compliant and ready to accept his subservient role, and the two girls were very soon treating him with the same condescending disdain they had hitherto shown.

Meanwhile, Gertrude's battle with the unfortunate Miss Marshall went on unabated. David had learned to hold his tongue, even though it upset him greatly to witness the rudeness and the insults the poor young governess was forced to endure. He did have someone to whom he could express his displeasure, for he had taken to wandering over to the area of the garden where Nelly Tovey often came in the afternoons to do some tasks for her father. At first, David was painfully shy, and he would gaze at her in dumb adoration, but her manner was so warm and easy that he soon relaxed, and basked in the sunny glow of her presence. He told her of his distress at the hard time Miss Marshall was having to endure.

'Them sisters of yours want their ears boxing!' Nelly exclaimed, frowning. 'You should never have let them get away with it, what they did to you.' She added warmly, 'And Miss Marshall's ever so bonny. Right beautiful! And so nice, too. She always speaks so friendly when you see her in the village.' She sighed and muttered darkly, 'They don't deserve to have such chances, them girls of yours! If only *I* could be taught by her! I'd be over the moon!'

'Is the village school not good then?' David asked curiously.

Nelly grinned down at him, her usual sunny mood thoroughly restored. 'Bless you, no! Mr Baxter's got the lot of us. I spend more time teaching the young-uns than learning anything myself. I'll be leaving next Easter, any road. I'm thirteen, coming up.' She smiled. 'I might even be starting work up at the house. How about that then? Be bringing your breakfast to yer on a tray. Mornin', Master David.' She bobbed him a deep curtsey, and he laughed in reply.

'That 'ud be wonderful!' he cried enthusiastically, and she eyed him quizzically.

'Would it now?' she wondered dryly, and David was suddenly embarrassed, without fully understanding why.

'Oh, blast this stupid thing!' Gertrude, her cheeks flushed, flung the embroidery away from her and sucked on the finger she had pricked. 'Why should we learn sewing? I shall never use it! I'm going to do some sketching, like Davy.'

David glanced up quickly, alarmed at the dangerous tremor in his sister's tone. He watched apprehensively.

'Now, Gertrude, you must make the effort. I want that border finished today. Come along. Get on with it.' The governess's voice was shrill, the kind of voice she assumed, without much success, when she wished to exert her authority. David wanted to cry out to her to leave it. Gerty was building up to a storm, he knew, and would challenge her teacher head on.

'What do we need it for?' Gertrude now protested vehemently. She paused fractionally, waiting to thrust home the blade. 'I can see it's useful for someone of the lower class – someone who has to depend on it for her living. P'raps that's why *you're* so good at it. But for us—'

'Be quiet!' Miss Marshall almost screamed, and David jumped. Her face was red, she was breathless with rage, and her voice quavered on the edge of tears. 'You are such a beastly unpleasant girl! There is no excuse for ignorance, especially in someone in your privileged position. I've never known such rudeness! Now pick up that work and continue!'

She was white now. She stood over Gerty, her eyes glistened with tears. For a second, the younger girl was taken aback by this display, but then the bronze hair shook in that characteristically defiant gesture. 'No! I told you! I'm not doing it! So save your breath to cool your porridge!'

'Oh!' Miss Marshall let out a gasp of sheer frustration. Her hand moved in a white blur and slapped Gerty lightly across the left side of her face. There was a micro-second of frozen silence, all four caught up in this instant of drama, then Gerty yelped in astonished outrage. She sprang up, a wildly transformed figure, almost as tall as her adversary. She seized Miss Marshall's upper arms and with a mighty thrust pushed her backwards. She fell over the low bench, in a rustling flurry of skirts, and the mesmerised David saw the gathered flounces of white petticoat, the highly polished, delicate black boots, narrow toes waving to the sky, and even the glimpse of a black stockinged calf, before Gerty turned with a piercing shriek and raced for the door.

'Mama! She hit me! She struck me!'

Miss Marshall was sitting sprawled ignominiously on the floor, gazing up at David and Clara. She looked as shocked by what had happened as anyone. Trying to recover her dignity, she scrambled up, shaking out her full skirts. The tears were spilling over, despite all her efforts. 'You'd better go to your rooms,' she managed faintly. 'The lesson's over for today.'

16

They waited together in the playroom. Clara was agog with excitement. 'She's done it now! She'll lose her job for sure!'

'But Gerty was rude,' David answered. 'And she knocked Miss Marshall flying.'

Clara giggled. 'I know! Did you see her?' Her hand shot out suddenly and grabbed David. Her fingers dug hard into his thin shoulder. 'You have to tell the truth now, Davy. You saw Marshall slap Gerty's face. You must say what you saw.'

He was troubled. When the two younger children were summoned to the drawing room, mama was sitting regally on a small sofa, her dark skirts spread about her. A dramatically tearful Gertrude stood beside her and, somewhat behind, the distraught figure of Miss Marshall, fingers twisting a tiny lace handkerchief. David wished miserably that he could be anywhere but here. He could feel the piercing stare of Gerty's eyes on him, even though he avoided looking at her. Whatever happened, he would suffer from a keen sense of betrayal. His gentle heart ached for the slim young teacher, but he guessed that even if he tried to lie for her sake, it would do her little good. He could imagine how convincingly Gerty had put her case, even down to the hotly flowing tears.

In fact, Clara did most of the talking. He was there merely to corroborate. His mother spoke in a quiet, tired tone, managing to convey a sense of long suffering patience. 'Is this true?'

David paused, staring at the carpet, delaying his answer, then nodded faintly. 'Gerty shoved her and knocked her down!' he added, almost choking, glancing at his sister with a rare show of defiance. She was glaring daggers at him.

They were packed off to the old nursery, which served both as school and dining room for the children, except on Sundays, when they ate downstairs. Soon, Gertrude joined them. She cuffed David across the back of his head, ignoring Helen's cry of protest. 'You sprog! Miss Raggy-drawers' favourite, aren't you? Can't even tell the truth!' She smiled with spiteful satisfaction. 'Not that your sticking up for her will do her any good now. I don't think we'll be seeing much more of your precious Miss Marshall. Mama's giving her her marching orders right now, I expect. And good riddance too, I say!'

Helen's old fashioned look, which Gertrude did not see, warned David that this was one occasion when silence was definitely the better part.

'Well, Sophie? What on earth possessed you?'

Enid Herbert's tone, of such mild restraint, was like a needle pricking the balloon of the young governess's pent up emotions. She collapsed in a flood of anguished tears. 'Oh, I'm sorry!' she wailed. 'It was so foolish of me! I shouldn't—' for a brief while she sobbed uncontrollably, her head bowed.

Enid observed the dark hair, the gathered, neatly pinned bun, the delicately sculpted hollows of the thin neck, with its curling tendrils. All at once a sudden and compassionate tenderness swept over her, with a long forgotten power she recognized. It was a feeling whose origins she could trace far back to her adolescence. She was fifteen when Cousin Hannah, a tall, intense girl, head and shoulders above Enid though they were both the same age, had come to spend the summer with them. In later years, thinking back over that tumul- tuous season, Enid found it hard to remember exactly how the sweet intimacy of their relationship had begun.

They had of course shared a bedroom. Their initial shyness was largely dissipated in the mechanics of such proximity – the dressing and undressing, the performing of ablutions. Her cousin would spend long minutes brushing out Enid's long brown tresses, while Enid sat on the low stool at her feet, both girls caught up in the strong bonds of their innocent affection. They became close, like the siblings and the confidantes neither of them had known, and both treasured the months of that long summer they shared, and wept bitterly when they were forced to part. They had clung to each other, their tears mingling, their lips closing in gentle, longing kisses, and vowed they would never allow anyone to supplant the cherished place each held in the other's heart. Now, when she thought of the passion of that innocent, ignorant declaration, Enid's lips twitched in a smile of gentle reminiscence, even as her eyes moistened. Neither of those two unschooled maidens had any idea of what shocks their conventional world held in store for them.

Mama talked vaguely and with extreme embarrassment about the duties of marriage, and gave Enid a pamphlet which discreetly and unsatisfactorily dealt with conception, pregnancy, and childbirth, and Enid, despite her new fears, embraced her parents' whole-hearted efforts to find a suitable match with pleasing filial obedience.

However, the marriage bed did nothing to dispel her fears. Sex with John at best suggested only the vaguest, most shadowy hint of a possible climactic satisfaction that remained torturously in the farthest distance; at worst, it was a brutally fierce invasion of her body, and her spirit, too, that left her drained and degraded, and utterly alone. In addition, the confinements were times of intensified fear, culminating in an agony that took her outside herself, made her long for an escape into that safe and private innocence of her girl-hood affection, which had so wonderfully excluded the world of men.

She had met with her cousin only infrequently since those long gone days. Hannah was soon married herself, and living in India, the wife of an army officer. After the birth of Clara, her second child, Enid was moved to write to her. With some delicacy, she referred to that fateful summer of their fifteenth year. *I was so sure*, she wrote, *in my ignorance, of what constituted right and wrong, of what my young dreams and expectations were. Now I feel the world is not quite so black and white. It asks so much of us as women. It seems unfair that we get so little in return. Of course, I should not speak of 'we' so freely. I have no idea how you feel about such things, though once (is it really eight years ago?) we were – can I say it? – close to each other.*

She had to wait over two months for a reply. Her fingers shook slightly as she opened the bulky envelope, with its exotic stamps. Hannah's tone was equally warm and friendly, and, towards the end of the long letter, Enid's cheeks pinked, and her bosom rose and fell a little more agitatedly at the words she read so eagerly. *I have never felt so close to* anyone *as I did in that wonderful summer of our love.*

'What news does your cousin have? Is it all excitement? Tiger hunts and that sort of thing?'

Enid started, blushed at her husband's light, bantering tone. 'Just girl talk,' she murmured.

19

The correspondence grew into a regular habit, until, for the first time since that far off summer, Enid felt she had a real confidante. And somehow it seemed even easier to reveal the most intimate thoughts on paper, without the constraint of the other's physical presence, yet with the knowledge that those thoughts were being shared with someone close and dear to her. She had written thousands of words to her cousin in the eleven years that had followed that first tentative letter, pouring out some of her most secret feelings, and she had a box full of equally intimate, revealing replies, which she kept locked and hidden at the back of her sewing closet.

They had met only twice in all that long time. Hannah and her husband had returned to England nine years ago. Enid was privately a little disturbed about seeing her again. Their spiritual kinship on paper was a valuable thing – one of the most valuable, she readily acknowledged. But how would that treasured closeness translate into their reunion in the flesh, in the physical world of husbands and offspring?

In the event, all passed off with perfect propriety. They brushed slightly pinking cheeks in the bluff presence of their men folk, Enid suffering from a sense of shock at seeing the voluminous loose drapery which betokened Hannah's pregnancy. 'Why didn't you tell me?' Enid exclaimed when, finally, they were alone. 'How far on are you?' She tried to keep a tone of reproach from her voice.

'Six months,' Hannah murmured. 'I *did* write, when it was definite,' she continued, colouring at her lie. For a number of strange reasons which she hardly understood herself she had not wanted to confide this significant news to her cousin. 'I assumed when you did not refer to it that you considered it a somewhat delicate matter—'

'I hope there's nothing we can't confide to one another now!' Enid burst out, then blushed, too, at her own vehemence, to which Hannah responded with a dazzling smile. Enid studied her. There were traces still of the darkly handsome girl, but the face looked worn and tired, the complexion somewhat sallow. India was not kind to the memsahibs, in spite of the pampered lives they led.

They spent a considerable time together, out of doors when the weather was fine, the drawing room, or Enid's little sewing room when they were indoors. Major Spencer seemed agreeable enough, though Enid knew that Hannah's feelings were remarkably similar to her own. Shy at first, they were able eventually to share a degree of intimacy in their conversation approaching that of their letters. Most comforting of all for Enid was the knowledge that she was not alone in her distaste for the 'pleasures' of the marriage bed. Painfully constrained as they were by the hidebound customs of their society, nevertheless, Hannah once bravely attempted to breach the wall that convention placed around this 'unmentionable' subject.

Her voice was unsteady with emotion as she murmured, 'I have never known in my intimate relations with Charles anything of what I foolishly imagined as a girl.' They sat for several long, tender moments, clasping hands, too charged to speak.

Hannah returned to her parents' home in the north for the confinement. It was her first child, and she did not recover well. She wrote to Enid that she hoped to remain in England with the baby once Charles went back to his regiment, but he insisted she accompany him, and so the cousins did not get the opportunity to see each other again that leave.

The Spencers returned to England four years later, not long after their little girl had died of tropical fever. Hannah had seemed almost a pale ghost, withdrawn, only half aware most of the time of what was happening around her. They clung, and wept, and kissed, but Enid felt all the love and compassion she directed towards her sinking into a blankness of despair. She tried, in the brief days they spent together, to break through to her, without success. Hannah went back with her husband. The letters became shorter, much more formal, and Enid wept over her loss.

She had never felt more lonely than during these past four years. The sight of young Sophie Marshall, the girl's fragile, vulnerable beauty, her distress as she broke down and wept before her now, roused such sympathetic warmth, along with all those distant but vividly recalled emotions, that Enid was uncomfortably close to tears herself as she gazed at the tragic figure.

Sophie's father was the vicar of a country parish, with a large family of whom Sophie was the eldest. She had felt obliged to ease

21

the financial burden of her parents by seeking some sort of employment in keeping with her education and station. Her admiration of Mrs Herbert, whose serene beauty had captivated her from the start, had increased at the gentle kindness her employer showed her. Which was why she was so distraught at her signal failure to carry out her duties, and why she sobbed so heartbrokenly before this dear lady she had wished so fervently to please.

CHAPTER THREE

THERE was no sound other than Sophie's low weeping. In those few minutes, the whole of Enid Herbert's life from its fifteenth summer had unreeled before her like the flickering images of the new cinematograph. Her heart swelled in sympathy with the desolate sobbing. All the sadness, frustrations, the might-have-beens of those intervening years rose chokingly, too, pressing on her with a constricting tightness like the rigidly boned stays that bound and held her upright in slender captivity. And all at once something within her gave, burst its tight confines, something that she had suppressed all these years, something in the very centre of herself that demanded acknowledgement at last. 'You poor child!'

She stirred, took hold of the slim figure, one arm about the waist, and moved her to the door. 'Come, my dear. You mustn't distress yourself like this. Come up to my room. There now! Shush! Don't cry.'

Still dazed by the swiftness of what had happened, and the looming despair at the picture of her return home in disgrace, Sophie allowed herself to be led across the hall and up the wide staircase to Enid's own bedroom and dressing room on the first floor.

'You poor thing! You'll make yourself ill. You must stop this crying. It's over now.'

Her cheeks glistening with tears, her eyes puffed underneath from her grief, Sophie stared tragically at her. 'But – my father! He'll be so upset—'

'What's your father to do with it, you silly girl? Why should he ever know of it? You surely don't think you're to be dismissed, do you?'

Sophie stared at her, utterly bemused, and Enid smiled through the prick of her own tears. 'I can't approve of you slapping my daughter, but I'm sure the little minx deserved to have her ears boxed.'

Sophie gaped now. 'But – but – Mrs Her—'

'No more! You've got yourself into far too much of a state about it already. We'll sort everything out in the morning. Now sit down here and don't distress yourself any further. You really will make yourself ill. You don't look at all strong.' She moved to the dresser, pulled open a drawer and took out a fragrant handkerchief to replace the sodden crumpled square Sophie still clung to. But when she moved forward to offer it to the girl and to guide her to the nearby chair, the anguished sobs increased in their abandonment as the shock of her relief flowed overwhelmingly through Sophie, who stumbled forward and flung herself half fainting into the arms of her beautiful saviour.

Enid's own arms reached out to enfold her, and the dark head nestled at her shoulder. She could feel the trembling of the thin frame against her. Deeply moved herself, she kissed the wet cheek and held the girl close until the violence of her grief had abated. Enid assisted her to the seat. Slightly giddy with her own emotion, Enid let her fingers caress the dark head, the fine, silky hair, to play with the stray tendrils that were escaping from the coiffure.

Without lifting her head, Sophie suddenly reached up, groped for that caressive hand and seized it, pressing it hard against her wet cheek. 'Oh, Mrs Herbert!' She still could hardly form her words, though the tears were falling quieter now. 'I can't thank you – enough! I swear – I'll do whatever you want—'

Enid bent, grasped the drooping shoulders in a tight hug and pulled the head once more to her proffered bosom. Her nose brushed against the sleek hair and breathed in its fresh, lemony fragrance. Her lips touched it lightly before she stood upright, blushing unseen at her own demonstrativeness. She gave a shaky little laugh. 'Then you'll oblige me by blowing your nose and drying your eyes and taking some tea with me while we discuss what's to be done with that forward madam of a daughter!'

*

David could sense that cook and the rest of the servants were not at all pleased with the children. Even Helen, who scarcely ever said more than three words without giggling, looked askance at them, and rattled their lunch things at them in a clear demonstration of her indignation. Gertrude merely put on even more superior airs, tossing her locks in that toffee nosed manner of hers, and making pointed remarks about servants who didn't know their places.

They were free most afternoons, unless Miss Marshall had planned an excursion, but this particular day Gerty showed an unusual reluctance to grab her hat and coat and make for the garden. 'I don't think I'll go out today,' she said affectedly. 'I don't feel very well after all the upsetment.' Clearly, she wanted to be on hand to savour to the full Miss Marshall's final humiliation. Clara, inevitably taking her cue from her older sister, also declined to go outdoors.

The house was broodingly silent, and David was glad to make his escape. He was feeling bad enough about things, and certainly didn't want to witness any more of the young governess's shame. He carried a heavy burden of guilt at having been forced to corroborate Gerty's story. He should have made a more spirited attempt to explain to mama what had really happened, why Miss Marshall had been driven to act in such an uncharacteristic manner.

Helen buttoned up his coat, and tugged his cap down on his head. 'It's none so warm today,' she chided, 'so don't go takin' 'em off, Master Davy, you hear?'

He ran off quickly. Once out in the open, he felt better, and pottered about down by the stream, then gradually headed down the drive towards the heavy gates. He had to wait a while, but he was rewarded with the sight of golden Nelly Tovey striding along in her jaunty manner as she came in to do her work in the garden.

'Hullo, Davy,' she grinned, and he felt much better for the sunny warmth of her smile. But she knew at once there was something wrong. 'What is it? What've you got to tell me?'

He gabbled out his tale, emotion causing him to stammer breathlessly over the words. 'And Gerty says she'll be dismissed for what she's done. Mama sent for her straight away. And . . .' he paused, blushing. 'We had to go down to the drawing room and tell mama what had happened.'

'Damn 'er!' David knew from the ferocity of the oath for whom it was intended and how deeply upset Nelly was. She stared at the boy in consternation. 'I've always said that sister of yours wants her face smackin'! Why didn't you tell your mammy what a devil of a time she's been giving Miss Marshall?'

David flushed painfully. 'I tried,' he answered miserably. 'I told her Gerty knocked Miss Marshall down. But that – that was after – mama just wanted to know about the slap she gave Gerty. I could- n't . . .' he stopped, close to tears, his heart full of gloom. He felt an added burden now, at having let this lovely girl down, whom he so admired. She knew he had made a poor showing. She was frowning fiercely, brimming with anger. He felt an obscure relief that Gerty was nowhere near the scene, for Nelly looked furious enough to carry out the violence she advocated for his sister.

It put a blight on their time together, which was usually such a delight. 'I'll let you know what happens,' he offered sadly, when she was ready to go off for a break with her father.

' 'Spect I'll hear all about it before then,' she sighed, favouring him with a little smile. 'Never mind. See yer tomorrer. Life's not very fair, though, is it, Davy boy?' He nodded his solemn agreement and turned back with distaste towards the house.

He found his sisters hanging about the landing that led down from the nursery. Gertrude looked a little uncertain for all her bravado. 'Helen says mama has got Marshall up in her bedroom. She must be giving her a real rocket! There's been no sign of her. And things are deadly quiet. We'll have to keep watch for her. Davy, you can go down there and have a listen outside mama's door. Nobody'll hear you. And if they do see you nobody will mind. Come on, get your coat off. And you can slip your boots off, too. You won't make a sound then.'

He didn't much relish the idea of playing spy for his sisters, but a knock on his shin, and a tweak of his right ear, persuaded him to do their bidding, so, with a few snivelling tears swiftly sniffed to silence, he padded off down the nursery stairs to the first floor landing, in his thickly stockinged feet. Everything seemed suddenly fearfully quiet, the ticking of the large clock on the old carved dresser startling him with its loudness. The afternoon light, slanting dustily on to the rich pattern of the rugs, and the darkly polished floorboards with their dangerous creaks, added to the atmosphere of solemn stillness. They were never allowed to linger in this part of the house, merely passing as quickly and, particularly in the morning, as quietly as possible on their way to and from their rooms and the nursery.

Mama's room was at one end, to the right of the main staircase. Her windows opened on to the rose garden. Her room always appeared full of light, and filled with a sweet perfume, on the comparatively rare occasions he had been allowed to set foot in there. Papa's room was at the opposite end of the passage, much smaller, and darker, and you had to go through his study, with its huge desk and formidable shelves full of books, to get to it.

Once, he remembered, he had been sick in the night, and very early next morning Helen had allowed him to go down to the kitchen for a drink. On his way back, he had been shocked and frightened to see papa emerge from mama's room, tying the cord of his red dressing gown. His father had glared rather wildly, his eyes wide and white, looking strangely furtive. David had wondered since whether daddies were not supposed to visit mummies in their rooms, but when he mentioned it to the girls they only looked and sniggered in their knowing way, as though they had some secret they would not share.

He thought about his father now, the familiar edge of fear colouring his feelings. Papa was away such a lot these days. It felt like weeks since he had been home. Again, David was obscurely relieved at his father's absence, for goodness knows what he would have done to poor Miss Marshall if he had been here today.

He felt rather than saw his sisters' impatient gestures from the top of the narrower staircase leading to the upper floors. He crept along the landing, heart beginning to thump now, afraid that the uneven floor would squeak too loudly, that mama or someone else would emerge suddenly and find him sneaking like a thief. Briefly, he hated

Gerty for her bullying ways with him, but he continued his stealthy steps along the passage towards the door of his mother's room.

In truth, he, too, was intrigued by the mystery of what was happening to Miss Marshall, and why this unnatural, brooding atmosphere hung over the house. The dark panelled door was solidly shut. He had no thought of knocking, but, trembling with fear, he crept as close as he dared. He could hear nothing except the thunder of his own pounding heart. He strained, listening intently, thought he could hear the faint sound of a voice, too muted for him to distinguish the words. Plucking up a desperate courage, shivering with apprehension, he moved forward, pressed his ear to the wood. There was a sharp, clinking sound, like the sound of crockery, the rattle of a teaspoon. Then voices, one overlaying the other, both low and musically feminine – and neither sounding angry or distressed.

'Oh, Mrs Herbert! If only you knew how much this means—'

'Now, now, no more, please! I'm only sorry for neglecting things so . . .'

There was a sound of someone moving, the soft creak of a chair, and David fled precipitately, his courage failing, and ran skidding back down the corridor towards the haven of the stairs. He only just made it to the girls crouching at the top when Mama's door opened, and they saw the dark gowned figure of the governess, her face a pale blur, glance round somewhat furtively before placing something on the floor and stepping inside the room again, closing the door with an audible click. It was a laden tea tray.

The three children stared at one another in bewilderment. 'What the devil is going on?' Gerty's expression changed, to one of a dawning fury, which made David's insides clench with all the resurrected fear he had known since the morning of this eventful day.

There was much speculation in the kitchen, too, though muted at the inhibiting presence of the children, who, in an indication of how different this day was from the norm, were allowed to take their tea there, seated at the thick, scarred wooden surface of the long table which occupied the centre of the room. Mavis, mama's maid, came in bearing the tray which the children had seen placed outside the bedroom door by Miss Marshall. 'Been in there hours!' Mavis said, lips compressed. In deference to cook's warning glance, she lowered her voice. 'Chatting away like bosom pals! Taking tea with the missus an' all! Quite the lady is our Miss Sophie! And the bairns there left to themselves all day long. Not right by a long chalk, if you ask me!'

The children were equally shocked, and at a loss to explain these strange events. Hitherto, mama had scarcely acknowledged the governess's presence in the house, let alone evinced any interest in her duties. Gertrude was pale and withdrawn, and David had the uncomfortable feeling that more storms were brewing.

The next morning the children were in the schoolroom at nine o'clock, waiting nervously to see what would happen, though Gerty muttered mutinously, 'I shan't let that savage anywhere near me. If she hasn't gone by this evening I intend to let daddy know everything that's happened.' She tossed the rippling mane of coppery hair.

Though they were left on their own, they were too anxious and subdued to get up to any real mischief. When nothing had occurred by nine-thirty, however, they were distinctly restless, and so were quite relieved when Helen appeared, even though it was to summon them once more to the drawing room.

Their mother was seated on the same sofa, though they were quick to notice she was not yet formally dressed, but wearing a house gown, high collared, and with a trailing, tasselled hem, and braided buttons up the front. It gave her a softer, less formidable air. Freed from the uncomfortable rigidity of her stays, she was able to recline more at ease on the cushions. One pale ankle peeped from beneath the ruffles of a petticoat, the narrow foot encased in the lightest of daintily embroidered slippers.

Sophie Marshall, dressed as usual in one of her severe, high necked, dark dresses, stood behind the sofa, but close enough to grip its high back with her thin hands, whose paleness showed, only inches from the piled and gathered tresses of her mistress. The girl's eyes were darkened with weariness or strain, and her pretty face was white as paper against the sombreness of her dress. She looked frightened, and David was more confused than ever. Even mama looked odd. Almost embarrassed.

'I called you all down,' she began quietly, 'because I want you all to hear what I've got to say. When your father and I engaged Miss Marshall we expected you to treat her with the respect to which her position entitled her. She is a young lady, of impeccable background, highly educated. Not a servant, but someone who has been employed to pass on her knowledge and skills to you – to educate you, and prepare you to take your place in the world. An important and responsible task, as I would have thought you would agree.'

Already, Gertrude's head was up. Twin spots of colour glowed on her cheeks, and her eyes were narrowed as she stared at her mother, sensing that what was coming next would not be to her liking. Mama's voice continued, growing stronger, and harder, all the while. 'Instead, I find you have behaved abominably, displaying a gross ignorance and rudeness that makes me thoroughly ashamed of you.'

David blushed and glanced down at his feet as she added, 'I do not include Davy in this reprimand. He is the youngest and yet he is far in advance of you girls in both conduct and civility. You would do well to learn from your brother.' He could almost feel the heat of Gerty's fury, heard the hiss of her indrawn breath.

'As the oldest, we expect you, Gertrude, to set the example. And what do I find? You behave disgustingly—'

'Mama!' Gertrude's voice was shrill, almost a squeal, of shock and indignation. 'I only—'

'Be quiet! How dare you interrupt me, girl?' Though it remained low, the intensity of Enid's tone cut through the girl's cry of outrage. Her mother's face was flushed, too, now. Her throat, revealed by the house gown, worked with emotion. 'You forget yourself altogether! That is precisely what I mean! Now – I have asked Miss Marshall to forgive you, and to accept your apology, which she has very kindly agreed to do.'

There was a terrifying instant of silence. 'Apologize! Me, apologize to her! She slapped me! She should be the one – it's wicked! And unfair!' Gerty burst into noisy tears, and dashed from the room, despite her mother's calling urgently after her.

The other two children stood there, miserably at a loss. Miss Marshall sniffled, close to tears herself once more, and their mother looked flustered, However, she managed to restore some sense of dignity and calm. 'You two will continue your lessons with Miss Marshall.' David noted with some surprise how his mother's hand came up and sought the whitened knuckles of the governess's fingers on the back of the sofa. She closed her hand comfortingly over them and gave them a small caress. 'As for young missy there, I'm afraid she must be taught a harsher lesson. You're not to have anything to do with her. Understand? She'll be kept in her room until she learns to conduct herself in a proper manner. Now go up to the school-room. Miss Marshall will be along shortly.'

CHAPTER FOUR

ONCE outside, Clara gave David a shove and a kick, but they were half hearted for she was too preoccupied with the events that had taken place in the drawing room. 'Gerty'll starve to death!' she told the worried boy excitedly. 'She'll never apologize! Never!'

After some time, Miss Marshall appeared in the schoolroom. She seemed to blush whenever the children caught her eye, and her voice, always musically gentle except when she was driven to remonstrate with Gertrude, was so faint as to be almost inaudible. No reference was made to what had happened downstairs. David tried to show by his demeanour where his chief sympathies lay, and Miss Marshall was pathetically grateful for the youngster's efforts to please her. Clara, robbed of her older sister's influence, behaved with a studied politeness which was patently false. All three were glad when the hands of the wall clock climbed up to noon, and lessons were over.

'This afternoon, I think we'll take a walk up to Bidulph Common. Have a look at the pond. There's some—'

The door opened, and Mrs Herbert's head appeared. 'Oh, have you finished?' She smiled at the governess. David noticed with a tingle of pleasure how full of warmth the smile was.

Miss Marshall was blushing. 'I was just saying – telling Clara and David. I thought I'd take them to Bidulph Common. We—'

'Oh, can't it wait until tomorrow? I was going to ask you to drive into Willerby with me. I'd like you to help me choose something for the Pattersons' ball. I have no idea of what's in fashion nowadays.'

'Well, er . . .' Sophie stammered, her colour deepening as she glanced at the children.

'I'm sure you won't mind being left to your own devices, will you?' their mother asked them. She did not expect or wait for an answer. Her face became serious. 'One thing I must remind you. You will not go near your sister's room. She is to remain there for the rest of the day, and also this evening. Clara, Helen will put out the things you need in the small guest room – the one next to papa's study. If necessary, you'll sleep there tonight. You'll be told later. Do I have your word on this? You're to keep away from Gertrude. Understand?'

'Yes, mama.'

Over lunch in the nursery, Clara said, somewhat indistinctly because she was still chewing, 'When mama and old Raggy-drawers have gone, we'll see if we can have a word with Gerty. Scout around a bit.'

'Why do you call her that?' David exclaimed hotly. 'I'm sure she's not – she's always . . .' He gave up. 'Anyway, we promised mama—' he was silenced by a swift kick on his shin under the table, as Helen reappeared with their pudding.

Despite Clara's protests, Helen insisted they put on their outdoor things and head for the garden. 'Miss Gerty's lunch was sent up to her room,' she informed them, in answer to Clara's pressing enquiry.

'Why can't we just sneak in for a quick word?' the girl pleaded. 'Mama won't know. Why should she?'

Helen sniffed. 'I've been given strict orders. You're not to go anywhere near her. Besides, she's locked in. Mavis 'as got the key, I think. I know *I* haven't, that's for sure!'

Locked in! Clara and David glanced at each other, wide eyed. Nothing like this had happened before. 'Do you think it's fair, Helen? Honestly? You heard what happened. Why should Gerty be made to apologize? She's done nothing wrong!'

The maid sniffed again, louder and more meaningfully. 'Dunno 'bout that! There's all sorts of funny things going on around here these days. Not my place to comment on what folks gets up to, is it? Now come on! Out you go, the pair of you! And don't let me catch you trying to sneak back in afore teatime, otherwise you'll be in hot water an' all!'

'Let's go round and see if we can see Gerty at the window. At least we can wave.'

Reluctantly, David followed his sister through the vegetable patch, to the stables where the carriages were kept. The narrow windows of the children's rooms, high on the second floor, looked down on the gravelled strip beyond the out buildings, that led round to the front of the house. 'Give her a shout,' Clara urged.

David stared at her in alarm. 'No! You! Somebody will hear us. We'll get into trouble.'

'Scaredy cat! Disgusting little coward! You're getting too big for your britches again, toad! How about if I take you down to the stream again and give you another thrashing? Sounds like you're about ready for one, I'd say.'

David tensed. He knew Clara was aping her sister, trying to assume Gerty's dictatorial role. He measured her against himself. She was not much taller, in spite of her three years' seniority. But she was heavier, more robust. In a fight, she would easily defeat him, he knew.

He had a sudden, stinging self-loathing at his own delicate, puny frame, with its smooth, milk white skin, which he so loved to caress and stroke when he was alone in bed. It made him feel strangely weak, yet shivery with delight. He blushed hotly at his secret imaginings: the touch of silks and ribbons and lace next to his skin, the rustling spread of beautiful, flowing gowns. He knew enough to be ashamed of his secret longings, the girlishness which made him shy away from dirt, and rough, boyish pursuits. And which ensured that Clara, though not much superior in physical strength, was quite capable of carrying out the drubbing she threatened him with.

However, he was poised for flight. He was not quite prepared to surrender himself up for punishment the way he had with Gerty. There was a certain inevitability about his subservience to his eldest sister. She was practically grown up. Beautiful. Far above him. Why, he had even noticed the slight roundings of her blouse, a hint of the exquisite feminality that would blossom into a beauty like mama's and Miss Marshall's some day. But Clara was too close to him. Still a child. He could not surrender himself to her in that way. Not yet.

Fortunately, she was diverted by the timely appearance of

Gertrude herself, at the high window. A white blur, and a mass of untidy hair, she waved forlornly, like a captive princess from her tower. They stared up at her, and she stared back. They did not shout, and she did not open the window. Perhaps it was locked, too. After a long minute or two, the figure gave a final, tragic wave and turned away.

'Bitch!' muttered Clara venomously. David knew too well to whom the epithet was applied. He would have liked to defend her, but dared not. Clara tugged her tam more firmly on the side of her head and kicked the gravel with a scuffed boot. 'You know why she's got away with this, don't you?' Clara went on. Feeling that some sort of response was required from him, David shook his head.

'Because she's made mama have a crush on her!' She stared challengingly at him, and frowned impatiently at his blank look. 'Girls can have crushes on each other,' she announced in worldly superiority. 'They go all soppy. They start to spark, just like a boy and girl. It's disgusting!' she added, in tones of moral condemnation. 'It happens between schoolgirls. That's all right. But mama's so old! Everyone's shocked. All the servants! You can feel it, can't you? Wait till daddy comes! He'll go absolutely mad if he finds out. Which I'm sure he will.' She smirked in triumph. 'I expect Gerty's already written the letter. So Miss Baggy-drawers will get her comeuppance yet, you mark my words!'

'Come in. Close the door behind you.'

Sophie Marshall obeyed John Herbert's quiet instruction. Her limbs felt jellyish as they carried her across the patterned carpet leading to the hard-backed chair placed in front of his desk, towards which he was gesturing. Her insides felt liquefied and her heart was thudding, as it had been all the way along the corridor to his study, after receiving the summons to attend him there. She even feared she might swoon, and clutched at the carved wooden top of the chair, onto whose hard, narrow surface she sank in what felt like utter exhaustion.

She stared waveringly at the dark, rich silk of his cravat, the quilted lapels of his smoking jacket with its black braided buttons –

anywhere except at those implacable dark eyes which seemed capable of piercing into her innermost being. Her gaze lowered further, to his hands, scrupulously manicured, sensitive looking, yet imposing on her reeling senses a frightening awareness of his masculinity, with the fine, dark hairs showing against the paleness of the skin over his knuckles, folded solemnly together on the tooled leather of the desk. She could see the thinness of his wrists, the impeccable white cuffs and the gleaming tiny chains of the links which held them together. The silence dragged endlessly on, until she wanted to cry out. Her nails dug painfully into the wet palms of her clenched fists held like stones in her lap.

'You know why you're here?'

She fought desperately to force out her whispered reply. 'Yes – I think so, sir.' Despite all Mrs Herbert's assurances that she had nothing to fear from the return of the master of the house, Sophie had remained deeply anxious, even though the brief interlude before he came home had been one of rare happiness, all the more treasured because of its total unexpectedness. That her mistress should display such warm tenderness and concern for her, after all those long weeks of Sophie's secretly cherished admiration, had left her dazed with appreciation and gratitude. The gentle but distant benevolence Enid Herbert had hitherto displayed was transformed to a closeness Sophie had never shared with anyone; a reciprocal closeness, she had discovered, which both embraced with heartfelt eagerness. And to think it had come about so swiftly and dramatically, through an event which Sophie had been convinced was to be her ruination.

Not that that problem had been truly resolved. Hence, the fear which gripped her now. After a further full day and a second night confined to her room, Gertrude, her young face closed stiffly but looking worn with exhaustion and paper-pale, had come with her mama to the schoolroom and, in the presence of her embarrassed siblings, had muttered a tight lipped, mumbling apology, the effect of which Sophie had almost cancelled by her own hasty and effusive outpouring of repentance. 'And I, too, am so sorry for my behaviour, Gertrude. Forgive me! I had no right to behave as I did. Forgive me, please! Let us start afresh!' She made an awkward movement to reach out, to take Gertrude's hand, but the girl's arms remained rigidly at her sides, and the look in the red rimmed, grey eyes gave clear warning that the forgiveness Sophie had asked for was not forthcoming.

'You were provoked beyond all measure!' Enid said hastily, to cover the embarrassment of the moment. 'But Gertrude has assured me she will never behave in such a manner again. And she knows the consequences should she ever break that promise.'

In the days that followed, Gerty had applied the letter of the law, and sat stony faced through all Sophie's efforts to ingratiate herself with her pupil. She accepted with silent contempt her teacher's careful concern not to provoke her into any further displays of rebellion. For David, every minute in the schoolroom felt like sitting on the crater lip of a rumbling volcano, and outside, he was assiduous as the governess in his attempts not to provoke his sister, though with considerably less success. 'Just wait till daddy gets back!' Gerty muttered through those tight lips, and he waited with dread.

Sophie finally managed to drag her gaze up to the darkly handsome features of her employer. John Herbert felt his body react like a spring, his blood throb with a primal exultation at the vulnerability and helplessness he read in the girl's eyes. He held them in his gaze, thrilled at the dark colour he saw steal up from the slim neck, and the eyes fall away once more in defeat, to stare at the delicate hands, which, in spite of all her efforts, had joined and now intertwined, twisting at her lap. He kept his voice soft and deep, carefully modulated, grave yet free from any menace. 'My daughter has been greatly distressed by what happened. I have no need to remind you, I hope, Miss Marshall, of the difficulties she faces at such an age. She is still a child but . . . on the brink of young womanhood. You understand me?'

Sophie felt the heat of her embarrassment damp beneath her clothing. Again she managed a faint whisper of assent.

'You are yourself somewhat young and inexperienced. Isn't that true?'

She felt as though he were extracting the murmured answers from her like a torturer, then was immediately ashamed of her thought at his undoubted measured restraint. The deep, compelling voice continued. She felt it like a physical force, an insidious sensation of thrilling fear. Its effect was so strong, and so primitive, a stirring deep within, that she had difficulty in distinguishing his words, making sense of them in her whirling mind.

'It was largely my sympathy for your father and for your situation that persuaded me to offer you the post in the first place, as I'm sure you are aware. And we have been pleased with your work with David. But perhaps the girls are a little advanced in age for your own youthfulness. You're – what? Twenty?'

'Nineteen, sir. I shall be twenty in March.' She felt her face burning, the threat of tears behind her eyes. 'Oh, please, sir! I'm sorry for what happened. I realize how wrong it was of me. I told Mrs Herbert – I promise it will never happen again!'

He gave a humourless little laugh, raised a hand in remonstrance. 'Oh, you have a champion in my wife, I'm only too well aware of that. She is very eloquent on your behalf. And very strong on Gertrude's lack of manners. In fact, I'm quite surprised at just how enthusiastic my wife is in your cause. I had no idea she had such strong feelings about you.'

Sophie once more experienced an uncomfortable warmth of embarrassment sweep over her at his words, and the underlying mockery – or was it contempt? – with which he spoke them. They made her feel a guilt she could not quite comprehend, and added to her wretchedness. The increased gentle reasonableness with which he went on only served to distress her more.

'But you were not hired as a lady's companion to Mrs Herbert. And I must ask myself, are you indeed suited to the role we *did* employ you for? Have you the temperament to deal with girls of Gertrude's age – or Clara's for that matter? Would you not be more comfortable with children of a younger age, like David, for instance?'

She felt despair welling up, settling icily at her breast, and the tears came even closer, she could feel the gathering wetness on her lashes. Her chin sank further towards her chest, which felt so constricted she could hardly draw breath. She could not trust herself to speak, her throat was closed. She was going to be dismissed after all!

'I know how disappointed your family will be. I have a great respect for your father, he is a good man. But you'll appreciate, Miss Marshall, I'm a father, too, and must consider what is best for my children, like any caring parent.'

She could hold back no longer. A deep shudder passed through her, her slender frame shook as a great sigh escaped, and she sobbed. The tears, hot with her shame, spilled over, splashed onto her clenched hands and she cried brokenly, what little pride and dignity she had tried to cling to dissipated in her grief and hopelessness. 'Please, sir! I beg you! Don't send me away! Give me another chance, please! I can't—' the words ran out, engulfed in her misery. She wept abandonedly, let her blind sorrow tear through her, the tears streaming now, soaking her face, falling thickly until she all but forgot the imposing, sternly handsome figure before whom she slumped so abjectly.

Until, all at once, she became aware of a hand, heavy and strong on her shoulder, of its fingers curling, pressing through the fabric of her dress, fitting to the delicate sculpt of her thin bone and the hollow beneath. Another hand pressing a scented cloth to her wet face, wiping at her tears, those hands, so strong, lifting her now, holding her, so close that she felt the silken stuff of his jacket brushing against her.

'My dear! Please – don't upset yourself so! There there!' The hands openly caressing her now, stroking, patting her, surely improperly, and yet in her desperation and need she yielded gladly, felt only their solid strength and comfort, luxuriating in her own surrender and weakness as the enveloping warmth of that soft, hypnotic voice flowed through and over her, the lips so close she could feel them brushing against her hair, the warm breath stirring her brow.

CHAPTER FIVE

To David the following three months were among the happiest he had known. Only days after the incident of 'Gerty's slap', it was announced that she would no longer be under the tutelage of Miss Marshall but would be attending a college for young ladies in nearby Saffron Walden. She would lodge in the town during the week and return home on Fridays for the weekends. Though she pretended to be put out by this arrangement, and to play a martyr's role – 'I'm the one who's banished and Miss Raggy-drawers stays on as mama's pet!' – in reality she was highly pleased with the arrangement. 'I suppose I should get used to being away from home,' she said airily to her brother and sister. 'After all, I shall be going abroad anyway in a year or two, for my finishing.' She added ominously, 'It's something you'll have to get used to as well, soon, little Davy. Papa will be sending you off to boarding school any day now.' Her words disturbed him greatly, but, child that he was, the future was not something he could dwell in for any length of time, and he basked in the present – lessons without the constant threat of Gerty's disturbances and disastrous eruptions. Clara was but a pale shade of her sister's dynamism, for which David was duly thankful. And the governess, freed from the terrors of Gertrude's remorseless antagonism, was transformed, too. David basked in the sun of her radiance and felt his child's heart torn between his love for her and his joy in golden Nelly Tovey's presence, whose company he sought in the garden whenever he could. But then things changed again, and his anxiety and sadness became all the worse because this time he could not for the life of him fathom the reason for it.

One winter's morning, so wet and gloomy that they needed the lamps lit in the schoolroom, Miss Marshall came very late, and her face, usually so lively and full of warm enthusiasm, was pale and pinched, stamped with anxiety, and something else. Could it be fear, David wondered? His own unease grew as it quickly became evident that something was seriously amiss, for she scarcely spoke, and set them tedious exercises for the whole of the morning, telling them to 'get on' with their work in silence, and spending most of the time standing by the rain-specked window staring out at the greyness and the black waving treetops.

Once again, David felt the weight of tension, that heavy brooding danger sitting on the household like the dark winter clouds. Helen was tight lipped, the other servants spoke in low tones and avoided looking at the children if they could. Miss Marshall had taken to eating her meals with mama and papa in the dining room, and spending a large part of her evenings with mama in her dressing room. David was delighted with the way she and mama had become friends – he was so happy for both their sakes. And he and Clara had seen far more of their mother recently, for she took a new interest in their lessons; was a regular visitor to the schoolroom, and had even accompanied them with Miss Marshall on several of their excursions about the gardens and to the common on fine afternoons. But this evening the governess remained shut up in her room, at the end of the nursery corridor. He had heard Helen murmur, 'Bleedin' cheek!' when they had seen one of the young downstairs maids carrying a tray past the doorway on the way to Miss Marshall's room.

'What's she been up to now, I wonder?' Clara surmised with malicious glee. Her eyes were on David to observe the effect of her words. 'Gerty said she'd pay her back in the end. P'raps she's found a way to do it at last!' David shivered. He felt a hot anger but he choked back any response. He was too upset for one thing, and, for another, he had no idea of what to say, only a painful awareness that, once again, clouds loomed threateningly over his small world.

Sophie had the feeling of being caught up in a nightmare. The feeling was so powerful that at times she even entertained a wild hope that she might yet wake up and find all her fears unreal. It was all one with that sick, clenching dread that trapped her in its web of help-lessness and paralysing defeat. How could it have happened to her? The question reverberated in her mind, all the more frightening because she found herself unable to explain her actions. Always that same hopeless entrapment, her powerlessness to do anything, like some shivering dumb creature mesmerized by its own impending doom.

He had been firm, and kind, too, in those first days, and nights; when she crept through the dim, night lit creaking silence of the sleeping house to his room, through the dark, book lined study, to that inner sanctum – and place of her destruction. The destruction of her purity, and honour, and everything she had always believed herself to be. She was lost now. He had revealed to her another self, a self she had no idea existed, and now every vestige of that former person, that character she had thought herself to be, had vanished, destroyed beyond return. She had tried to plead her innocence, to see herself as the victim of his utter wickedness, but even on her knees in the solitude of her room, she could not form the words to pray for forgiveness but crouched despairingly, crushed by the weight of sin.

From that first night, when she had broken down – the irony of it scourged her now when she thought how foolishly she had imagined her troubles could not be worse. she had been torn by the looming disgrace of being sent home dismissed from her post, without the means of procuring another position. If only she could return to that fateful moment, accept her failure and take the punishment of her dismissal, never to see him again, to be free of him. If only! Most terrible of all was the knowledge that she had dearly earned, from the very first embrace: the touch of his hands and lips, the whispered endearments, the shocking declaration of his passion for her, the devilishness for which he made not the slightest excuse. The seeds he had sown sprang to life within her, came from some taint inside herself, unworldly maiden as she was, and condemned her from the first.

How had her innocent mind, and her virgin body, been so swiftly and completely corrupted? She had not known the meaning of depravity, had not the slightest notion of the ferocity of that throbbing rebellion in her blood, which he had mercilessly opened her to, extracted from her. With consummate cruelty, only when she was lost in his power over her had he told her, with that devil's smile, 'Some women have this heat, Sophie. This fever and passion which is normally the prerogative of the male species. Fallen women, you might say. But why condemn them? You might as well blame them for an ugly wart, or a squint, or crooked teeth. I felt it in you the moment I set eyes on you, despite that mousy, demure look, those virginal blushes. It's a passion I thoroughly acknowledge, and recognize. Unfortunately, many women, *virtuous* creatures, of whom Enid is one, lack it entirely, or never acknowledge it, and become those crabby, thin lipped wives and spinsters that abound in our society. So God bless the fallen, I say! Sisters of Joy, we salute you!'

And now she was his, bound to him by chains all the stronger for their invisibility. She feared that God's retribution was to follow swiftly on her downfall, in spite of her seducer's wicked knowledge and advice. Her menses had ceased – 'Don't be overanxious, my sweet. You have only just become a true woman.' But now she was overdue again, and she knew beyond all doubt she was carrying his issue, the mark of her sin, within her. Her fall, and the flowering evil he had released in her, had not made her any less religious. She believed more firmly than ever in God, and in His terrible justice. She must pay the penalty for her sins.

The torment was refined by her additional role of traitor. For while John Herbert possessed her body with a demonic power, her spirit was shattered by the pain of an equal betrayal, of the woman with whom he was bonded in the eyes of the Almighty, the sanctified bearer of his children. And Sophie could not deny that this was a betrayal of love; a love unfettered by flesh and by the world of men, for she did love Enid Herbert, who had taken her to her bosom in pure, unadulterated friendship. Sophie could not sustain such wickedness any longer. It was too much even for the depths of degradation she had so quickly allowed to swallow her. She must tell him. She would go to him this very night, even though no rendezvous had been made. She glanced at the clock. After ten. Another hour and she would creep down the stairs and along the corridor, past the betrayed wife's room to his own den. She felt the scourge of her shame once again as she thought of how many times she had made that silent journey, with only a thin shift beneath her dressing gown, her body bared, perfumed and hot for the perfidy she had become enslaved to. This time, she would be fully dressed. This time she would not yield to those hot, whispered words of blazing sin, or the hands which drew her down to that shame and made her trembling, weak limbs open to their own consuming fire.

He was waiting for her. 'I am in trouble,' she declared, but all her previous steely determination came to naught as she failed to meet his gaze and the red heat of shame swamped her. Somehow she forced the words out. 'My courses – they have failed to appear again. I fear . . .'

'You are with child?' He finished her sentence for her. He had not approached her, had not offered to embrace her, made no move to usher her through from his study to the bedroom. She was stunned by his coldness. It shocked her, even though she had always sensed the hardness beneath his passion. 'You haven't been careless, have you? You've always done what I told you?'

She felt pinned down, like a specimen sliced open for inspection. The tears came, choked her, she shook her head miserably, and the ripe tears fell down her cheeks.

'Never mind. No use to weep over the spilt milk! We must get you to a doctor quickly. See if you have indeed fallen. And put things right, while there's time. I'll take care of it.'

She might have taken hope, searched out a spark of tenderness from this last sentence, except for the tone in which it was delivered. The spark was not there, not the slightest flicker, in the hard and practical selfishness of his concern.

'I know a man. A good man, not a back street quack, who'll take care of things, if necessary. And I know a place – in London. You'll have to leave, at once. You can't stay here. Pack tonight, be ready to leave in the morning. I'll furnish you with everything necessary. An address in town. You'll stay there.'

At last he came round the desk towards her, put his hands on her shoulders and drew her close. Part of her wanted to twist from under his grip, to thrust him away from her and cry out as the victim of his animalism, but in the weakness of relief it was smothered like a weak flame and she sobbed, wilting against his strength.

'I'm not going to abandon you, you goose. But you know things have gone beyond what may be tolerated under this roof.' He gave a low chuckle, which she felt as deeply as any blow. 'Things have got entirely out of hand. I refer of course to your entirely unseemly affair with my wife.'

In spite of her grief, her head jerked up, she stared, her face agleam with tears, in complete surprise.

'It's becoming a matter of gossip below stairs, I'm told. Even scandal, I might say. Gertrude has protested most strongly to me.' He shook her playfully again, and gave another hateful, dry chuckle. 'She tells me you spend all your time in my wife's company these days. She says you neglect your two charges, go off gallivanting with Enid like a lady of leisure. And as for the night time! She tells me you're in her bedroom half the night. You've been seen coming out, late at night, in your night things. That you are as tender as lovers with each other. In fact, the servants believe that you might well be. They're convinced you share the same bed!'

He was laughing openly now, highly amused at the almost ludicrous expression of amazement on Sophie's face. 'Oh, come now! Don't tell me a girl like you isn't aware of it! You're not going to claim such ignorance as the old queen, God rest her soul, once displayed?' He ignored the tiny mews of confounded protest, and carried on, letting go of her as he moved to the desk once more. 'As a matter of fact it suits our purpose admirably, however ridiculous it is. It can explain your sudden disappearance. There'll be no trace of you. And I'll play the poor dupe of a husband cuckolded by your Sapphic charms! A delicious irony, don't you think?'

The heat of her shame was replaced by paleness again. She sank down weakly on the hard chair before him. 'But – I can't – I mean, what will happen to me?' Her eyes were big, shone with her need and helplessness.

'I've told you. I'll do the decent thing by you. The place I have in town. It's small, humble even, but respectable. You'll be fine.' She heard the hardness creep back into his voice. 'But there'll be no more pretence between us. You'll be there as my mistress. You understand. I'll keep you, in comfort. I'll continue to pay a stipend – I'll even inform your father that you've found another post as governess. They shan't suffer by the change in your circumstances. And they need never know. Provided you accept my terms. You *do* accept them, don't you, Sophie, my sweet? I don't want to lose you. But I won't have you trying to ruin me or turn my life around. I'll break you if you do.'

She felt the blood draining from her, was powerless to make her limbs obey her. 'Well, Sophie? You do agree, don't you?' She couldn't speak against the thunder of her heart, but she nodded, the imponderable weight of her subservience pinning her to the chair.

'Please, John! Just tell me what has become of her! Is she all right? What's happened to her? Has she gone back home?'

Enid's voice was beseeching. John Herbert felt the inner surge of brutal excitement, felt his flesh throb with response to his power over her. Its novelty was as stirring to him as it had been in the old, early days of their marriage. His desire for her body was rekindled. 'You're still pining for your little friend? I've told you. I've sent her away, my dear. It's better you don't know her whereabouts. Her inversion is a sickness. She abused your trust. You'll never see her again.'

Enid swallowed hard to ease the choking lump in her throat. She fought to suppress the tears stinging at her eyelids. Whatever Sophie had done or said to convince him of her wickedness, or, rather, whatever the vindictive Gerty or the gossiping servants had said of her, she prayed that he would not extract, had not already extracted, too terrible a revenge on the unfortunate girl. She was sure that he was right in one thing. She would never meet her again. He would ensure it.

Her life had changed in the all too brief period she had shared with the lovely young girl. And now John had made their attachment seem like some crippling disease, tainted it with a shocking obscenity. Servants, family, all except poor young Davy, were aware of the smear of unnaturalness. The girls – she saw it on their eyes whenever hers chanced to meet them. And something else, too, in her eldest daughter's gaze. Gerty was undoubtedly the chief instigator of Sophie's downfall. Stronger than the contempt was that heady triumph her daughter could not hide, the conquest of a thirteen-year-old who had ousted her mother. And John encouraged it, reflected it in his new found intimacy with her, his complicity in her triumph.

He had his own triumph, too, in his responsibility for Enid's demeaned status. Once more, he controlled her entirely, mind and body. She was again his possession, his thing, for him to use as he pleased. And he would use her, she was sure, as he had before, both sexually and spiritually, to demonstrate his mastery of her.

Within weeks of Sophie's leaving, this mastery was amply proven. Her monthly flow did not come, she felt that strange heaviness, the dull ache in her belly, the first faint hints of queasy awakenings that foretold her pregnancy. She was alarmed, in spite of her doctor's assurances. 'You're only – what? – thirty three, my dear. As long as you take care, we'll ensure the best of attention. Everything will be fine.'

'I couldn't be more delighted, my dear,' John said, when the news was confirmed, and he came to her where she lay in bed. He sat on the edge of the covers. She felt their tight restriction, pinned beneath them by his weight. He picked up her hand, lifted it gently to his lips and kissed it lightly. She smelt the subtle cologne, the clean, masculine aroma of him. He was handsomer than ever, she thought, his features stamped with the authority of his years and his success. Suddenly, she felt a strong flickering pulse of her bodily hunger for him, and blushed with shock at her waywardness. It was almost as though he could read her mind, for his mouth curved in a smile which, for all its gentleness, seemed to hold an underlay of quiet mockery.

'Well, my love, I'm banished to my narrow bed once more. But I bear it gladly. We must take every care of you until the blessed day. I'll bid you goodnight. Sleep well.'

CHAPTER SIX

ENID felt ill throughout the whole of her term, her physical discomfort compounded by an apathetic lethargy which made her a voluntary prisoner in her room. She could find out nothing of Sophie except the little that John had finally and grudgingly vouchsafed; that she had obtained a situation in the north country somewhere, and that, against his better judgement, he had not informed her family of the true circumstances of her leaving his employment. 'Put her from your mind. She's not worthy of any pity you may still feel for her. Besides, you have other, more important concerns now. I really don't see why your condition should give you so much distress. It's a perfectly natural function of the female body.' And he added with that smiling cruelty against which she had no defence, 'Perhaps that's why it causes you so much disturbance.'

'I think I have done my duty by you,' she answered faintly.

'Yes. You've always fulfilled your obligations, my dear, no matter how difficult or unpleasant you have found them. Though I think you must also grant that my observance of my rights has been far from excessive.' And it was true. In the eyes of the world he had been a most undemanding partner. Besides, she was too weary and dispirited to argue the point.

For a long time, there was scarcely any outward sign of her condition, only that dragging inner heaviness low down within her, and the tiredness which seemed to inflict her permanently. One day, as she roused herself around mid-morning to leave her bed and take her bath, Mavis appeared with another capped and gowned figure in maid's uniform behind her. 'I've been speaking with the master, mum,' Mavis declared, in the off-hand way she had adopted more and more openly since the governess's departure. 'He says Nelly can take over some of my duties up here now. Seeing as how you are confined up here so much, and I'm looking after so much downstairs. Cook's no good on her own, mum.'

Enid nodded resignedly. She recognized the tall, sturdy frame of the girl behind Mavis. The yellow tendrils of hair poked rebelliously from the white mobcap. Nelly Tovey, the gardener's girl, had been taken on only a month or two ago, as kitchen and downstairs maid. She was about Gerty's age, yet a head taller, and taller, too, than the smug Mavis, who departed with a perfunctory bob, in an aura of triumph. Yet another snub for Enid, another of the endless reminders of her stumble from grace. Wryly, Enid recalled Mavis's bursting pride when she had first assumed the role of personal maid to her mistress. Now, she could hardly be bothered to hide her insolence and her contempt.

'I don't know much, mum, but I'm willin' to learn. I hope as how I'll do for you, mum.'

Enid smiled at Nelly's robust confession. The sleeves of the gown were pushed up to her elbows. The forearms were brown, tanned from their exposure to the sun, while her square, strong shoulders, even under the looseness of the gown and long pinafore, indicated the strength of her young frame. More suited to milkmaid than parlour maid, Enid reflected. She pushed aside the bedclothes and swung her feet down to the carpet. She sat for some seconds, feeling the giddiness swell then recede.

Nelly was familiar with the bedroom only from the laying of the fires and the cleaning of the rooms after their occupants had left them. She had little knowledge of the work involved in being a lady's maid, but, as she said, she was willing to learn. And, most of all, Enid appreciated the young girl's straightforward approach to her. Respectful, but friendly – a little too friendly for some, Enid was soon aware – young madam Gertrude often carped on about her, and, in particular, her over-familiarity with David. 'She treats the little wart like a chum,' Gerty observed. 'She needs to be taught her place.' Enid knew that Gertrude would never waste any opportunity of reminding the youngster of her lowly status within the household.

Enid herself felt constrained to warn David about his attitude, more for his sake, and Nelly's, than as a mark of her disapproval. 'You mustn't be too friendly, Davy,' she said gently. 'Remember, she *is* a servant after all.'

'Yes, mama.' He blushed. He was embarrassed on Nelly's behalf, and hoped no one would reprimand her. He made an effort to be a little more distant in the company of others, especially his sisters. It worried him deeply, though, that she might feel hurt, and, when he was able to speak to her alone one afternoon, waylaying her during her hour off when she went out to the garden to see her father, he tried stumblingly to explain.

'I hope you don't think I'm – well, not – you know – friendly. It's just I don't want Gerty or Clara – they can be beasts—'

'It's all right, Master Davy.' Her smile was so warmly sympathetic it wrung his heart. 'I know what you're a-saying. I'm only a parlour maid, like. I know that. I hope you don't think I've been disrespec'-ful?'

'No, not at all!' he answered quickly. His face was hot. He had a sudden, startling urge to throw himself into her arms, to hug her tightly, even though she'd probably box his ears when she'd recovered from her surprise. 'You've always been – so nice.'

'And you'll always be a young gentleman to me. I know my place, Master Davy, I really do!'

He swallowed the lump in his throat, and blinked rapidly, dismayed at the unexpected pricking of tears. He recalled vividly the words she had said those months ago, when the trouble with Miss Marshall and Gerty had first erupted. 'Life's not very fair.' He reflected on their bitter truth as he turned away sadly from her.

Enid's fourth surviving child was born in the summer of 1910, on the last day of August, ten weeks after Gertrude's fourteenth birthday and three weeks before David's tenth. A serious heart defect made it certain that the infant, a tiny girl, would not live long. In fact, she clung to her fluttering, irregular life for three months, and long enough to be christened Olwyn Elizabeth. The branches of the trees around the churchyard were a skeletal black, dripping, their stripped leaves a dark, soggy mould underfoot. A cold, damp mist shrouded them when baby Olwyn gave up the struggle.

David was taken in with the others, trying not to show his fear, to see the delicate waxen doll laid out on a narrow bed of white silk and ruffled lace in her tiny coffin, on the sideboard in the morning room. Her skin was almost transparent, her closed, dark eyelids glistening.

When they came out and were alone back in the nursery, David burst into an anguished sobbing. 'It's nuh – not fair!' he gasped.

Helen was damp-eyed herself as she tried to comfort him. 'She's gone up to Jesus, Master Davy.'

'You're such a baby!' Gerty exclaimed disgustedly. 'A bigger baby than poor Olwyn. What are you snivelling for? You heard papa. It's a merciful release. She should never have been born alive. She wasn't. Not properly!'

As usual, he had no defence against her harsh attack. In some strange way, he felt she was right, and that his tears were yet another shameful sign of his feebleness, but he could not help himself. As she grew older, and in his eyes more beautiful, Gerty remained as spiteful and as dictatorial towards him as ever. After Miss Marshall's sudden disappearance, their father had decided to have no further truck with governesses. Instead he engaged a newly appointed curate to a nearby parish to come in as tutor. Mr Calderfield, a plump, unworldly young man whose pink cheeks bloomed with childlike innocence, was malleable enough in Clara's twelve-year-old hands, and David shuddered to think how Gerty would have ladied it over him if she had still been taking lessons with them. Meanwhile, David strove to glean what lean pickings he could from the curate's efforts. He knew better than to complain, and at least there were few ructions in the schoolroom these dreary days.

Their father absented himself for long periods again, often return-ing home from the city only at weekends, sometimes not even then, while, after the baby's death, their mother seemed almost totally withdrawn from the life around her. She kept to her room, leaving the capable Mavis and the cook, Mrs Hewson, to run the house and the children, who were, apart from the few hours at lessons, left largely to their own devices. Davy was cheered by the sight of Nelly's warm grin about the place, and tried to snatch conversation with her whenever he could, but her work, and Mavis's sharp eyes, kept her busy from morn until night. And Davy had learnt to be wary of letting his sisters see how he felt towards her.

Days went by, weeks, seasons. Sometimes a series of days would pass without them catching a glimpse of their mother at all, for they were no longer summoned for an audience with her after tea. On the rare occasions when his father was home, life became something of a nightmare for David. Sunday lunch was the greatest ordeal. The children dined with their parents. His mother sat like a ghost. Her face had sharpened, the flesh had fallen from her, she had nothing to say to anyone. Her replies to the few questions launched at her like little bullets from her husband at the other end of the table were dry, rustling whispers, which induced in David a savage urge to cover his ears to avoid hearing the sound.

'Come to the stables after lunch, David. I want to take you riding.'

David stared at his father, his heart racing with fear. He wanted to speak, but he was dumb. A year ago, the carriages had all been replaced with the motor. Now, only a couple of horses remained, and the ponies. Gerty and Clara had, a long time ago, taken some interest in them, had gone out riding, leaving him behind. He detested the smell of the animals; the heavy odour of the dung, and the urine tainted straw, the rank sweat. Lewis, the groom, and the stable lads all stank of it, too.

'I don't know – I haven't . . .' Davy wheezed, his terror forcing the words out.

'Exactly! Good God, boy! How old are you now?' His father had to repeat the question before David could stammer out an answer. 'Coming up twelve! And you can't even sit a horse yet! You're a pansy, boy! Is that what you want?'

Davy hung his head, his face partly hidden by the ringlets of his dark gold hair. The thin shoulders shook as he wept. He heard his mother clear her throat, as if speaking was somehow painful for her. Again the dry whisper, and his father snarled her into silence. 'Look at him! He's as much of a girl as his sisters! That's what you've turned him into. Or perhaps that was your intention all along?'

It was every bit the nightmare he had envisaged. He stared at the unfamiliar clothing: the hacking jacket, the corded jodhpurs and gleaming boots. He had no idea where they had come from, could only surmise miserably that his father had planned this, had procured the clothes in advance, for he had never seen them before. Though approximately his size, they were a poor, loose fit.

To his surprise, and initial comfort, it was Nelly who came to assist him after both Gerty and Clara had left, with cries of glee. He was too frightened to feel ashamed or embarrassed at her seeing him stripped to his vest and drawers and thick socks. She helped him into his gear. All at once, he burst out sobbing again. 'I can't! I'm scared, Nelly!'

'Oh, my love! Come 'ere!' He felt himself enveloped, crushed against the buttoned front of her dress, and her stiff pinafore, and he flung his arms gratefully around her waist. He could feel the soft, cushioning embrace of her bosom, and it distracted him powerfully, if only momentarily, from his grief. 'Be a brave boy – for me, Master Davy. You got to go through with it. Don't you let 'em see you're afraid. Come on, now. You'd better go.'

Her hands were gentle on his shoulders, and he released his frantic hold on her. He saw that her blue eyes were awash with tears, too, and he felt a great sense of gratitude and tenderness for her. He nodded and gulped. 'I'll try,' he promised.

He did, but he failed. His father made him get up on Monty, a sturdy hunter whose broad back seemed as tall as a building. Davy clung there, leaning ignominiously forward, frozen with his fear. He could carry out none of the commands necessary to make the patient animal move. His father, mounted also on his own horse, led him out of the yard. Davy tried his utmost, but his fear was clamped on him like irons.

'Well, if you want to act like a girl, we'll treat you like one. You, boy!' John gestured at a stable boy, scarcely bigger or older than David. 'Get up behind him. Show him what to do.'

'Yes, sir!' The boy scrambled agilely up, squirmed into position behind Davy, thrust against him by the confines of the saddle. Davy could feel the thighs, the knees, fitting into his, feel the body pressed close to him, the arms encircling him from behind, taking hold of his thin wrists, guiding them to the reins as though he were a baby, moving his limbs in the mechanics of control. The boy's chin rested on his shoulder, his breath warmed his neck, the lips tickled his ear. 'Dig in, Master. Just flick the rein, like that. Talk to him easy, see?'

They moved slowly along the path to the gate out into the pasture. The stable lad's body curled round him, thrust more intimately against him because of the horse's movement. Davy felt a weakness that was almost shamefully pleasant. His spine collapsed, the muscles of his slender frame seemed to dissolve. He leaned back against the boy, surrendered to the spoon shape holding him, the arms about him, the warmth of the breath on his cheek.

A few minutes later, back in the stable yard, the boy had to help him down, clutching him around his waist as Davy slid down into his arms, his own flung over the boy's thin shoulders in the coarse shirt.

'Well, Miss! A fine performance! Your sisters have more spunk in them than you'll ever have! Unless we can knock some into you! Over here!'

Davy whimpered as John Herbert plucked him by the lapels of the jacket and hung him over the bars of the nearest stall. The coat's cutaway flap was tossed up, exposing his backside. His father's crop made a sharp whistling disturbance as it cut through the air to land fierily across the proffered rump. Even through the stretched, thick material of the britches the pain was flaringly intense, a thin, burning agony that made Davy jerk and scream. Only his father's grip held him down as, under the gaze of the stable hands, he was whipped until his behind scorched with the torment inflicted on him, and he begged abjectly for an end to his suffering.

John Herbert stemmed the regurgitating anger at the boy's snivelling tears and the smothered sniggers of his sisters, as he felt the thin, trembling body under his grip. He snipped relentlessly, and the rich curls fell all about those shaking shoulders, and onto the carpet of the morning room. Let the public circumstances of the boy's shame be a further lesson to him, just as the flogging in the yard had been.

Coming up thirteen and still the milksop he had always been. By God, he should never have allowed Enid to influence him so much when the boy was young. He should have been sent away to school years ago before he grew in this namby-pamby fashion. Well, it was not too late, even now. He would go to school, to Riponcourt, in September. They'd lick him into shape there, all right. Make a man of him, as they had his father. Even if they had to flay the skin off his backside to do so!

The ticking of the clock on the dresser plucked at David's stretched nerves. He stood there in the haze of the mote-laden shafts of sunlight pouring through the long windows at the end of the first floor landing. The faint sounds drifting up from the distant kitchen served only to highlight the overall silence of the brooding house. He stood, listening intently. This late August heat was enervating. It pressed visibly down on him, making the thick stuff of his clothing, the heavy woollen knee socks, the Norfolk jacket and the knicker-bockers, the heavy boots, cling with oppressive stickiness to him.

The costume was obligatory for the shooting practice he had just been forced to endure, under Mr Bolton's scornful tutelage. Davy hated, was terrified of, the heavy shotgun, the fearful noise it made, the brutal kicking of it against his frail shoulder and ineffective grip. 'Reckon you'd be hard put to hit the side of a barn, Master Davy!' Bolton told him contemptuously, before dismissing him. It was only because of his absent father's strict orders that these wretched daily lessons were taking place.

Gerty and Clara had gone off somewhere in the car. Mama was, as always, in her room, which was just behind him as he stood there on the landing. But she would not make an appearance, of that he could be sure. She wouldn't emerge until this evening, to take a turn around the garden before eating alone in her room again.

He caught a glimpse of his pale face in the mirror over the dresser. Involuntarily, his palm shot up to smooth his newly shorn hair. He felt the softness of it, in spite of the close crop. Reeman, who liked to think of himself as the 'butler', even though the household was not grand enough to warrant such a title, and who was more realistically

John Herbert's personal manservant, the masculine equivalent of Mavis's role with Mrs Herbert, had tidied it up, after David's father's brutal severing of his locks. Reeman cut hair for some of the staff, female as well as male, Nelly had told him. Davy turned his head to the side. Though it looked strange still, he had to admit that Reeman had made quite a good job of it. He was sad to lose his long tresses, but at least it would be one less thing to worry about when he started school in two weeks.

At the thought, he felt his belly churn with the fear of what lay ahead. What little contact he had had with the stable lads and garden boys, and those of the village, had convinced him long ago that he was not equipped to deal with such a rough and ready species. Now, the idea of going away from home, of living day and night with hundreds of such creatures, made him almost faint with dread at the prospect. His rioting thoughts were full of desperate alternatives, such as running away, or causing himself some fearful injury, which would make such a move impossible. But of course they remained only thoughts. He trembled and left it at that.

His heart thumping, as loud, it seemed, as the clock, he moved on, powerless to control his steps. His sweating hand rested on the handle of Gerty's room. He slipped quickly inside and closed the door behind him. At once, his nostrils were filled with her sweet scent. It hung dizzily in the air. He lifted her hairbrush. The coils of thick, bronze hair clung to its bristles. He moved to her wardrobe, turned the key in its lock and eased the door open. He gathered one of her flounced dresses, pressed it to his face, breathing against its cool smoothness.

Gerty was a young lady now. She scarcely recognized his existence. Even Clara had recently reached that mysterious state of being 'grown up', a process he gathered was steeped in mystery, vastly different from that of boys. Neither of them took much note of him now, they had grown distant and remote, whispered together. He was excluded from their world and, in spite of the tyranny they had always exerted over him, he found this exclusion hurt him. And now he was to be banished altogether from them, and from the familiarity of this small, secluded world he had lived his entire life in.

He held the gown close, clutched it to his face and felt his tears wet on the silky material. In a swoon of weak delight, he breathed her fragrance, and a spasm of pure physical pleasure shook through him, a quiver of sensation that left him soft and weeping in the silence of the heavy, sun-drenched afternoon.

CHAPTER SEVEN

'**Y**OU'RE absolutely mad, darlin'! You know that? I'd a been up and off ages ago! Girl with your looks. Your posh voice and education! There's lots of old codgers what'd treat you like a first class lady. Not like that sick bastard!' Clemmy Lucas nodded at the fading bruises, pale yellow and misty blues now.

As Sophie wrapped the towel about her arms and shoulders and thus hid the offending flesh from view, she thought ironically of how appalled she would have been three years ago at the very idea of any other person, of either sex, seeing her so exposed. Now, it was only the evidence of John Herbert's roughness on her tender skin that drew from her even the slightest tinge of reticence, and that not from any notion of modesty, but rather from the glaring proclamation it made of her subservience towards him.

She never thought of him in terms of his Christian name alone, even after all this time, when he knew so well every inch, every curve and hollow and mark of her surrendered body as well as she knew his. And why not, when he owned her entirely? There were times when she felt he possessed her mind and its troubled thoughts as conclusively as he possessed her compliant flesh.

At first, when the shame and disgrace had fallen upon her, she had submitted to all the degradations he had heaped on her in a kind of numb horror: the brutal examination to confirm the fact that she was in the early stages of pregnancy, and the swift harsh measures to ensure its termination, which had left her wretched and ill and unfitting even to serve as his concubine for some time. He made good his word to keep her disgrace secret, fabricating a fictitious employment for her family, and ensuring that the regular stipend she had sent to her home should continue. But he left her alone, in a totally alien world, in the two shabby rooms at the top of the terraced house just off Ebury Street, amid the grime of countless smoking chimneys. The rest of the rooms below seemed to be occupied by young women, too. It gave her a kind of bitter amusement to think back now on her staggering naïvety, but she had had no idea what these girls did, nor the role of the fat, middle aged landlady, Mrs Evans, who lived on the ground floor. The girls, rough and uneducated for the most part, befriended the hapless stranger. The buxom blonde, Clemmy Lucas, in particular, had taken her under her wing, until soon, the despairing Sophie came to realize that she had no closer friend in the whole of her confined world.

In those early days, Sophie had thought of death as an escape, many times. When he left her to lie weeping in the befouled and tumbled bed, she dwelt on it, envisaged ways of doing it, tried to imagine the final peacefulness of it. In vain. She was too afraid. It was too great a sin. Somehow she thought she might yet find a way to atone for her sinfulness. She was young, the spark of life enfeebled but not spent. But still her shame and her guilt tormented her. She would lie, still sore from his use of her, writhing at the ultimate disgrace of her own treacherous body's complicity in the evil they practised; the perverted skill he used upon her helpless frame to rouse her to ungovernable excitement, the final scourge of his quiet chuckle after she lay shivering and weeping in its aftermath. 'You love it, don't you, my little whore?'

And she was, exactly that, just as Clemmy Lucas, and the other girls who inhabited the old house were, though Sophie was just one man's harlot. It lessened in no way the degree of her sin. The other girls seemed freer to her, bound as she was by his complete mastery over her. 'If your poor daddy could see you now, eh?' he would murmur as they sprawled naked, and the weight of his words were like a slave's chains about her slender person. She would sob bitterly, until she could no longer weep, then rise and clean herself, striving to wash away the stain of him from her in the chipped enamel bowl she placed on a towel in the middle of the floor.

The bowl she picked up and carried now to the washstand, where she finished drying herself, comfortable under Clemmy's gaze. 'He doesn't even keep you in decent togs!' Clemmy declared, eyeing the plain underwear, and the black, darned stockings.

It was true. These days he gave her hardly any money. He liked to have her ask, to beg, for every penny. Not that she needed it. Her food and lodgings were paid for, supervised by the corpulent Mrs Evans whom, for all her easy humour, Sophie looked upon as her gaoler and Mr Herbert's faithful spy. For a long time she had actually been confined to her room and the tiny recess that served as a kind of kitchen on the landing, and locked in at night, just like the prisoner she felt she was. Only gradually had she been granted a greater amount of freedom, to fraternize with the other occupants, and eventually to accompany some of them on their walks around the neighbourhood, when they were 'off duty'. Mrs Evans maintained the fiction that she was innocent of any underhand activity. 'I only rents them rooms, dearie,' she said challengingly, her hard eyes daring Sophie to contradict her. 'What they gets up to when they're entertainin' their guests I have no idea. Of course, *you're* different, ain't you, my dear? Your gentleman is very particular about what you does. He looks after you proper, he does. You're a lucky gal an' no mistake!'

She was 'lucky' again, that very evening, for he came visiting. After the prolonged and turbulent bout of their intimacy, she stood again at the washstand, and when she turned, after her hasty ablutions, he stared with pleasure at her down turned eyes, showing the long, flickering curl of her lashes, and the rose-tint stain rising from her slim neck, which gave him a quivering after-thrill of delight. He thrilled, too, to her passiveness as she drew a wrap over her nakedness and stood waiting, an indication of how completely he had broken her to his will. She was completely his creature. 'You remember your charges back home? Your golden haired little angel, young Davy?' He saw her glance up, her shame temporarily forgotten in the new tension he could feel as well as see. 'Those lovely long golden ringlets he wore, that made him look more like a darling little girl than a boy?' He smiled sadistically. 'The last of the litter – and the runt!'

He pushed away the stinging reminder of his lie, the tiny coffin with the waxen doll they had buried, three years ago now. 'The little milksop is thirteen. He's off to school. Who knows? They might even make a man of him yet!'

Davy stood there, in the foggy steam which belied the shivering cold wetness of the bathroom, with its streaming, rough stone floor. The three high sided tubs stood companionably in a row, with the communal shower stall a few yards behind them. He hunched forward, shivering and weeping, his hands cupped over the offending member, until his thin wrists were plucked away and his shame exposed.

'Tom Thumb!' someone sniggered.

'No! He's far too pretty for a Tom! And that tiny excrescence is miniscule! How about Thumbelina?'

And Thumbelina he became, or Thumbs for short, in the merciless exposure of that chilly bathhouse, pinned on a rack of public shame which would scarcely leave him during the interminable two years that were to follow. He learned the art of survival painfully and slowly. He learned like any coquette to plead his lack of boyishness, to trade on his softness in that hard growing masculine world; so that, eventually, he became tolerated by many with an almost affectionate contempt. There were one or two others like him, which made his life only slightly easier. He still had to fend for himself, despite a few whispered intimacies and shared tears of understanding.

The staff, too, had to be dealt with, their bullying more subtle but often crueller than that of his fellow pupils. And there were other, stranger relationships, whose complexities David only half grasped yet was able to negotiate with some almost instinctive part of his nature. His assistant housemaster, Mr Gregory, became his protector, frequently rescued him from the more brute tyranny of sadistic boys. But at a price.

'We must somehow endeavour to make more of a man of you,' Mr Gregory would say, the dark eyes staring piercingly, while David lowered his gaze and blushed. At a nod from the slight figure, David would bend over the small table until his chest and stomach rested on its surface, forming a right angle with his straight and quivering legs. His hands would grip the far edge of the table, his chin rest on his taut knuckles. He would feel Mr Gregory lift his pupil's coat tail, fold it over his bent back, and Davy would tense for the fiery strokes which would follow.

But not too soon. There would be what to Davy always seemed to be a long interval of silence while he lay there. Then Mr Gregory would come round to his lowered head, and place against his right cheek a large white handkerchief, soaked in a dizzying perfume, both pungent and fragrant, which, in far less penetrating quantity, could be faintly and habitually discerned about Mr Gregory's person. The aroma would fill Davy's senses, make his head swim with its dizzy, rapturous power. Then, and only then, would come the swishing blows, the sharp, thin cuts, so that burning pain and reeling pleasure fused, and he would gasp and flinch and bury himself desperately in that cloying sweetness until the blaze of pain was over, and only the steady throbbing remained.

There were boys, too, usually senior to David, who would, in exchange for his subservience towards them, offer him protection and even a certain amount of affection. So he learned this art of survival, in a world which nevertheless remained detestably alien to him, offending his sensibilities in countless ways.

He was the same age as the century when the outbreak of war brought into even more prominence the inculcation of those manly virtues which now prioritised killing and being killed for one's country. Boys flocked to join the 'Corps', to put on khaki, and to drill, and handle the heavy service rifles, so that Davy and the few of similarly unmanly demeanour became even more odd. After a year of slaughter, the nation's thirsty desire for more of the same had in no way abated, and David was glad when the long summer holiday came round again, and he could look forward to the comparatively peaceful, quiet sanity of his home for ten blessed weeks.

The jostling boys cheered loudly at the sight of the ranks of self-conscious, grinning men, who made an awkward attempt to march in some semblance of formation onto the narrow station platform.

They were led by a single khaki clad figure, of advancing years, with three stripes on his sleeve. His prominent cheekbones, and the droop of his grey moustache curving down the sides of his chin, added to his air of resigned gloom, in great contrast with the group of new recruits. Their civilian clothing emphasized the mixture of backgrounds. There were several dark suits and stiff collars, one or two bowler hats, though the majority of the headgear consisted of cloth cap or straw boater. Many were in coarse rural garb, with collarless shirts and moleskin or corded trousers.

Though the war had been raging for a year now, and had already consumed so many young men, there was no dearth of eager volunteers, as this latest batch indicated. 'Well done, lads!' the boys of Riponcourt yelled, and waved their striped and tasselled caps aloft in encouragement.

The end of term meant that the normally quiet country halt was flooded with their numbers. Their boxes and trunks were piled high at one end of the platform, and cases and grips, with an assortment of tennis racquets, cricket bats, or canvas shrouded fishing rods attached to them, littered the rest of the floor space, as the noisy clusters of pupils stood about waiting for the train to carry them to the mainline terminus. When it came, there was a scrum around every carriage doorway, while the station porters and the guard bellowed for order. Somehow, the seething mass forced its way into the first class carriages at the front of the train. Each compartment was packed, with some boys standing in the narrow space between the bench seats, straddling the luggage between their feet.

David closed his eyes against the pungent swirl of humanity enveloping him, and prayed for the locomotive to jerk into motion, for the uncomfortable journey to be over, for him to be safely delivered for an almost unimaginably heavenly two months from the boisterous crudity which surrounded him. It astonished him to reflect that he had somehow survived two years at Riponcourt, that he had in some ways become inured to many of its discomforts and worse.

A raucous voice called out, 'Hey, Thumbelina? What are you going to be doing for the war effort in the hols? Knitting comforts for the troops?'

There was a burst of laughter. 'You don't have to knit the kind of comforts Thumbelina has in mind for the Tommies, eh, Thumbs?'

'No! He wants to be a VAD, don't you, Thumbs, darling? Wear a pretty uniform and stroke the fevered brows of the wounded. Sit and hold their hands – or something!'

To David's alarm, the taunts built to more threatening proportions. It was on just such occasions, when spirits were roused to abnormal pitch, by the start of the holidays, and in such public gatherings, that the greatest danger lurked. The general air of excitement and uncertainty the troubled times had brought increased the danger even more.

Eager hands reached up and pulled him down into the forest of limbs, stretched him on the dirty floor. His shrill cries of protest were drowned by the buffeting noise all around him. In seconds, the 'scragging' was completed, his clothes ripped and hauled off his limbs, over his head, until he was left in nothing but his short summer drawers. His kicking form was tossed aloft by those eager hands until he almost touched the curving roof and, to his disbelieving terror, he felt a sudden rush of cold air, the slipstream tearing at his feet and legs as they were passed through the open window.

He screamed in sheer horror as the hands clawed at him, thrusting him through the narrow aperture. The breath was torn from him and he hung there, his pale body spread like a star against the wooden surface, held only by the imprisoning hands which he prayed sobbingly now would not let him go. The rush of air swept over him, and then a blinding, choking, soot infested cloud of smoke. He was scarcely aware any longer of what was happening in his utter panic. He found himself lying curled in a shivering, sobbing bundle on the floor again, his knees to his chest, his hands about his shoulders, gasping and coughing, his lungs full of the engine's smoke, his face and body grimed like a chimney sweep with it.

'All right, you brave and doughty warriors. You've had your fun! Now where's his clothes? Get them quick, or I swear I'll scrag some of you to make up any deficit!'

There was a yelp of pain as a stinging hand shot out and cuffed the nearest head. Bodies collided as Davy's tormentors sought to distance themselves from the strong avenging arm reaching out to them. Sam Ellington, cricket and rugger captain, and deputy head boy, was exercising his last authority as a senior. His prowess on the games field had earned him adulation. His modest and quietly contained manner had cost him, some said, the post of Head of School, a post which many vociferously asserted he should have occupied during the past year. With typical diffidence, Sam insisted he was quite content with his rank of deputy and that, as far as Head of School went, 'the best man' had got the job. All of which served to confirm the universal opinion that he was without doubt 'an all-round good egg'.

The pupils of Riponcourt, including Davy, were glad to hero-worship him. He never courted popularity, and though he didn't seek the limelight, there was something about him, apart from his athletic prowess, a quiet strength, which marked him as a leader and one who would achieve much. Although he could have stayed on an extra year at Riponcourt before going up to Cambridge – and perhaps attained the most senior pupil rank after all – characteristically, he had cut short his academic career to take up military duties. He would soon be serving as a junior subaltern in an infantry regiment.

Davy was both dazedly grateful and amazed at Ellington's dramatically timely intervention on his behalf. The senior thrust Davy's bundled clothing at him, and ordered him abruptly to get dressed. 'Cut along to the lavatory and get yourself cleaned up,' he advised Davy brusquely, seeing the runnels caused by tears on the soot streaked face gazing worshipfully up at him.

David's emotions would have been doubly roused had he known how Sam was feeling as he watched the slender form depart through the ranks of the now shamefaced pupils. That face, those delicate features! So unnervingly like those which had fixed themselves so vividly in Sam's consciousness, which had sweetly haunted his dreams and so many of his waking moments over the past term. Ever since he had caught his first glimpse, and become firmly smitten, by the beauty of the enchanting Miss Herbert, who had accompanied her father to the Founder's Day celebrations and the dance held that memorable evening in the school hall.

He had even touched her, held her exquisite gloved hand, while the other rested on his shoulder and his own reclined decorously at her silken waist. He had stumbled round in tongue tied, hot faced silence, furious with himself at his inability to speak, let alone shine, while she had gazed politely over his shoulder, and no doubt thought what a surly oaf he was. Until, that is, she forgot all about him five minutes later.

It had startled Sam that such an effete wart as Herbert should have an angel for a sister. He had scarcely spoken to the sprog, for he was already a fifth year monitor and member of the first fififteen when Herbert joined the school. But after he had fallen under Gertrude Herbert's spell, he found himself surreptitiously studying young Thumbs, noting his innate gracefulness, acknowledging, with a secret sense of shame, the youngster's remarkable beauty. He had acted without thinking, springing to the aid of the hapless Thumbs – like a knight to the rescue of a fair damsel . . . he thrust the burgeoning comparisons from his reluctant mind.

CHAPTER EIGHT

SAM waited beyond the barrier, enduring the handshakes, the backslapping and urgent good wishes of the other pupils as they streamed by him, until he saw the slim, still bedraggled figure making its lonely way down the platform under the high vault of the station's roof. 'I say — Thumbs — er—' Sam strove to recall Herbert's Christian name. His cheeks flushed at his failure. 'You all right now? Got everything?'

Davy seemed not in the least offended by Sam's use of his nickname. Indeed, the sensitive face was pink with the thrill of being singled out by his hero, whom he had long admired from very far. He stammered in his shy pleasure and excitement. 'Yes – I'm – it's fine, honestly. I'd like to thank you – it was wonderful – what you – sticking up for me.' The long fair eyelashes fluttered as Davy murmured with disarming candour, 'I was absolutely terrified. I really thought they were going to let me go.'

Sam frowned, shook his head. 'Idiots! I'm sorry I didn't get there sooner. Listen.' He glanced around in faint hope. 'Your folks not meeting you?'

Davy shook his head. 'I have to catch another train. The branch line to Willerby. Essex. We live not far from there.'

Sam reached over, took Davy's brown suitcase from him. Unlike most of the others, there were no sporting items attached to it. 'Here. Let me get that for you.' Sam flushed again, suddenly struck by the oddness of what he had done, but Davy surrendered it, pinking with delight, his heart skipping a beat at the gallantry of the gesture. He felt giddy now with rapture that Sam Ellington of all people should be squiring him like this. And at the tall figure's next words, he almost quivered visibly with joy. 'Look, have you time for a drink? I mean lemonade or tea or something? I've got masses of time myself.' He was blushing a little, too, and felt impelled to add, 'I've got to make sure you get off home safely. I remember meeting your folks. Your father, at Founder's Day.' There was the slightest pause. 'And your sister. Gertrude, isn't it?'

'That's right!' The brown eyes widened with further astonished happiness that Sam should recall his family. 'She's lovely, isn't she?' His ingenuous admiration startled Sam, who could only nod, and murmur his acquiescence with the boy's statement.

It was as well the school blazer identified them, for they were a greatly contrasting pair. Sam was a head taller than Davy. His hair was dark and was cropped short about his neck and ears, swept back in tight waves from his brow, unlike Davy's soft, dark golden unruly curls, which, because it was the end of term and through Mr Gregory's Nelsonian blind eye, were clustered thickly about his stiff collar. The taller figure's athleticism was evident even in the clothing he wore, so different from Davy's frail looking slimness.

David could hardly believe in the reality of his sitting across the table from the handsome, smiling fellow he had so often peeked at with hidden adoration. He found his cheeks reddening yet again as he thought of Ellington seeing him unclothed and helplessly captive like that, even though he had doubtless observed his naked frame numerous times in the showers or the rough and tumble of bath nights, when thirty or more boys shared the swiftly scummy, grey water in the three tubs. A duty monitor always supervised the boys on such occasions. And, unlike that of most of his contemporaries, Sam Ellington's presence ensured that the horseplay prevalent in the bathhouse was kept within reasonable limits.

'How *is* your sister?' Sam asked presently, with an awkward attempt to sound casual, which did not at all fool the perceptive Davy.

'Gertrude, you mean? I have another sister. Clara. She's seventeen now.'

'No, no — I mean it was Gertrude I met . . .'

Davy was well aware of Sam's embarrassment, and was well

aware of its cause. His own heart was smitten with a strange admixture of sudden, sinking disappointment and spontaneous pride in Sam's appreciation of Gerty's beauty. 'She should have come out last year, but with the war.' He smiled wryly as he recalled the fury, the simmering resentment and stormy tantrums. 'She was quite put out at missing the season. All the balls and things.'

'Please give her my regards when you get home. She won't remember me, I'm sure, but we had a dance at the Founder's Day. And I hope your mother is fully recovered now. She couldn't attend, I recall.'

'Mama never goes anywhere nowadays,' Davy said. But then he added, 'I'm sure Gerty *will* remember you. She remarked on how handsome you were. She'd already noticed you in the match against the Old Boys.'

Sam's eyes widened suddenly, and the colour flooded up once more into his face at the embarrassing fervour of Davy's remark. He seemed completely at a loss how to answer, and all at once Davy felt a deep surge of tender affection for his idol. And suddenly much closer, too, on a level of intimacy he would never have dreamed possible mere hours ago.

'What is she doing now? Is she still at home? Or at college or anything? I mean – with the war and everything—' Sam's face was growing redder by the second. He floundered on, exuding embarrassment, yet unable to drop the subject which so fascinated him.

'Well, she's been helping with the war work in Willerby, of course. And she's talking of training to be a nurse. She wants to do her bit. If she can persuade papa.' A whimsical expression of regret passed over his dainty features. 'I expect she will. She's nineteen now.'

Sam nodded seriously. 'The war's upset so many lives.'

'When do you join up?' Davy felt constrained to ask, though he felt a fastidious distaste in discussing anything to do with the war.

Sam shrugged deprecatingly. He flashed a smile at Davy that sent the young heart bumping again. 'Next month some time, I think. I have to wait for an officers' training course to start.'

'They won't send you over there straight away, will they?' Davy's face betrayed his genuine anxiety. 'You have to be twenty, don't you?'

Again the shrug, and charming smile. 'If I wait that long, it might all be over before I get there. It depends how short of men they are. I've heard there are ways round it.' He quickly changed the subject, for which Davy was grateful, and moved with admiration.

They chatted on and on. To Davy's amazement, Sam seemed reluctant to end their conversation, and before too long his heart raced anew with a daring plan which was forming. 'Listen,' he said, his cheeks glowing, and his short breathed lisp becoming more evident in his anxiety. 'I hope you don't think I've got an infernal cheek and all that, but – would you consider coming down to our place for a few days? It's – rather nice – there's some decent shoot-ing. We've even got a couple of hunters left if you'd like to ride. I know my people would be delighted – and Gerty would be thrilled, I'm sure.'

Sam gazed at him with such an open glance of dawning pleasure that, once more, Davy felt that curious blend of tenderness and concern, as if he were at least as old and worldly wise as the young man smiling so dazzlingly opposite him.

'Come on, Master Davy! Have some of this pie, eh? You haven't eaten more'n a mouse!'

'No, thanks, Nelly. I'm not hungry.'

'You'll fade away if you don't eat more hearty,' the maid admon-ished him fondly, after first glancing round to make sure that none of the others could overhear her. But John Herbert was engrossed in his paper. He was sitting back in the low canvas camp chair, his legs spread wide, bare feet planted in the soft white sand. He had rolled his baggy old white flannels up to his knees, and his shins and ankles looked delicate and incongruously youthful, despite the long, fine dark hairs which stood out against the paleness.

Davy's dark golden curls flapped damply across his brow. The hair was still neat at the back of his slender neck. Nelly recalled the scathing tone of Mr Herbert that first breakfast of the holiday, which had resulted in Davy sitting on a low stool in the stable yard that very same day while his locks were sheared inexpertly all about him by Marion, the cook's assistant.

Reeman, the onetime amateur barber, had departed to join up months ago. In fact, the male staff, indoors and out, had been seriously depleted since the outbreak of the war, whose first anniversary had passed just a week ago, on 4 August. Not that Nelly was worried. Neither men nor boys, or the lack of them, bothered her very much. She was generally disgusted at the stupid fuss her contemporaries made over them, even those who were old enough to know better, including Miss Lah-di-dah Mavis Cockeridge, who was putting on all kinds of airs and graces now that she was practically running the whole household. Mavis was supposed to be walking out with a fellow who had been head footman over at Tynedale, a neighbouring estate, until he'd gone off and joined the colours, just after Christmas.

Nelly was glad that her dad was too old to be off. It was bad enough having to worry about her older brother, Joe, who was doing his training still, somewhere over in the west country, and who couldn't wait to be sent overseas to fight. She thought everyone had gone crazy this past year, the women almost as bad as the men. Even her ma went on about how proud she was of Joe, and how dashing he looked in his uniform. She'd paid for him to have a studio portrait taken in Willerby, and she had it mounted and framed, in pride of place on the dresser.

Mr Herbert was always chuntering on about how he wished he could be taken on, and that at forty-four he was 'more than fighting fit'. As it was, he spent more time than ever away from home, didn't even get back for weekends usually nowadays, with the war work he was involved in up in London. Poor Mrs Herbert. She was one of the very few who didn't seem caught up in it all. But then she scarcely knew or cared what year it was, never mind day, these days!

With a pang of compassion, Nelly followed the direction of Davy's gaze, to where the distantly small figures were splashing and yelling in the shallows near the black line of rocks. She could see the wistfulness in his gentle face, which, unobserved as he thought he was, he could not disguise. At least not to someone who knew him as well as she did.

'Why don't you go down an' and join 'em?' The words popped out before she could think, and she saw the characteristic tide of colour pink his lightly tanned features. The fair curls shook, then his eyes lifted, caught hers nakedly for a second, and she saw in their helpless luminosity all the pain, the inner suffering he strove to hide from everyone.

'They don't want me,' he murmured softly, shaking his head once more. He turned away from the distant figures, his head bent, shoulders, too, and trudged off up the beach. In the garish hoops of his bathing togs, his frame looked even slimmer and frailer than usual. She had a powerful urge to rush after him, to grab his arm, pull his head down to her breast, and she blinked back the prick of tears as she knelt and busied herself with gathering up the remnants of the picnic and stowing them in the hampers.

That bloody little cow! she thought mutinously as she worked. She wasn't happy till she had all the men young and old within miles of her twisted hopelessly round her little finger. The wonderful, high-and-mighty, fairest-of-them-all Miss Gerty Herbert! And that tongue-tied, foolish young oaf, Mr Sam, was her latest in the long line of conquests. Red faced, stammering, mooning after her like a sick calf. Another one who seemingly couldn't wait to enlist and get himself shot, or blown up!

But what angered her was that he had no time for Master Davy at all. Supposed to be his chum from school. Miss Gerty would never have met him if it hadn't been for her brother inviting him down here. Davy had been so pleased, and proud as punch of his new friend. Even Mr Herbert had been impressed, and pleased for once with his son. And now Miss Gerty had captured the young man and had him trailing round after her like a puppy dog, with no thought for anyone or anything else.

All right! Nelly had to admit to herself that it had struck her as odd, to say the least, as it had everyone else, that someone like young Mr Sam should be a special chum of Davy's. Talk about chalk and cheese. Mr Sam was grown up. Loved to ride, good shot, captain of the football and the cricket. Then of course the penny had dropped. Soon as she'd seen him that first time in Miss Gerty's company. He'd practically collapsed at her feet there and then – and no time for Master Davy at all, from that moment on. It made her blood boil.

And young missy had known right away. She'd twigged on at once, and loved every minute of it, loved especially cutting poor Davy out, rubbing his nose in it.

Again came that uncomfortable feeling when she thought of Davy's secret sadness, and she argued fiercely with her own sense of disloyalty to the boy. Why shouldn't he be hurt? Why shouldn't he have special feelings for someone like Mr Sam? He was a lovely looking lad – the kind any boy would look up to. And Davy was different, she wouldn't deny it. Gentle, soft — in looks and in nature. More like . . . a girl. Well! All right! So what? He'd no doubt grow out of it. Be forced to.

It was no different to herself, really. She didn't have any truck with lads, either up here at the house or in the village, couldn't abide their sniggering, oafish ways. She'd rather have someone as gentle and kind as her Master Davy was, even if others did think him odd!

As for Miss Gerty! She could well box those pretty ears of hers for her, try to knock some sense of decency into her – and some of that preening selfishness out of her. How many times had she just itched to do that since she had begun working at the house? The way she treated Davy, too! The disregard, the contempt! And him, poor lamb, not standing up to her at all, so ready to give in, taking all her nastiness without hitting back. Like now, watching her steal his friend from him.

But then she had always been, always would be, a spoilt little bitch. Nelly recalled the great song and dance she'd made a while back, just because some fancy petticoat had gone missing. She'd accused someone of pinching it. Nelly and all the other maids had had their rooms searched, the laundry room and everywhere else turned inside out, for one stupid frilly lace petticoat. A few days later it had turned up, screwed up in the bottom of one of the clothes baskets. And the little bitch had still said someone must've taken it and put it back again. She'd flung it out, refused ever to wear it again. God help those poor sick Tommies if she ever does finish this training course and gets to be a real nurse, Nelly reflected. They'll be cured double quick if she ever gets let loose upon them!

*

73

'Will you promise to write to me?' With a boldness that came purely from desperation, Sam Ellington reached out and took hold of Gertrude's cool hand, held on tightly to it. He had thought he would never have this treasured moment. Treasured but poignantly painful, too, for in less than three hours he would be leaving her, leaving this place. There was a consciousness of melodrama in the thought that he might never see it, or her, again. It embarrassed him, yet there was a romance in it which moved him powerfully.

He would not have believed he could fall so readily and so heavily in love. The first and only girl for him. Of that he was quite certain. He looked back now on his fascination with her after that brief dance on Founder's Day as on a nostalgic memory of childhood. How feeble that emotion had been compared with the torrent of love which surged through him now, after this also brief yet eternal week of happiness he had known. He knew each moment of the many they had shared must be stored up, held in his heart against the desolation of separation facing him.

That sense of urgency hovered at his shoulder now, mixed with the profound gratitude that a relenting God had after all vouchsafed this last minute opportunity. The chance he had thought miserably he should never have.

He had kissed her once, or tried to, on their way home from a walk through the woods north of the village. Clumsily, a hasty smack at her quickly turned cheek, after the dizzying pleasure of feeling her in his arms, his hands about her waist when he caught her, lifted her bodily as she stepped down from the stile. He thrilled to the touch, the feel of her hard, slim litheness, the thick stuff of her shirt tucked in tightly to her waist, above the broad navy leather belt which divided it from her dark, flaring skirt. 'Sam!' she had protested, outraged, according to her tone. But even in his hot confusion, he had seen the sparkle in her grey eyes, the cheeks flushed with plea-sure, and she hugged his arm tightly into her as they completed their journey.

I must tell her! he had urged himself so many times during those last hours relentlessly ebbing away. Tell her this is not some silly schoolboy crush. This is the real thing! But his shyness clamped him, sealed his lips, his hammering heart, while, almost cruelly (except that he could not think such unkind thoughts of her) she had mocked him with that gently teasing manner. 'I think you've been making sheep's eyes at Clara, you naughty boy! She's quite taken with you. Of course, she's such a beauty, isn't she? She'll be the toast of London when she comes out. So lovely! And still a schoolgirl! It's not fair!'

He had once again tried to tell her of his feelings, but again she evaded the issue, and he trailed miserably in her wake. But now, this morning, his bags already packed in his room, he was determined to snatch this reprieve from the gods that had led to their seclusion on the terrace. 'You know what I think of you!' he blurted, like a hero going over the top.

Her eyelids fluttered. 'Oh dear! Don't tell me! I'm sure it can't be complimentary.'

'I'm in love with you! I love you!' he amended with instinctive wisdom.

Gertrude was wise enough to know when to draw the line, as far as badinage went. Besides, her heart was racing, her stomach fluttering with the strength of his passion. 'We hardly know each other,' she whispered, suddenly meltingly soft. She stood very still, waiting.

'I know how I feel!' His face was close now, red still, working with emotion. His dark eyes blazed at her, and she shivered, deep inside herself, quivering with a sweet yet truly frightening sensation that, it seemed, was not part of her brain at all, but something deeper, more primitive, and physical, which gripped her, raw and damp and fiercely compelling. Her mouth opened, they kissed, worried and sawed at each other, and his tongue plunged into her, drowning her, engulfing her, so that it was dire necessity that made her arms come up to encircle his neck. Then she was thrusting herself madly against him, striving to crush herself against his hardness, all propriety forgotten at the flame of desire that wrapped itself hungrily about them.

PART II

A MAN'S WORLD

CHAPTER NINE

DAVY lay back in the water, let his knees and thighs fall slackly outward until his legs rested against the sides of the bathtub. He settled his shoulders more comfortably against the curve below them, rejoicing in the private solitude, sliding down until he was almost horizontal, his chin on his chest. He felt the quiver of sexual arousal, the beat of its tiny pulse stirring his flaccid penis in almost imperceptible movement. He studied it and the small tuft of brown hair, darkened and moss-like at his belly. He clenched his teeth, forced his hands to remain under the water, palms uppermost at his sides, still. He continued to regard his body, with its smooth, hairless skin, its delicate features of slender shapeliness.

He remembered the glossy photographic plate Mr Gregory had revealed to him, the heavy volume open on the master's desk, the light of the lamp falling on it, the statue of the breathtakingly beautiful figure, the realism of every smooth curve and plane, despite the cold hardness of the marble. *The Boy David*, Mr Gregory had told him, in his hushed, repressed voice. David had flushed at that shocking yet familiar nudity. Gregory's hand had fallen on his shoulder, the thin fingers pressing painfully upon his collar bone, holding him in some strange, encapsulated instant of intimacy as shocking as the nakedness they both gazed at. 'Beauty, my boy,' the whisper had continued at his ear. 'True beauty. Nothing to be ashamed of. Above our sullied world, Herbert. Far above. Never forget it in this human slaughterhouse we're creating.'

David recalled the lamp lit insulation of the room, the heavy black curtains, the stout wooden door closed, sealing them together in the stuffy, tiny interior. The strange, haunted look on the ascetic features, the carefully repressed sensualism that beat so stirringly beneath the surface.

Gregory was looking old; his hair, sparse on top now, was lank and long behind his ears, was streaked liberally with grey. It was as though Davy was noticing him for the first time. It would be the end of a long and extraordinarily intimate relationship. There were other boys, too, whom Gregory had singled out in this way. Befriended was hardly the right word. Davy had never mentioned it to another soul. And yet he had classified it rightly in applying the term intimate. It was probably the closest he had been involved with anyone during the whole of his four years at Riponcourt.

Gregory recognized the significance of this meeting, just as Davy did. If Davy returned – and already there was doubt, which he had expressed to the master – he would be in Lower Sixth. Hardly eligible for any more of the strange treatment Gregory meted out to him in these tête-à-têtes. There was something different about Gregory this time. Or so the hypersensitive Davy thought as soon as he entered and closed the door behind him. An added element of contained tension, confirmed when Gregory had motioned him over to the open book, and placed his hand on the boy's shoulder. 'We've known each other a long time, Herbert, have we not? I've tried to guide you along the path of righteousness, of decent standards, painful though that guidance has been. Don't you agree?'

'Yes, sir.' Davy tried not to tremble against the fierce intensity of the master's grip.

'You're leaving boyhood behind now. Approaching manhood.' His gaze seemed to direct Davy back to the picture pooled in the lamplight. 'You must be on your guard. You will face temptations. *Have* faced them, here, already, I think. There is a propensity in you, which you may not realize, David –' Davy was startled at this first use of his Christian name – 'to attract a certain . . . type of admiration, of an unhealthy, not to say deviant, nature . . .'

Davy thought of the endless jibes, and worse, he had endured, the insults, and more violent degradations, recalled the shame of that day two years ago, when he had been stripped, held crucified in the choking smoke to the wooden side of the train. Unbidden came the vision of Sam Ellington's dark beauty, the glow of his smile, the tenderness and longing which had filled so many of Davy's conscious and unconscious thoughts this past year. 'I'm not queer, sir, I swear!' He blurted out the words, his voice trembling on the brink of tears.

'You must be resolute. Resist temptation, at all times.' Both hands seized his shoulders, in a strange kind of embrace, then were gone. Mr Gregory swung abruptly away, nodding towards the table as he did so. 'Prepare yourself, my boy.'

There was only the slightest pause before Davy moved, in obedience to the time honoured ritual, bent in obeisance over the wooden surface, tensed his muscles to receive the beating.

David stirred, winced slightly in the cooling water, his buttocks still slightly sore, though the thin stripes had faded to a pale pink insignificance, in the week that had passed since the caning. He wondered if he could persuade his father not to force him to return to Riponcourt for another interminable year. He would soon be seventeen. He fervently hoped that pater would see the uselessness of making him endure another year, when he could study far better alone, to prepare himself for going up to university. Expense was Davy's most powerful argument, for his father was constantly pleading reduced circumstances since the war had dragged on for three years now.

His thoughts drifted on, turned inevitably towards Sam, and, equally inevitably, Gerty. The two were inextricably entwined in his brain, his heart rather, where the two of them reigned supreme, each the epitome of all that was beautiful in their sex. Sam had written four times in all, in the year he had been away overseas. Short notes, never more than one sheet, deprecatingly self mocking, joshing. The affectionate tone of an elder brother. Davy knew every word.

Thank you for your latest literary epistle, Sam would write. Davy would detect the implication of embarrassment in the jocular phrasing. Davy wrote reams – he had to discipline himself not to post more than one letter a fortnight, though scarcely a night would pass when he did not snatch time to scribble at least a few lines. Embarrassed or not, he felt sure Sam derived a strong comfort from his writing, from the home world trivial intimacies he strove to create for him. *Better go. Snoopy Mirren is on duty tonight and the midnight oil is spluttering. 'Night and God bless.* He probably wrote more than Gerty, damn her, even though Sam was hopelessly in love with her. Though it caused Davy acute pangs of what he guessed with dismay must be jealousy, he hoped for Sam's sake that when she *did* write, her words were as ardent as Sam would wish for.

His heart began to beat more agitatedly at the direction of his thoughts, and he stood and dried himself quickly, drained out the water. He peppered his body with the light floral scent of talcum powder, slipped on his robe and let himself out of the bathroom. The house had its ticking, deserted air. After the awful noise and relentless non-privacy of Riponcourt, he revelled in the lonely stillness. Compelled by a force he could not resist, he went to Gerty's room, shut himself in. He found the key on her dresser, slipped it in the door and turned it, locking himself in the fragrant sanctuary.

She was away in London. She came home once a month now, if that. His mouth twitched in an involuntary smile, half admiration, half admonition, as he recalled the ending of her training to be a VAD, and the brief storm it had caused in the household. She had got no further than the local hospital in Willerby. 'Wiping up vomit and worse besides! Scrubbing out stinking lavatories on my knees!' Her voice had shaken with disgust, her fiery copper hair, pinned on top, had trembled with her incredulous indignation. 'How on earth can such peasants' work help to win the war?'

He had felt for her, yet part of him had derived a mean satisfaction from the very notion of her performing such menial tasks. Papa had been angry of course, especially at the scathing tone of the letter he had received from the matron of the hospital: *Your daughter is a thoroughly spoilt and undisciplined young lady who has far too elevated an opinion of both her rank in society and her value as a person in this troubled world.* But, of course, she had got round him, gone off instead to learn to drive an ambulance, which she had been doing for some months now, ferrying the endless stream of wounded officers from the mainline rail termini, and even from the Channel ports on occasion. And very fetching she looked, too, in the dark green uniform she wore the last time he had seen her, almost three months ago, at the beginning of term.

He was speared by guilt as his eye caught the small photograph of Sam, framed by its dark embossed leather, which stood at one side of her dressing table. He fancied he could read shocked and sad accusation in that soulful, dark eyed gaze, in spite of the reflective smile on those features, which sent, stronger than his guilt, a shaft of love and anxiety through Davy's tender heart.

Davy stared at his pale reflection in the mirror, then sat on the cushioned stool, feeling the caress of its soft surface through the thin robe. His hands moved with shameful, practised knowledge to the drawer, the second, deeper one on his left, drew it open, lingered sensuously over the silken daintiness of its contents before they sought out under the fragrant garments the solid wooden box hidden at the back. He pulled it out, searched again, this time along the narrow ledge at the top right of the drawer, to find the small black key.

His fingers shook as he fitted it into the lock. His heart was still racing. Yes, the pile of letters, mostly in the special envelopes denoting HM Forces, was much thicker than when he had last invaded here. His fingers flicked nimbly through. The most recent lay as he had expected nearest the front of the carved box. There were at least six which he had not seen before, all with her London address on – she must have brought them up with her on her last visit. Goodness knows how many more there were, so Sam was an equally prolific correspondent, though not to him. At least she was keeping them, treasuring them he hoped as *he* would. Evidence that his friend really did mean something to her.

Friend? that taunting voice mocked inside him. He was never your friend, you simple fool! He was already smitten with Gerty. You were the only way he could ever get to her. And get to her he has! He remembered the way Gerty had teased him the last time they had met, before he had left for the new term.

'Oh, don't worry, my little brother! I'm in touch with your darling Sam all right! We met up in London just after he finished his training at Oakshott. That's when he gave me that photograph. My! He's handsome in his uniform, isn't he? No wonder you've got such a crush on him, Davy.' She had stared levelly at him as she added, 'He's not the tongue-tied schoolboy he was when you first brought him to me.'

The recall of it eased the sting of his guilt. Until he began eagerly to devour the close written contents of the letters held in his trembling hand. Their passionate truth gnawed at him. He had no idea how long he had been sitting there, scanning page after page, when the door rattled and he heard a voice cry out. He started in drumming panic.

'Hullo! Is anyone in there?'

The handle rattled again while he sat, his head twisted round, staring in hypnotic dread at the key still in the lock. He heard Nelly's retreating steps, her voice calling out, 'Miss Gertrude's room's locked. Who's got the key?'

He sprang up, stuffed the letters hastily back in the box. His fingers were shaking so badly he could hardly fit the pages back into their envelopes and restore them to their secret cache. He was keening softly to himself. It seemed to take an eternity for him to do so, and to thrust the box back into its recess, to cover it once more with the clothing that concealed it, to fumble the key back into its ledge.

Nelly's steps were returning. Was she alone? He prayed desperately that she would be. He grabbed at his displaced robe, pulled it to him to cover his nakedness, and dived towards the door as he heard someone trying to fit a key into the other side.

'Master Davy!' Nelly gasped, her blue eyes wide with shock, then she saw the fright etched onto his own features. She pushed her way in, banged the door to with her hip. 'What are you doin' here?' She took in his state of undress, saw his bare ankles and feet. He was still staring, his eyes so wide and fearful, his mouth open. 'Oh, Master Davy! What are you up to, eh?'

'Nothing! Nothing, Nelly, I swear it!' His expression belied his vehement protest. 'I just – came in here. Wanted a bit of peace – I do – sometimes. When she's away. Just – to be on my own. To hide away.' He flung her a look of agonized appeal, naked in its plea for understanding.

Suddenly Nelly recalled the incident of the long-ago missing petti-coat, and for some reason she felt her face flame with colour. 'You haven't touched anything, have you, Master Davy?' Her voice was urgent, and he stared at her in helpless shame. 'I mean any of her things? You haven't moved 'em? We've had a telephone call. She's comin' 'ome. Tonight. Don't let her find anything—'

He nodded, glanced at the dressing table, turned back to Nelly. Those intense eyes held hers for a second, then lowered in shame and admission. Nelly had not missed the direction of his glance, nor his expression, though she had misunderstood his shame. 'She won't know. Nothing's disturbed. Unless . . .'

She gave him a deeply wounded look. 'I won't say anything!' she answered passionately. 'I never would! You should know that, Davy!'

His eyes were still shining with tears. He nodded once more, cleared his throat. 'I do,' he said, even more quietly. He reached out, took her large red hand in both of his, and lifted it to his lips. He kissed its roughened skin, held it to his mouth until she snatched it away from him.

He moved past her and hurried out. She stood stock still, gazing after him, her own eyes misting, and she raised her hand to her own lips, touching them to the still damp spot where his had rested.

CHAPTER TEN

NELLY came into the morning room, her eyes lowered, not quite meeting Davy's gaze. He glanced up from his solitary breakfast. Father was of course away. As was Clara, sent off for the summer to their aunt's in Weymouth, no doubt to stop her endless pleas that she, too, might be allowed to 'do her bit' for king and country in the conflagration. She was, after all, old enough to volunteer for one of the women's auxiliary services, such as the Ambulance Corps, in which her sister was already serving. However, her zeal for duty seemed to have, temporarily at least, been blunted by the demands of a flourishing social season in the seaside town. Unless being squired at the various balls and other entertainments by a host of young officers qualified as serving the cause.

'Mornin', Master Davy.' Nelly's golden head, with its white cap clipped to its crown, bobbed in the gesture of respect which always caused Davy such acute embarrassment. 'Miss Gerty says she's sorry she missed you last night an' could you go up to her room when you've finished your breakfast, as she'd like a chat with you?'

Her cheeks were red, her rapid speech a little breathy. Davy stood at once and laid aside the newspaper, which, before her entry, he had been reading with quickening interest, despite his detestation of the war and everything that it entailed. The headlines blared blackly about the huge new and hopefully conclusive offensive being launched at a place already bloodily infamous in the annals of the war, Ypres. 'I've finished. I'll go up now.'

His heartbeat quickened as he mounted the stairs. He had been glad enough after his unnerving encounter with Nelly yesterday to avoid seeing Gerty when she arrived late yesterday evening. But perhaps she had brought fresh news of Sam from London.

She was lying in bed when he knocked and, on her invitation, entered. Her long hair streamed down in its rich, thick profusion over both her shoulders. She had not bothered to don her bed jacket, so that her shoulders and arms were bare. The upper rounds of her breasts swelled from the lace-fringed bodice of her nightgown. He could see the tiny deep brown of a mole on her inner left breast, rising then falling as she smiled a greeting at him from her propped pillows.

'Hello, Davy.' She held out her arms commandingly, and he moved obediently. He felt her hands on his shoulders pulling him in close as her lips claimed his cheek. He smelt the faint perfume and newly wakened body smell of her. The wisps of her hair brushed ticklingly against his face, and the white slopes and valleys of her breasts bobbed under his nose for a magical second before she released him.

His face was hot. He was angry with himself at the effect she had on him. 'Have you seen the paper this morning?' he asked. She was far too cheerful, he thought resentfully. She should be as sickly worried as he was.

She waved her hand dismissively. 'Oh, not more bloody war news!' He knew she delighted to shock him with the strength of her language. 'I never look at it now. Besides, I see more than enough of it for myself. *I* don't need to read about it.'

He noted the emphasis on the pronoun, and its clear condemnation of his own refusal to condone the slaughter. He had resisted joining the school cadet corps, even against his father's vituperative scorn. Had been kicked and cuffed, and scragged, and had yellow paint daubed all over him. He was afraid, deeply, of what would happen to him if the war went on much longer, for there were moves to bring in conscription, to force men to fight. 'That'll sort the conshy cowards out!' his father had declared belligerently when he had read of the proposed Act of Parliament in the paper. His eyes had burned into David.

'I'm not old enough, father.' But soon he would be, unless the madness could be stopped.

'There was another bombing raid on Tuesday,' Gerty said. 'We were out in it. Air planes, not Zeppelins.' She shuddered dramatically. 'Why should I want to read about it when I might be blown to bits any day?'

'But Sam's—'

'We can only pray for him.' But his mention of Sam's name sparked off a disquieting sense of guilt. She felt a kind of nostalgic tenderness for the handsome boy, who was so besotted with her. She looked back on the brief time they had shared as part of the distant innocence of adolescence. It was an innocence she might well have lost during that last, two-day rendezvous with Sam before he had embarked for France. Had it not been for his diffidence and her nervous fear of what was still the unknown, for both of them, she might well have surrendered to the raging urges she was sure his body as well as hers was experiencing that grey afternoon.

It was as well that there was no convenient sanctuary for such a consummation to take place. The Army and Navy Club would not countenance the decadence of its members taking unescorted single ladies to their rooms. She could only be grateful now that Sam's unworldliness had made the notion of booking some anonymous hotel room literally unthinkable to him. She doubted if in such private circumstances she would have had the strength to resist their shared passion. She was convinced she loved him, truly and deeply. The secret soreness of her body now reminded her of what a terrible mistake that would have been, and stirred once more the wickedly powerful thrill of much more recent memory.

Gordon Pearce was no schoolboy: a captain, stationed at the War Office, doing a vital job at the vital centre of things. Wounded, too, thankfully not seriously, and long before she had known of his existence. He had already done more than his bit, served at the Front, in the far-off hell of Gallipoli before he was invalided home. While Sam and his contemporaries were still sweating on the rugger field, chasing a bit of leather about for their honour and glory! Gordon was no school boy virgin, tormented by a passion he could neither contain nor fulfil. And neither, any longer, was she.

Not that she needed any reminder, she reflected, as she raised her knees gingerly under the light bedclothes, and felt again the ache of battered bone and tender flesh surrendered this time so gladly. She should feel wicked, for indeed she was! A fallen woman! Fallen both in soul and body, for she loved Gordon madly, with every part of her, against which her feelings for Sam were but the first stirrings of undeveloped girlhood. Their furtive, improper gropings had been, she recognized with a new honesty, the first faint sparks of a progress towards that shattering climax of bliss she knew only now since coming together with the splendour of Gordon's possessed and possessing flesh in hers.

She struggled to meet Davy's worried gaze. 'I must write to him as soon as possible. I have something of such importance to tell him. I hope he'll be happy for me. As I hope you will be, Davy, my pet. I'm in love. Truly, magnificently, in love, for the very first time!'

Again she hesitated, then forced herself to go on, her chin lifting challengingly. 'His name's Gordon. I can't wait for everyone to meet him, to bring him home. He's a captain. So wonderful – and handsome!' She faltered slightly, aware of every stabbing word from the mounting pain on Davy's face.

'You can't!' he cried, at last, fighting against his breathlessness to get the words out. 'Sam adores you! You know he does! He worships you—'

'And *you* would know, wouldn't you, little sneak?' She spat the words out, unable to withold the release of her venom, because of the guilt she felt at the pain so clearly reflected in Davy's horrified face. She had not meant to accuse him yet, though she had been convinced for some time that it was he who had been going into her drawer, reading the letters. She had even set a trap for him. She saw him start, saw his protest blocked before he could properly pour it forth. 'Oh yes! You need look guilty, and blush as red as the little pansy you are!' She sat up, letting the sheet fall away from her breasts, whose rounded shape was contoured by the thin stuff of her nightgown. 'You think I don't know about you sneaking in here, going through my things – my most intimate things – reading his letters to me?'

Though Davy's lips moved, no denial would come forth. In any case, his wide-eyed horror, the helpless gaze of a rabbit who sees its fate at the predator's poised claw and ripping teeth, was a blatant proclamation of his guilt. 'I know you've read every one of his love letters to me! You've been at it for months, haven't you, you disgusting little pervert? You couldn't even put things back properly.' She gave a melodramatic shudder of distaste. 'Your grubby hands pawing at my things, too!'

She had risen, pushed aside the blankets, and was kneeling up in the bed. He shook his head wordlessly. 'Get out of my way!' she hissed, scrambling off the bed carelessly. He turned, almost stumbled as he made for the door. 'What will your darling Sam think of you when I tell him what you've been up to?'

'No!' he cried, turning back, his eyes pleading with her. 'Please don't! Don't tell him anything! And don't tell him about this chap. This captain! Please, Gerty! I beg you. I'll do anything!'

All at once, she was regally calm once more. She crossed to the window, pulling back the heavy drapes further, letting the strong sunlight come flooding in. She shook out her mane of hair, ran her fingers through it, stood gazing out at the sunny prospect. The light poured hazily through the whiteness of the net material next to the glass. Bathed in its brightness, the thin cotton of her nightdress showed the dark outline of the body beneath. The fiery glow of her hair was a halo as she turned, tilted it judiciously, regarding him. 'No. I really must write. Today. It's so unfair to allow the poor boy to go on living with such false hopes.'

'Please! You mustn't!' Davy's cry was torn from him, he took a step towards her, his hands held out pleadingly. 'He lives for you, Gerty! You know he does! It's probably what keeps him going – out there. It could make all the difference. Don't tell him!' He gestured wildly. 'I don't mean about me. Tell him what you like about me, I don't care! But not about you. Not yet! Not while he's out there. When he's safe – when he's home. Then . . .' his voice cracked, her slim shape shimmered before him.

It was the resumption of the despotic reign she had held over him during their childhood. 'Don't worry, I'm only home for a week.

You'll accompany me down to Weymouth on Friday for the weekend, and escort me up to London next Monday.'

On the second morning she again commanded his presence in her bedroom, then sent him to collect her breakfast tray, much to the giggling surprise of the two young girls helping in the kitchen. Nelly, who was waiting on the mistress of the house, met him in the corridor outside Mrs Herbert's room. Her own arms were full, but she stared at Davy with undisguised anger.

'What on earth d'you think you're adoing with that, Master Davy?'

He blushed. 'I was just — I was coming up to see Miss Gerty. I thought I'd — I know how busy you are on a morning—'

'Dear oh dear!' Shaking her white-capped head in shocked disapproval, Nelly quickly put down the things she had been bringing from his mother's room and seized the laden tray. 'You give me that at once! The very idea! Go on with you! I'll bring it.'

'But—' he stammered, still red faced, with a presentiment of disaster as he followed in Nelly's wake. At Gerty's door, she nodded for him to precede her. Once again, Gerty was sitting up in bed, her shoulders and arms uncovered.

'Oh!' she exclaimed, in startled annoyance when she saw Nelly bearing the tray. Involuntarily, her hand rose to her breast, and she gathered the sheet a little more decorously in front of her. 'What do you think you're doing, Nelly? I didn't send for you.'

Davy winced as he detected the truculence in Nelly's deep tone. 'I found Master Davy bringing your breakfast, Miss. There's no need for that. 'Tisn't suitable.'

'I asked him to bring it. To save some of you maids the trip. We must all be democratic nowadays. I know how busy you are since staff shortages—'

'We can manage fine, Miss. All you need to do is ring down. There's always somebody to hand below.'

'When I want your advice I'll ask for it!' Gerty hissed. Spots of colour stood out like rouge on her cheeks. Her bosom heaved with her agitation. 'Is that clear? You're right. I *will* ring if I need you! Now get about your business!'

Nelly's face flamed, while Davy stood in agonized dumbness. 'Yes, Miss. Sir.' She bobbed to Davy after making obeisance to the angry girl, her accent on the last word detectable to Davy's sensitive ear.

'That great, ham fisted oaf!' Gerty said as the door closed. 'She's altogether too big for her massive boots, the clod! I'll have her taken down a peg, you'll see!'

Davy wanted to intervene on Nelly's behalf, but wisely he knew that if he attempted to defend her, it might well cause Gerty to be all the more determined to carry out her threat. Better to deflect her rage his way if necessary. 'Here. Have your breakfast.' He picked up the tray and stood humbly while she rearranged herself and smoothed the blankets over her thighs. He placed the tray on her lap. She patted the bed beside her and he sat, watching her begin daintily to eat. When she came to the fatty edge of the bacon, she cut it off, then picked it up delicately between thumb and forefinger.

'Open!' She held it and he obeyed again, taking it in his mouth from her outstretched fingers, hiding his quiver of distaste as he felt its slipperiness cold on his tongue.

'You must love your chum very much,' she observed maliciously, but with genuine curiosity, too. 'Aren't you glad I've given him up?' His eyes met hers. The blood spread delightfully over his unblemished skin. 'Tell me the truth, Davy.' The grey eyes held his compellingly. 'At school – were you his catamite?' she asked levelly.

The big eyes widened, the rosy lips trembled, as he shook his head. 'You know I wasn't,' he answered huskily. 'You know he's not – he never – he hardly ever spoke to me . . .' his voice tailed away, remembering the stinging shame of his private solitary thoughts, the visions that assailed him. 'He's not like that.'

'Would you have liked to have been?' Her tone of detached enquiry was the same. Dumbly he shook his head, his throat working as he swallowed. 'You must tell me the truth, Davy. That's part of our bargain, too. Do you like boys? I mean, you know. Instead of girls?'

He shook his head desperately. 'No! Not like – not like that! Not those oafs at school!'

'But what about Sam?' The low, vibrant tone held him. 'He's so handsome, so strong. Don't you adore him?'

'No – I – it's not like that!' he repeated. His voice caught on a sob, he couldn't hold it back any longer. 'I do like him – admire him – so much! I would do anything for him.'

'But not *die* for him, eh, Davy? Not enough to follow him, and all those other brave lads, to fight for what's right. There's boys younger than you over there. Boys who know what's right, ready to lay down their lives.' She thrust the tray aside suddenly and flung back the blankets. She sprang out of bed in a careless flurry of limbs and strode over to the stand beside her wardrobe. She laughed and began to fling garments at him: a camisole, a lacy bust bodice, a pair of fashionable, elaborately worked cotton knickers, white stockings. They fluttered snowily about him, fell across his body, some onto the bed. 'No! I think we've found what you're good for, haven't we, my little Davy? Or should I call you Thumbs?'

Through the scourge of her trilling laughter, he felt the deep wound of betrayal tearing at his heart.

CHAPTER ELEVEN

DAVY squirmed uncomfortably on the plush banquette of the first class carriage. Gerty was flirting away with the two young midshipmen, much to the disapproval of the middle-aged man in civilian clothes in the corner, who crackled his *Times* admonishingly. The war had changed many things, Davy reflected, not least the degree of freedom as far as social etiquette was concerned. Though he supposed that in a way he could be regarded as Gerty's chaperone, even though she had virtually ignored him since so boldly striking up a conversation with the two junior naval officers.

They had eyed him rather warily, but soon forgot him under the spell of the lovely girl sitting opposite them. And Gerty had never looked lovelier, Davy thought. He found himself gazing, as had the pink-faced sailor youths from time to helpless time, at Gerty's slender ankles, superbly on show in the black stockings, silk of course, above the shining patent black shoes. That was another thing the war had brought about: a transformation of the female dress code, which had allowed hemlines to rise, in some cases, as in this instance of Gerty's dark green wool skirt, half way up the calf. And underneath, even more startling changes, with many young women going uncorseted, and wearing undergarments of unimaginable brevity.

Davy and Gerty had spent the past four days at their aunt's house in Weymouth. Four days of torment, as far as Davy was concerned, being dragged round various parties and balls with his sisters and a crowd of other bright society things, ostensibly passed off as part of the do-gooding war effort, but in reality the excuse for a wild excess of hedonism, a *morituri te salutamus* gaiety, which, in the case of the young men, the majority of whom were already in uniform, he could understand, but which only served to make him feel all the more isolated and out of it. The drinking, and the sparking, and worse besides he surmised, had that desperate nature to it which revealed how uncertain and frightened people were, in spite of their frantic effort to hide it. It saddened and sickened him. No one, after the three dreadful years of warfare, could deny the crazy and appalling cost, in terms of human suffering, and for what? No one seemed to know any more – if they ever had. Davy had only seen the flickering images on the cinematograph screen, but his vivid imagination could fill in the horror of the smashed up terrain, like some fearful alien planet, the pathos of the scurrying little black figures, the smiles of the blackened faces for the camera. Hundreds slaughtered over that pock marked waste, victory the taking of a few hundred devastated yards. It truly terrified him, the scale of such madness. He was wise enough, though, to keep his mouth firmly shut these days.

And now, he and Gerty were on their way up to the capital, where he had been promised he might meet the heroic Captain Pearce, with whom Gerty seemed totally besotted. Davy cursed his own cravenness for not refusing point blank to meet the man who had usurped his dear Sam's place in her perfidious heart. However, Davy was not merely journeying to London at Gerty's whim. Something far greater and more worrying was bringing him up to town – the summons of his father. It had been preying on his mind ever since the terse order issued over the telephone. His stomach fluttered in the all too familiar state of queasiness as his troubled thoughts dwelt on the reason for the command.

Victoria was full of uniforms, as usual. Davy was aware of countless male eyes ogling Gerty's beauty, and of her poised acceptance of them. 'Don't forget, you're to meet daddy at Brown's at two o'clock. Now put me in a taxi, there's a good boy, and be on your way.' As she stepped into the cab, she leaned in close, dizzying him with her perfume, and let her lips brush his cheek. 'And remember, be back at the hotel by seven. Gordon's picking us up there.' She gave her gurgling, musical laugh as she stared up at him mischievously. 'Best bib and tucker. And best behaviour, too! I don't want you letting me down, mind.'

But now he had other worries to trouble him. His father was waiting for him in the foyer of his club. Significantly, he had not invited Davy to lunch with him, nor did he enquire whether he had eaten. It wasn't until they were seated in the enclosed intimacy of the taxi that John Herbert abruptly broached the purpose of their meeting. 'Quite frankly, David, I'm damned worried about you. About the way you're turning out. And I'm not the only one. The whole family finds you odd, to say the least. And at school you're no better. The only reason young Ellington palled up with you is because he's dotty about your sister. Your masters tell me you've made no real chums at school at all. I won't have you turning into some namby-pamby artist type.' He gestured disgustedly, waving the cigar, whose blue smoke was making Davy's eyes sting. 'Look at your hair! All over your collar, curling like some damned girl! Time we made a start. Making a man of you! That's what you're here for.'

Davy was only further alarmed at the sudden embarrassment, so untypical, which appeared to grip his father, whose eyes were directed out of the window to the busy scene beyond, as he spoke next.

'There are some things – we have to acknowledge, my boy – that demand our attention. Feelings. Basic instincts, which we as males have, even in our advanced civilisation. You know what I mean, don't you? Urges – needs . . .' he gestured impatiently, though the tide of colour mounting in his son's face indicated that Davy was at least beginning to have some inkling of what his father was trying to say. 'These urges – while we must certainly not give way to them, do demand, as I say, attention. Indeed, can't be ignored. You'll agree, I think, I've always provided — been a conscientious parent — an honourable partner to your poor mother—'

Davy nodded hastily, writhing himself now on the spit of his mortification, longing only for an escape from this torture — a terrible accident, anything, to put an end to this.

'She isn't well. Has not been for some years, as you know. I've always been patient, understanding. Never made demands of her . . . even though to do so would not have been beyond the bounds of proper conduct . . .' all at once, he seemed to give up the struggle, and Davy felt his body jerk as he growled and coughed, his arm waving in exasperation. 'I'm going to see you are initiated into the ways of the world, David. The ways of the flesh. There are places — and people — who can accommodate them. You'll see. You'll thank me for it, I know. You have to know these things, my boy. For your own relief.' He lapsed into silence, gazing out of the window, while Davy's mind spun in helpless conjecture and trepidation.

His anxiety increased when they alighted, at a street north of the river. The narrow properties had once been fashionable. Now they had a distinctly seedy air. The high steps leading up to the front doors were dirty, strewn with litter, among which scruffy infants played. On others, shifty looking men sat about in shirtsleeves and braces, smoking and spitting. Some were clearly worse the wear for drink, even though it was still early in the afternoon.

Then Davy noticed the women and young girls. The bold directness of their stares made him burn, cast his eyes down. But not before he had noted their provocative dress, painted faces, their challenging manner. Unworldly as he was, he knew these were females of ill repute, the district one far from respectability. He was startled at how assured his father seemed, and familiar with it. He strode out quickly, confidently, until he turned up the steps of a tall building as shabby as its neighbours.

A well-made, blowzy woman came into the dim hallway. 'Hello, Mr H. Saffy's expectin' you. She said you'd be coming . . .' her voice tailed off. She was staring at Davy, who felt himself blushing furiously.

'This is my son, Mrs Evans,' John said, with heavy irony. 'Time he grew up a little, learnt something of the world, eh?'

Mrs Evans gave a wheezing chuckle. 'Yes, indeed, Mr H. Lovely boy, intee?' She paused. 'Anything partic'lar in mind for him?'

'Oh, I think my Saffy will do very well for him, don't you? She's a gentle girl. Don't want to scare him off. He's shy. A boy still.'

Davy's heart beat wildly. There could no longer be any doubt of the horror that lay behind his father's words, or what this place was, and why they were here. The dim light seemed choking, he felt sick and faint. He was seized by a fit of trembling. He would have liked to turn and flee, but his brain was numb and his quivering limbs would not have obeyed him. 'Come on, Davy. This way. It's on the top floor.'

Somehow, he got himself in motion. 'Father!' he gasped. The banister rail felt tacky, soiled. He shuddered with revulsion at its slimy touch. 'Please! I don't—'

'Come on, my boy!' John Herbert said. There was a new, deep note of salacious encouragement in his tone. Novel as it was, it did not help Davy's distress.

'I don't – please, Father! I'm not ready . . .'

'Rubbish, boy! You're seventeen. Boys no older than you are dying for their country. You'll love it, I promise you. Just let your body, your feelings, take over.' He chuckled lewdly, reached out and punched Davy on the arm. 'Besides, I've got a great surprise for you. You will love it, I swear!'

No! Davy's senses reeled in panic. He thought of the big-breasted woman downstairs, visualised with horror the flowing acres of her naked, ivory coloured flesh, then, worse, his own slender body connected with it, smothered by it. His father gripped his elbow tightly, hauling him up the last flight of stairs, with its narrow landing, its dirt encrusted window. John Herbert's knuckles rapped on the faded grimy surface of the door.

It was hard to say who was the more astonished, as Sophie and David faced each other for the first time in eight years. Yet, despite the long gap, each recognized the other instantly.

'David!'

'Miss Marshall!'

Although he had been fully prepared to find some painted whore at the top of the dark stairs, it took more than a few seconds for the reality of these dingy surroundings, and of what his former governess had become, to sink in. Her life over the past years had indeed left its mark on her. Yet under the mask of paint and powder, her sensitive beauty could still be traced. He gazed at her in dawning horror, while she seemed to have been turned to stone. The dark eyes glittered, remained tragically fixed upon his face.

John Herbert broke the spell of immobility by seizing her by her bare upper arms and thrusting her back into the interior of the room. 'I've brought you your former pupil, Saffy. Sorry, Sophie. You'll have to explain the allusion to him, my dear. As you'll have to explain so many things. You sadly neglected his education before. Now you'll have the chance to make amends. I want him to learn how to be a man.' He smiled, slid his arm around her waist, pulled her close with unmistakable claim. 'And who better, my love?' He bent and slowly covered her lips with his. She made no resistance, remained limp in his embrace, neither repulsing him nor responding to the long kiss. Davy was continuing to stare in dumbfounded horror.

'I'll leave him in your capable hands. Till six. Put him in a cab.' He turned to Davy. 'Naturally, this is our secret, David. Man to man, eh? Not a word to anyone. The consequences could be dire, not least to our lovely Saffy here – and her family,' he added with deep signif-icance. His smile indicated his cruel enjoyment of his son's dismay. 'I'll be back later tonight,' he said to Sophie. 'After supper some time. You can tell me all about the boy's initiation. A progress report.' He laughed cruelly again and went out.

'I'm sorry, David,' Sophie murmured into the tortured silence. 'I swear I had no idea — that he — that you were coming. He's never mentioned — any of you. I've known nothing of you — or the rest of your family.'

Davy swallowed hard, looked around. The neatly made bed had its blankets turned down, only a clean white sheet drawn up to the pillows. 'I didn't, either,' he whispered. 'Know anything about you. About this.'

'I'll make us some tea. We can talk.'

It was painful for both of them. Sophie could not bring herself to hold his gaze all the time, but bravely, against the tears, she fought on to tell him the truth. 'He was kind to me, at first. Gentle, even. Loving.' The last word was a whisper. Shocked, Davy realized she was talking about his father. 'But then — I saw how terrible it was. Your poor mother — she was so kind to me. And me living under the same roof, deceiving her so wickedly. I couldn't go on like that. He grew angry with me. Then he made plans, to get me away.' She glanced about the shabby room, as though seeing again the sordidness of her surroundings, her situation. 'I had no choice – my parents. My father would have been destroyed – I could never have found another post. I was with child. I even thought of – of ending it all, I was so frightened.' She could not keep the bitterness from her voice. 'He said he would take care of everything. I could see no other way out. And then it was too late. I was trapped here. All these years, I've been his mistress.'

David told her of the family. When he mentioned the birth of Baby Olwyn and her short three months of life, Sophie's head bent. She cried softly, but stirred with bitter anger, too, at the thought that the man who had possessed her countless times both before and after that tragedy should have said nothing at all about it to her. Davy was moved at her distress. 'Please, don't cry, Miss . . .' he stopped in embarrassment. Miss Marshall seemed somehow a sadly inappropriate title for her. To help ease her distress, he said, 'My father called you Saffy. Why. . . ?'

She blew her nose, and dabbed at her eyes. His question *did* alleviate her sorrow, but not in the way he had intended. She coloured, but raised her eyes to meet his directly, so that he saw the rekindled bitterness in her look. 'Yes. He told me to enlighten you, didn't he? It's his pet nickname for me. You've heard of the Ancient Greek poetess, Sappho? You know of her?'

'Wasn't she the one who lived on an island? With a crowd of girls?'

'That's right. The isle of Lesbos.'

Her emphasis on the last word helped him to recall the salacious schoolboy sniggers and the blood rushed hotly to his face, but Sophie's voice continued, with new hardness. 'That's what he alludes to. He accused me of . . . of harbouring illicit feelings for your mother. It was a wicked lie — I loved her, but only for her kindness to me, after that business with Gertrude. There was nothing improper—'

'Why do you let him — why do you stay here?' Davy cried passionately, as the awfulness of his father's conduct, the cruelty he had perpetrated by bringing Davy here, fully struck him. 'Why don't you just go — far away from him?'

She gave a twisted smile. Her shoulders seemed to droop in acknowledgement of defeat, and already he regretted his outburst, for in that gesture he felt an instinctive recognition of her weakness, her inability to resist, and he felt, too, a deep sympathy with it. 'Where to?' she said simply. 'I wasn't brave enough. I didn't want my parents to know – about me. He still sends money. They think I'm still a teacher.' Her eyes dropped, to fix on her hands, clasping and twisting in her lap. 'He even sends me home every year.' In spite of her resolve, her voice trembled, almost broke. 'That's the hardest thing of all. To see them – that other world I can never be a part of again. To deceive them.' The eyes, brilliant with tears and pain, swept up to meet his once more. 'He pays for these lodgings, for my clothes, my food. I am his kept woman, David. I can never leave.' The grief and the torment in her voice became strident, ugly. 'And now he wants me to play my role with you. To initiate you in the sins of the flesh, David! In the sins of the father!' She could not hold back the anguished sob, and she shook her dark head furiously.

His voice was thick with revulsion. 'I couldn't — in any case, I . . . I'm not like others. I don't feel . . . I couldn't.' The last words were whispered, a fresh confession of shame. There was a long pause, during which neither of them moved. They could hear the faint street noises, and distant movements in the house below them. Something forced him to speak again. 'I don't think . . . I could play the man's part.'

The words hung between them, until she rose suddenly, with a soft rustle of her skirts, and came round the small table. She came close, took his hand, her other hand rested lightly on his shoulder. Then she bent and very gently kissed the dark gold of his bowed head. His shoulders quivered, a huge sob shook him. She remained standing, her hands on him, so close he could feel the skirts of her dress brushing against his knee. 'There are many different forms of love, David. Not all need to be physical. I told you. I felt love for your mama. Women can share love for one another, just as men can. It's hard sometimes for men to understand women.' There was the briefest of pauses, and when she spoke again her voice was an intense murmur, filled with her emotion and repressed disgust. 'What happens in here, in this room, is not love! Has nothing to do with love! I don't condemn your father alone, David! I condemn myself also. There is passion, sexual feelings, in both male and female.' She turned away abruptly, moved over to the dirty window once more and kept her back to him. 'I believe you will find love one day. True love.' She spoke softly, and there was another silence, before she turned back towards him, equally abruptly.

She gazed at him squarely. 'I've always been his creature. I'll go on being his. But I'll defy him in this. I'm asking you to lie for me, David. I shall tell him we went to bed together, that we made love.' Again there was a painfully bitter smile. 'If you'll forgive the expression. Please tell him the same. For my sake, if not for yours.'

'Can I see you again?' Davy asked desperately.

'Not at your father's bidding.'

He blushed. 'If he insists?'

'He won't. I'm sure of it. He has had his pleasure out of bringing us together like this, out of forcing me to be the instrument of your corruption. That will suffice, I am certain.'

'Then can I come without his knowledge? On my own. To see you?'

She stared at him as though weighing in her mind how to answer. 'I'll give you this address. And a telephone number. But you must always write or ring first. Never come without warning me. You understand? It's important.'

He saw the intensity of the look she gave him, and he acquiesced. At the door she took his arms and drew him in close. 'My dear David,' she murmured. Her face was close to him, and he watched those expressive eyes fill once more with shining tears. 'My lovely boy. Take care. I'd like to see you. You're my true friend.' He saw her lips closing, felt their moist coolness touch his, press gently against him, holding the kiss, and his body trembled in response.

When he had gone, she tidied up the cups, and moved to the bed, which had not been disturbed. She took off her outer clothes and lay back, reflecting on all that had happened. She lay until the room was almost in darkness, then she lit the lamp and stripped off the rest of her clothes, before washing carefully in the bowl she stood on the towel on the floor. She changed into her silks and sat brushing out her hair, before applying the liberal make-up ready for her master's visit. She had thought she could no longer be shocked by anything he did, but the refinement of the cruelty he had inflicted on her that afternoon, to say nothing of the beautiful boy who had the misfortune to be his son, had truly appalled her. And as she readied herself to receive him, to subject herself yet again to his will, she began to plan a revenge on him that had taken eight long years to be born.

CHAPTER TWELVE

When Sam Ellington came out of the line with what remained of his battalion he was too exhausted and too stuffed full with the horrors he had witnessed to care whether the battle was being won or lost. They staggered, half dead, half asleep, too numb for the moment to be thankful that they were, unlike so many of their comrades, half alive. Before the rain-smudged, grey ruins of the village of Passchendaele, more than half their number had been killed in the first few days, mostly scythed down by deadly machine gun fire as they advanced through the rapidly miring ground and became caught up in the seemingly endless swirls of wire. Guns and wire which they had not expected to be there, after the barrage of shells which had been laid down in front of them.

The rain blurred things. At first, they almost regarded it as God-sent, for it hid the full scale of the horror from them. But once they had become bogged down in the enemy forward trenches, and the shuffle of attack and counter-attack drove them back and forth across the mad moonscape of torn ground, it became almost as much their enemy as the chattering bullets and screaming shells, and the crazy violence of the plunging, stabbing hand to hand encounters of desperate charges.

It clogged up mechanisms, made hands slip at vital moments on greasy gun butts, or running feet slither and lose their grip. Field guns stuck, buried to their axles, wild-eyed mules struggled and heaved and, presently, men and animals drowned in the glutinous mixture.

Cut off in the midst of a night attack, Sam spent hours of darkness in a shell hole filled with icy water the colour of milky tea. Bullets whined relentlessly inches above the crater's rim, pinning him there. Shells whooshed by higher overhead. The surreal nightmare was lit periodically by flares, which spread a pale dead brilliance that made the dark, so feared only seconds before, like a welcome extra blanket on a frosty night.

Opposite him, their feet touching now and then under the water, a young private lay dying. He was not from Sam's company, though Sam recognized his face. It was filthy, yet, under the dirt, it carried already that sheen of death Sam knew. There was a smell of death, too. The water about the young soldier's waist had kept staining black. Oily slivers of blood seeped through the scorched and torn clothing of his battledress.

His rifle and webbing had been discarded. Sam had scrabbled in the soldier's kit, and his own, to try to render first aid, to stop the wound, but one brief look had told him it was a useless gesture. Half the boy's side had been blasted out, just below the rib cage. The black seepage was thick, tissue and guts oozed, the blood flow thickened. Only the burnt remnants of cloth and leather seemed to hold him together.

At first, he had groaned and wept softly, had struggled to talk, in a wheezing whisper. But then his cries got louder, shriller, until he began to howl, and Sam was frantic. He wanted more than anything to stop that tortured noise. He contemplated pulling out his revolver and shooting him. Put an end to his misery. A kindness to the dying boy. He couldn't do it, instead snarled, 'For God's sake, man! Pack it in! There are Jerries crawling about all over the place!'

He was startled by the sudden, complete return to awareness, the frenzied cry shrieked back at him. 'I don't give a fuck, you stupid sod! I'm dying here! Help! Help me!'

Sam wanted to crawl away, wanted to bury himself in the stinking coldness of their watery bolthole. But the effort had proved too much for the wounded man. He began to cough, then to jerk and shake violently. Black phlegm stained his chin, then he slid down, until only his head was still clear of the water. Sam was not sure of the time of death, but no more sound came from him, or movement, and he was stiff before the greyness filtering through the steady rain marked the dawn.

Sam was so cold, so weary, that he scarcely cared any more for the machine gun fire, except to pray that it would be quick, and final, when he bought it. He did not want to die like his companion of the night. He wasn't even sure in which direction he should crawl. But he made it at last, fell into a trench full of British soldiers from another regiment, who dragged him over the parapet with a string of welcoming oaths.

All that seemed a dimly distant memory now, as he stumbled along in the ragged column. Sleep walkers, all of them, trudging, heads down, the rain drumming on their helmets, streaming off their capes, those who were lucky enough still to have them. They stared at their mud encrusted boots, the liquid ooze and pale tea puddles of the pocked roadway, until, a few miles back, a military policeman herded them off the road like a sheep dog, into the empty farmhouse and its outbuildings, which had been commandeered as a rest and recuperation centre.

The men sank down into the straw of a barn. Most removed nothing except their helmets and were asleep in seconds, sodden, dirty bundles of rags. Sam was shown into the farmhouse itself, and the luxury of a wooden pallet with a thin, stained mattress. He slipped off the cape and his helmet and haversack. Half way through pulling off his boots, he keeled over and sank into oblivion.

Six hours later, he was savouring the incredible luxury of a bath in warm water. He didn't give a second thought to its grey scumminess, the result of both a captain and lieutenant having enjoyed a soak in the high metal tub first. A grinning orderly was adding more hot water from a steaming bucket. Sam recognized the knowing grin, and his immediate dislike of its fawning familiarity. Private John Dixon had got himself attached as servant to the captain who acted as signals officer, and, as a result, had spent little time in the trenches.

As Sam kicked off his filthy underclothes and sank gratefully into the grey water, Dixon said chirpily, 'Good to see you back all right, Mr Ellington. And everything intact, I see,' he added cheekily.

Sam, still a little muzzy from his deep sleep, did not return the smile. 'Any news of Craine?' Craine acted as servant for himself and a fellow second lieutenant.

'Posted missing, sir,' Dixon answered. 'Easier to put down who's still here, I reckon. Still, never mind, eh? You made it. And there's mail waiting, and all.' He added slyly, 'Fat letter or two for you, sir. I'll fetch it up for you, shall I?' He moved away without waiting for Sam's reply.

Too cocky by half, slimy toad! Sam thought, but then felt his heart thudding in anticipation. A letter from Gerty. Must be. Just the ticket! The very thing above all he needed after . . . It took him by surprise. His head dropped, his body shook at the sobs which came wailing out of him, tearing at him. He heard Dixon thumping up the stairs again, and he doused his face savagely with water.

He forced himself not to rush, to scrub at his grimy body, as though he could wipe the memory of the last days from his pores, as well as the accumulated dirt. He wanted to be clean, as pure as he could make himself, before he immersed himself in Gerty's letter, in that wonderful, sweet world he could so gladly lose himself in, of drowning kisses, of fragrant flesh, and whispered love. He rubbed at his short hair vigorously with the carbolic soap, ducked under the water, then soaped and rinsed again, his fingers probing at his scalp, cleaning all the dross away.

'More water, Dixon!' he called blindly. 'Cold will do. Surely no one else will want this water after me?'

'Right you are, sir.'

He gestured and Dixon poured the bucketful of water slowly over his sleek head, and Sam gasped and laughed breathlessly. He rose with a great splash, shaking the liquid from his black locks. 'Very nice, too,' Dixon leered, as he handed him his towel. Sam glanced down at his tumefying penis and covered it quickly. For a second, he experienced a stab of anger, then pushed it away. He wrapped the towel about his waist as he stepped onto the wet bare boards. He picked up the pile of letters from the table and padded barefoot across the cold wooden floor of the landing to the room where his cot had been set up. It was alongside four others, one of which was occupied by a subaltern from D Company, who nodded a wordless greeting then turned his back.

In spite of the chilly damp, Sam did not dress, revelling in the freedom of his unclothed, fresh smelling body. He lay back on the narrow bed, smiled at the neat, square writing he loved, studied the other letters. One from Davy – of course! He wrote more than Gerty. Sam felt that edge of embarrassment, as well as affection. Gerty was always teasing him about Davy's hero worship of him. There was one from his own family. And a typed envelope from his tailors. No doubt a bill. They would seek you out no matter where, even in the most forward observation trench.

For a second, he toyed with the idea of reading the others first, savouring the most precious correspondence, saving it till last. But he knew his will was not strong enough. He raised the envelope to his nose before he opened it, tracing avidly the faint scent of her perfume, which would rise more powerfully as he slit the gummed down flap. He did so, thrust his nostrils into the gap, drawing in deeply. He lay back, felt his manhood stir vigorously. How the lascivious Dixon would approve, he thought. With a great thankfulness at being alive, and with a deep sense of love and gratitude, he slipped out the folded sheets and began to read.

My Dearest Sam,

I hope this finds you safe and happy in your billet, wherever it is. I'm sure things are almost as safe over there as they are here these days. Have you heard about all these air raids we are having? Terrible, I've been called out twice now. It's terribly scary. I'm afraid I'm not at all like you. I'm an awful coward and shake in my boots at all the terrible bangs and crashes. I'd be no good at all in the trenches, would I?

However, I have other problems equally worrying on my mind just now, and far more personal. Please don't be angry with me, darling – I can still call you that, can't I? In fact, I hope you'll be unselfish enough to wish me happiness. The thing is – I've fallen madly and passionately in love. Head over heels stuff. I couldn't help it, Sammy, it just hit me out of the blue. He's a captain. Fusiliers, a great regiment, he says! Gordon is his name. He was wounded in the Dardanelles campaign. Should have got a medal, so I'm told. He's fine now. Brilliant brain, apparently, which is why they've kept

*him at the War Office, though of course he's champing to get back on active
service.*

*There now! I've spat it out to you, as they say, and I feel better already.
I'm sure you'll understand, dear boy. I'll never forget you, and I hope we
can still be the best of chums, for, after all, you still mean a lot to me. I
hope you don't think I'm one of those fast girls after all the liberties I
allowed you take with me. But I'm sure you knew that I was just an innocent virgin – we both were, weren't we? And at least I can be proud that I
never lost my honour, and that Gordon is the first and will be the only man
to ever have me completely, body and soul.*

*Yes, Sammy, the dread deed is done, for I am truly his. I don't feel fallen,
except in love. We all know how dangerous are these times we live in, and
we must do what we know is right, and to hell with outmoded conventions.
Do you think I am very wicked? I cannot believe it, and I hope that soon
you meet the right girl for you, my dear, and live happily ever after, as I
intend to.*

*My little brother begged me not to tell you, but I'm sure you understand
that I could not go on letting you hold false hopes. I'm too honest for that.
There now. I know how sad this news will be for you, but try not to let it
get you down, and try to be happy for me. You are still a dear friend to me.
One whom I would trust with my life, and therefore I can send my love with
a clear conscience. Write soon and tell me there is no resentment. Take care,
my dear. I hope you will be home for our wedding, which we have not
planned yet,*

Yours affectionately,
Gertrude.

'I say! Steady on, old boy. Get a grip!'

Sam stared up in bemusement at the figure clad only in his drawers, who was shaking him vigorously by the shoulder. Sam blinked,
felt the tears soaking his face. A huge sob sent his rib cage heaving,
and he realized he must have been sobbing abandonedly. He had no
idea how long. The subaltern, who had been occupying one of the
other cots, padded to the door, and called out. Private Dixon's boots
came clumping up the wooden stairs.

'Better get him over to Sick Bay. He's cracked up, I think.'

Sam fought to control his weeping, wiped at his streaming face with the edge of his towel. The pages of neat handwriting were scattered about him, and he clumsily gathered them up. 'No, no!' he gasped, shaking his still damp head. 'Just some bad news — from home. Caught me on the raw.' Appalled, he found he could not suppress the tears.

''Sall right, sir. I'll sort it. You come along o' me, Mr Ellington. You'll be all right, I guarantee.' His tone was soothing, as if to a child, as was the way in which he took Sam's arm and led him firmly from the room, Sam clutching at the towel, which was all he wore to preserve his modesty. 'Nobody about, sir. You let it all out. You'll feel better for it.'

Again, Sam shook his head helplessly, and fought to stem the flow of his tears, without success. He found himself sitting at a rough wooden table. A small glass of strong, rich spirits was thrust under his nose. 'Drink up, there's a good lad.' A heavy hand fell on his bare, quivering shoulder. Too bereft to register this gross familiarity, of tone and gesture, Sam raised the glass obediently, gagged and coughed at the fierce heat and bite of the thick rum, then swallowed it off. Dixon filled his glass again at once. 'That's the ticket. Get it down you.' Once more, Sam obeyed.

In less than four minutes, he drank four glasses of rum. In less than an hour, he was head whirlingly drunk. The tears had stopped, but the desolation, though dulled by his befuddlement, hovered like a thick, drifting fog on the edge of his consciousness. His head lolling, his jaw slack, he poured out his pathetic story to the unctuously sympathetic Private Dixon, who, though not keeping pace with Sam, knocked back several glasses himself during the unfolding of the sad tale.

'Show you a picture. Beautiful. She's beautiful.' Sam mumbled, his speech slurred. He groped, his hand scraped across his bare chest, and he gazed down with comic amazement to discover he was naked but for the towel.

'Why don't we get you upstairs?' Dixon suggested. 'A bit more shut-eye, that's what you need. Come on, sonny. That's the ticket.' He got the swaying figure to its feet, guided him with one arm firmly round the slim waist. Half way up the narrow staircase, Sam stumbled, the towel slipped, then fell at his feet. Dixon quickly snatched it up, helped the nude figure to complete the trip to his cot.

'Sorry – sorry – don't normally – get this—'

'That's all right, sir. Don't you worry about it. I know just what you need. Have you sorted in no time. Leave it to me. You just go to sleep, there's a good lad.' He swung Sam's feet up, struggled to slip a blanket over him. 'Sweet dreams.'

When Sam woke, his head was pounding, his stomach was burning, and his mouth was dry and foul. The pain of his grief was there, there was nothing else except its blackness pressing upon him. Blearily, he lay back, in the near darkness. He never wanted to move again. The room was empty. He could hear distant laughter, and a strong smell of cooking almost made him gag. He wondered vaguely how long it was since he had eaten a proper meal, knew only that he could not face food, or the company of his fellow officers.

'Mr Ellington? You awake? Blimey! At last! I've been calling you every half hour for ages. Come on, up you get. I told you I'd see to you, and I keep my word. Come on.'

Sam's mind was still disorientated enough not to be shocked at the urgent way Dixon pulled the blanket off him, began to tug at his arm. 'Get dressed. Here. Have a quick wash. I've laid some clean kit out. Be quick. It's all fixed.'

Outside, the air was heavily damp, full of the autumn smells, but it was warm, the rain had actually stopped. The war was a constant flicker of lights to the east, and the still loud rumble of the guns, which he could feel translated faintly through the soles of his boots. 'Where are we going? What the devil's going on?' He still felt giddy, somehow helpless under Dixon's familiar control.

'In the barn, over there, Mr Ellington. What you need more than anything to make you forget that party of yours. All the same under their kecks, eh?' He nudged Sam's arm, chuckled softly. 'You can settle up with me later. I've arranged everything. Only don't be too long. And don't be too noisy. In you go.' He thrust him bodily through the narrow opening of the wide wooden door, which immediately swung to behind him.

'Bonsoir. Ça va, monsieur?'

Sam blinked in surprise at the woman dressed in the black skirt and a shawl wrapped over a lighter coloured blouse. Her outfit looked typical of the farming folk of the region. She had set a lantern on a wooden shelf, over a pile of fresh straw which someone had arranged invitingly. She laid her shawl down carefully, began to unbutton her blouse. He saw that she was tall, but very thin. Her face was a deep brown against the white of the chemise she wore beneath the blouse. Her hair was black, coiled thickly on the top of her head. She was not old – Sam's racing brain guessed perhaps in her thirties – but her features were hard, with sharp nose and prominent cheek bones. She looked like a gypsy, Sam thought.

She sat, swiftly unlaced and pulled off her muddy boots. She flicked up her full skirt, to reveal a clean, embroidered underskirt, which she hauled up, too, exposing a pair of long drawers. They were old fashioned, with ruffles of lace around the knees, and, again, very clean looking. Her brown hands scrabbled under her clothing, untying the strings, and then she wriggled and squirmed, to ease the drawers down off her limbs. Above the black, gartered stockings, her thighs looked startlingly full. He caught a glimpse of a thick triangle of black hair at her belly before she fell back in the hay and held out her arms impatiently. 'Vien, vien, vite! Baisse-moi, alors!'

CHAPTER THIRTEEN

S AM formed his words with care, striving hard to hide his drunkenness from the sergeant, who was staring at him suspiciously. 'Looking for the signals officer. From the Foresters. Up ahead somewhere.' He nodded confidently towards the reverberating thumps and the flashes. The supply column was sitting by the side of the road, its animals nervous, soothed by the low voices of the men.

The sergeant shrugged doubtfully, shook his head. 'Don't know, sir. But you be careful. Gets tricky from here on. There's a communication trench about a hundred yards along. Get down there fast as you can. I would.'

Sam nodded in turn, grinned cheerily, returned the sergeant's salute. He felt the low-clouded night sky whirling above him, and he concentrated on walking steadily until he was well clear. He realized his uniform was sodden. The rain had begun to fall again some time ago, but it was softer this time, more like the fine summer drizzle. It clung like sweat to his face, yet he welcomed it. It was cleansing, too.

He gave a shudder, felt the stale stickiness inside his clothing, thought he detected the faint sea fish smell clinging to him from the woman's body. The revolting, crawling memory of her touch on him returned, the rasping hair of that heaving, searching belly. Her gaping rawness made his gorge rise with loathing. He pulled the bottle of stolen wine from his pocket, swigged at its acidic bitterness. It was almost empty.

He relived the shame of his buckling failure, soft and wet as he lay on her, thrusting, felt the cruel grasp of her, trying to force him into her, the belly and thighs jostling, striving to capture him. Pictured the ridiculous, obscene image, his ankles bonded in the tangle of his trousers and drawers, between those black woollen pincers of her limbs, the long muscles of her hard, working thighs. Until he had rolled off, fought clear with a despairing gasp, and she had thrust him away, curling up her legs, hiding them in her skirts, reaching for her white, delicate undergarment, hauling it on, all in a cold fury. 'No jig! Pas bien! Tu payes! You pay. Tommy tell me. Je suis mariee, moi! Je suis femme, n'est-ce-pas? You pay!'

Duplicitously, she flourished her hand under his nose, rubbing thumb and fingers together expressively. Sam had restored his dress just as hastily as the spitting woman. Now he dug out his wallet and frantically began to pull out the flimsy notes, then, in a spasm of utter disgust, he dragged out the entire wad, flung it at her and made for the door.

He had gone straight to the mess, ignoring the greetings of the clustered groups, most of whom he did not know. He found the store of bottles, selected the first that came to hand and marched out with it. He had been wandering for hours, resting and drinking now and then, avoiding the snaking columns which filled the roadways under cover of darkness. With gradual calmness came despair. He was vaguely aware that he had been heading towards the Front, drawn like a moth to the display of lights, the flickering lightning of death. Along with his revulsion for the defilement of his body came the painfully sweet memory of Gerty's half proffered flesh.

He laughed aloud now, in the chattering, rumbling, flashing dark. He recalled the phrase in her letter. *At least I can be proud that I never lost my honour.* 'Neither did I – my love!' he shouted, thinking of the fiasco in the barn. 'Faithful to the end!' But he had lost far more. He thought suddenly of David, saw the delicate, youthful face so clearly, remembered all the cloudy emotions the boy's devotion had caused. Maybe it's you I could have loved, Davy, he thought, without, for the first time, feeling any trace of embarrassment at the notion. It matters not.

He reached the first communication trench, slipped into it. Steady on. More bodies, still alive. Lines of silent men carrying the supplies up to the forward trenches, the odd muttered curse at a collision or lost footing. The duckboards were greasy, the mud churned to new slipperiness by the gently falling rain. Too many men here. Too cluttered, stinking with humanity, the detritus of war. He hauled himself out, carried on quickly now, slipping and sliding in the pockmarked hillocks, veering to the left, to escape being seen.

There were visible explosions ahead, and he caught the strong whiff of rolling cordite. He must be close to the Front Line itself. It was a ramshackle affair, as he well knew. Startled, he recalled that he had left this sector only at dawn on this very day. He came to the entanglement of wire and the sandbagged remains of a deeper entrenchment, which had until the start of the attack belonged to the enemy. He slipped through easily, crouching, taking care not to be observed, crawling through the depressions made by countless shells from both sides in the last days.

He was in no-man's-land. He knelt, swigged off the last remains of the bottle, flung it aside. He held up his face to the rain. The sector was almost eerily quiet. You sometimes got these lulls, as if both sides had simultaneously recognized the madness for what it was. Maybe they'd just fought themselves to a temporary exhaustion, a surfeit of blood. All at once he remembered how good he had felt that morning, in the tin bathtub, his joy at the thought of Gerty's letter. So good to be alive.

He wanted to be clean again, to be free of the taint of the whorish farmer's wife. He stripped quickly, scattered his clothing around him. He took his service revolver from his holster, stood upright. He felt the rain on his nakedness. It felt good. He set off, walking steadily, the whines and crashes growing louder and more frequent again, the light flickering on his pale body. He stumbled, slipped, sometimes sank almost to his knees in the cold mud, so that it looked as though he were wearing dark stockings. But the mud felt good, too, no longer the defiling filth he had previously thought it.

He came to the wire. Rags of clothing flapped softly, heavy with rain. Long white streamers rustled also, symbols of some earlier attack, encouraging men onward to their fate. Plenty of gaps. He moved carefully through. There was a rush, like game birds being set up, and he knew it was rifle fire. The rattle of a machine gun started its blind probing. He was close now to the enemy lines. Cry God for Harry . . . he laughed, almost merrily, and began to run, the ground rising slightly, and saw the redoubt. He was on the parapet almost before he realized it, and saw the amazed faces, pale blurs under their heavy helmets, gazing up in wonder.

Mustn't be captured, he remembered. Might give away vital clues. Code of honour. Must do the decent thing. Immediately below him, someone held up a long rifle, its bayonet gleaming in the dimness. Oddly hushed voices called up to him. He laughed again, pointed his revolver down at the men at his feet and fired. Several rifles crashed at once, and blasted the terrifying, naked spectre away, off the lip of the trench.

To describe her revenge as clinical could hardly be more apt, Sophie thought to herself, with a wry touch of gallows humour. She came out from behind the screen, to where the doctor and Clemmy Douglas were waiting.

'I'm afraid there's little doubt,' the doctor said. He was young. There were rumours among the prostitutes who formed a large part of his patients that he was a medical student who had failed to qualify. But they all called him 'doctor', and his surgery, handily close to the houses where the whores plied their trade, was always well attended. 'The rash on your chest, and the chancres on your private parts . . .' he paused eloquently.

Sophie could feel her cheeks warming, and she scolded herself angrily. She was way beyond such maidenly prudery. To divert her thoughts, she considered the word chancre, with an inward shudder. Fastidious as ever! she mocked herself. But it was an ugly, repulsive word, for what were no more than hard little spots, scarcely noticeable, and not to be seen at all, unless, as just now, she laid herself open to examination. 'How long have I been infected?' she asked, pushing aside her embarrassment, and meeting his gaze squarely.

'Well, the rash and soreness have just appeared, you say? Probably no more than a month or two. Don't worry,' he continued, injecting a note of hearty encouragement into his voice, which immediately made Sophie think he was being optimistic. 'I'm sure we've caught it early enough to have you cured completely. Though treatment will take a while. And of course–' this time it was his turn to fight against embarrassment, in spite of the numerous times he had imparted similar or identical news to his patients — 'you must refrain from any sexual activity until we can be sure the disease is no longer present.'

'Of course.' I will not blush! she urged herself fiercely.

'I'll give you some ointment to apply. And also there are some pills now. They're new. A new mercury compound. Very effective, it's been found.' Now the tone changed to one of apology. 'Rather expensive, I'm afraid.'

'That's all right, doctor,' she answered. 'I'll pay you now.'

Outside, as they linked arms for the short trip back to the house, Sophie said, 'You must keep my secret, Clem. No one must know. I don't want to risk Mr Herbert's finding out.'

Clemmy stared at her, her face clearly expressing her shocked delight. 'He's got no idea? And he's still having a go? Doing it as usual?' She could not repress a giggle.

Sophie nodded. 'He's coming again tonight. Probably staying over!'

'You little bitch!' Clemmy declared admiringly. 'So your scheme's bound to work. It probably has already! I never thought you could be so wicked. You of all people!'

Sophie smiled, hiding her own sense of shock at her deviousness. Her plan had worked, all too well. Clemmy and the other girls in the know had been astounded when Sophie had confided in them that she wanted to 'trade' as they did, but as discreetly as possible. Clemmy had even tried to argue with her. 'Come off it, gal! You're no brass! Not like the rest of us! You're too decent for that!' But Sophie had convinced her otherwise, by persuading her that she wished to prostitute herself simply as a means of secret revenge on her keeper, Mr Herbert. Once Clemmy had accepted that as the motive for Sophie's action, she had become instrumental in helping Sophie achieve her aim.

Sophie herself had been plagued by doubt that she would find the courage to go through with her plan, but she was spurred on by the depth of John Herbert's sadism in forcing the corruption of his

117

sweetly innocent son on her. Davy had visited her several times. The incongruity of their taking tea together, in what was no better than a brothel, while she acted like the perfect lady she had ceased to be all those years ago, was never lost upon her, and served to spur her on in her own depravity. She had even, to her own surprise, found that the hasty, commercial sex with strangers was, if anything, less degrading than her role with John Herbert. The growing hoard of coins and bank notes hidden in her room, while it literally constituted the 'wages of sin', made her feel in no way more defiled than when she surrendered her body to her master for his continual pleasure in her submission.

And now her desperate plan had succeeded, far beyond her expectations. Not that she was not frightened at its success. When she had first devised her revenge, her thoughts had not gone beyond the secret satisfaction to be had from knowing that he was entirely ignorant of her infidelity, her casual depravity with the bodies of her anonymous strangers. He believed her his creature, thoroughly corrupted to his will alone, craven in his possession of her. The bittersweet pleasure of his coming to her unaware of all those other casual possessions, some only hours previously, was reward enough.

The news that she was infected with venereal disease from one of her 'clients' was justice, in more ways than one. She was still being punished for her sins, even if she had sought the punishment herself. God was still in His vengeful heaven all right. But now she prayed to that God that vengeance would also fall on the chief architect of her ruin; the man who had kept her in utter sexual submission all these years, who had been so vindictively cruel as to bring that young, innocent boy to be initiated by her hand into the world of animal sexuality his father inhabited. True, she was afraid. But not too afraid to pursue her course, however dire the consequences.

He had no inkling of her treachery. It gave her a deep sense of bitter satisfaction when she heard him railing against Davy for his 'conshy cowardice' and his own trumpeting about the importance of 'doing your bit' for the country, that she could claim she, too, was 'doing her bit' for the war effort, for the majority of her customers were in uniform. Some were nervous young virgins, afraid of their own 'deflowering', yet more afraid of dying without ever having experienced one of the elemental forces of their young lives.

She had often wondered how long she could go on deceiving him, for more and more of the girls were aware that she was doing the 'business' now, and though those she had confided in had all been perfectly amenable to the idea, with no hint of any professional rivalry, Sophie felt it would not be long before Mrs Evans learnt the truth, and then her situation would be precarious indeed, for Mrs Evans had always acted as a kind of supervisor on his behalf. In any case, he *must* learn of her perfidy if the disease she carried within her was to be transferred to him. There was of course always the chance that he might believe he had been infected from another source. She had no idea whether he used other whores to satisfy his urges, though, according to Mrs Evans, and the girls of the house, he had never indulged in vice with any of their number. 'He likes to own his girls!' Clemmy had said darkly. 'He don't like sharing with no one. Except his own son, poor kid!' she concluded disgustedly.

Sophie could not deny the clutch of fear she felt at the thought of her future. What would he do when he learned the truth? She had seen plenty of examples of his cruelty towards her. Her greatest anxiety was that he might tell her parents the truth at last. It might well destroy her parents spiritually, if not physically. But then there were others now to help carry and ease the burden. She had younger sisters who were grown, to support and care for them. And her father was still extremely active, not yet sixty. But he was naive in the ways of the world, for all his advancing years – a country parson. The news of her sin would surely maim him in one way or another.

Still, she could not truly regret her action. John Herbert was coming again to her, tonight. And she would take the same keen, wicked pleasure out of deceiving him, welcoming him to her bed, as she had so often during these past months, with her body still marked and sore from her copulation with a stranger. She would once more play the licentious mistress to the hilt. She knew what enjoyment he derived from seeing her caught up in passion, revelling in the fact that he was responsible for the transformation from virgin to wanton.

And then there was his poor wife: another powerful reason why he should be punished for his crimes. Sophie had learned from Davy's ingenuous talk during their secret meetings together how completely isolated Enid's life was. 'He never visits her room,' Davy confided. 'In fact, he's hardly ever home now. I think mama is seriously unwell. Her mind. She shuts herself in her room, she sees no one, except her doctor. She eats alone, goes no further than the garden.'

Sophie had looked forward to Davy's visits, few though they had been, and only at long intervals. She dressed soberly, and they sat at the small round table, with the tea things spread before them. He was shy at first, but gradually relaxed – she had been at pains to make him feel at ease – until their talk had become both confiding and free. 'You realize that Mrs Evans and the girls assume we are in bed together? If your father should ever find out about your visits you must convince him that that is what you come for.'

He had blushed vividly. 'Of course! I know — he thinks — that first time — it—'

She nodded, putting him out of his misery. 'Yes. He was delighted. I told him what he wanted to hear.'

Davy talked of his own worries and feelings, and of the family. He told her of Gerty's behaviour, her attachment to Gordon Pearce, and his own fears for his friend, Sam. 'I begged her not to write and tell him, to wait till he can come home, out of there.' His face expressed the depth of his fears. 'But I know how selfish and headstrong she can be.'

Sophie was well aware of it. She knew just how big a part the spiteful girl had played in her downfall, the malicious lies she had told to her father. She leaned forward, put her hand lightly on Davy's wrist. 'You're very fond of him,' she said tenderly.

The look he gave her showed the strength of his feeling better than any words. 'I just want him back home safely,' he said simply.

CHAPTER FOURTEEN

DAVY was surprised at the speed with which his father acceded to his plea not to be sent back to Riponcourt. Capitulated was not the word to use, for John Herbert did not put up any opposition to Davy's nervous request. 'You're absolutely right to say it would be a waste of time. The four years you've been there have been a waste of time from what I can see. You've never even tried to fit in. You might as well drop it now, you've been nothing but an embarrassment to me the whole time you've been there.' John Herbert stared at his son in cold contempt. 'And what do you propose to do for this next year? Sit at home and embroider?'

'I want to study for going up to university next year. Perhaps do something useful here, around the estate. With you being away so much—'

'Huh! Study what? Greek and Latin, and love poetry, I suppose? So you can go up to Cambridge and chat with other longhaired nancy boys while the real boys your age are out there dying for you! And what about the National Registration Act? Or do you consider yourself too delicate even to be conscripted? I'm sure there must be something even you could do in the army. Push a pen or something!'

'That's not for another year, sir,' Davy muttered, his face glowing. 'My studies won't be wasted, even if I do get called up.'

His father seemed to tire of the argument all at once. 'Oh, stay here, if that's what you want. Leave it to your sisters to show a bit of spunk and fight your battles for you. You always have, it seems to me.'

A few days later his father had departed, and Davy was still euphoric with relief that he would not have to face the rigours of school again, when Nelly brought a large envelope to the morning room. It was addressed to him. He recognized Gerty's handwriting. A single folded sheet fell out, together with another sealed envelope — a letter of his, written some time ago and addressed to Sam.

Davy felt his heart give a great lurch. It seemed to close his throat, and he gave a soft, smothered moan of fear. Gerty's note shook in his hand.

Dear Davy,

It gives me great pain to have to tell you that Sam has been posted missing in action, they think around 20 August, in a night attack on the German lines. Although his body has not been recovered, they say there is no doubt of his death, and that it would be wrong to hold out any hope. I know how deeply upset you must be, as indeed I am. You know how dear he was to me. It is such a comfort to know he died bravely doing his duty.

I received a letter from his company commander. They found my last letter to him opened in his billet. Also the enclosed letter from you which was still unopened, and which they forwarded to me. No doubt he hadn't had time to read it before the attack.

I know how hard this news will hit you, but you must try to bear up. Perhaps it will encourage you to think a little more about how you can play your part in the war, as so many of us are doing. Believe me, you can't feel any worse than I do, especially as I had just written telling him the truth about Gordon and I. On the other hand, I'm glad now that he did know before it happened, so that at the end everything was honest between us. He was such a decent chap. It seems that this war takes only the best from us.

The final lines danced and dissolved in his tears. The sobs which erupted seemed to scald his lungs, as he let his head drop into the crook of his arm on the pristine white table cloth and let the grief tear at his heaving body.

He felt a hand clutch urgently at him, then he was standing, his head pressed to Nelly's shoulder, her arms circling him, hugging him tightly to her, leading him past other shocked faces, out into the corridor and up the staircase towards the sanctuary of his room. They lay together on his unmade bed, Nelly soothing his head as it burrowed into her breast. She stroked the dark gold, into which her own tears fell, while she murmured the age-old formulae of comfort.

'She killed him, Nelly!' he gasped finally, his tear ravaged face lifted to her. 'She killed him!'

Nelly stayed with him. Eventually, he was able to quell his grief sufficiently to give her what meagre details he had, and to point out the significance of Gerty's confession that she had told Sam about her relationship with Captain Pearce. 'That's what did it, Nelly,' he wept. 'I told her – begged her not to do it. He just lost the will to survive, I know he did. I knew what it would do to him.'

Nelly did not know what to say. There was nothing she could offer, but her presence was a deep comfort to him, her compassionate arms and body a solace in his despair. More than he realized at the time. She was still holding him, a long time later, when there was an impatient knock at the door, and Mavis Cockeridge's penetrating voice called out, 'Nelly! I don't know what you're up to, but can I remind you you have other duties to discharge? Mrs Herbert's breakfast things want clearing, and there'll be her bath to run before long. *If you wouldn't mind!*'

Davy stiffened in her arms. Nelly stood, shook out her apron and her skirts, adjusted her white cap. She moved to the door and opened it only a little way. 'Master Davy has had some terrible news, as I'm sure you've gathered by now. Mr Sam has been killed. I'll be down as soon as I can.'

Davy had risen also. He rubbed with a childlike gesture at his tear-besmirched face, with the back of his wrist. 'No, look. You go, Nelly. I don't want you getting into trouble. I'm all right now, honestly.' He smiled at her through his grief. 'You're a brick, Nelly. My only true friend.'

She glanced towards the door, then back at him, her open face showing the distress she was feeling on his behalf. 'If you're sure, Master Davy. I don't want to leave you—'

'I'm all right now. Thanks to you. You go now.'

But he wasn't all right. The sadness crashed in on him, again and again, in great waves which battered his strength. He fell back on the bed, lay in the indentation his and Nelly's clinging bodies had made. It was still warm, and smelt faintly of the fresh, simple soap she used. He pressed his face into the counterpane, while his body shook with the weeping which engulfed him once more.

Worn beyond endurance, his conscious mind finally granted reprieve, and he fell asleep. And into a dream of such erotic power every touch, every sensation, remained vividly with him. Sam was there again, rescuing him from those tormenting boys on the train, only this time there was no restraint between the two of them, no manly reticence. Sam smiled tenderly, a loving smile, dazzling in his glory, and led him by the hand. He could feel every movement, as Sam embraced him, and folded him joyously into his loving strength.

He woke, once again weeping softly, as the overwhelming happiness of the dream drained away, leaving him utterly bereft at the head pounding reality awaiting him. He could not bear to stay still, to be in that haunted room a second longer.

He ran downstairs, out into the cloudy, humid daylight. He had started to learn to drive during the summer. Now he went to the old stables, most of which had been converted to a garage. He took out the 'Tin Lizzie' Ford, after filling it from the precious store of fuel Bolton jealously guarded, praying that the overseer of the estate would not appear while he was doing so. Davy was filled with a frantic urge to get away from the house, to put a distance greater than any he could manage on his own feet between its peaceful serenity and his painful emotion and memories.

He was by no means expert as a driver, and, in his distracted state, he drove more erratically than usual, but fortunately the roads were scarcely more than rural lanes, and traffic was light. All the other vehicles he passed on the road to Willerby were drawn by nervous, startled horses. But by the time he reached the edge of the market town he had come to his senses enough to realize he was a danger to himself and others. Besides, this was far enough. He was anonymous here, as long as he kept out of the shops where the family was known. And he had every intention of doing that.

He parked the car on an open patch of ground behind the cattle mart.

Compelled by an urge he hardly understood, he made his way across to a pub called The Beehive, a rough looking establishment frequented by labourers and cattlemen. He had never been in such a place before, though he recalled seeing large groups of noisy revellers sitting about its cobbled frontage. It was busy enough today. He could see a group of khaki clad figures sitting at the rough wooden benches and trestle tables in the yard. This was what he needed.

Inside, the low ceilinged bar was as he had imagined: filled with smoke, and the smell of bodies, of stale beer, and the menacing rumble of loud voices all around him, bellowing with coarse joviality. He edged and insinuated his way to the dripping counter. He stood for so long that he could feel his face burning in a blush, before the barman noticed him. 'Yes, young man? What can I get you?'

'How much is your whisky?'

'How old are you? Old enough to be drinkin' whisky, sonny?'

'And if you are, why ain't you in uniform?' One of the broad, flannel-shirted backs, divided by the broad, grubby white canvas of a pair of braces, turned to face him curiously. The red bewhiskered face stared boldly.

Davy's blush deepened. 'I will be soon,' he answered, trying to disguise the tremor in his voice, to round and deepen it. 'Can't wait!' he added, loathing himself for his craven grin.

'That's the ticket, son! Give the lad his drink, George. This young buck's gonna be killin' Fritzes by the score in a week or two, incha, boy?'

Davy guessed that the chorus of laughter flung up at this remark was not kindly meant. He knew that his slim frame and delicate features were anything but martial. However, he grinned, and nodded self consciously, picked up the small glass and took a great gulp at the contents, which burned fiercely and caught his breath, forcing him to gasp and cough as he turned away from the rack of stares round the crowded counter. He convinced himself that the tears were simply on account of the burning spirit. It was gnawing at his guts now, its bite easing, the warmth spreading in his stomach. He escaped outside, took another tentative sip, striving not to shudder, or to cough.

He was totally unused to strong drink, and even the one small measure made his head slightly dizzy. But, somehow, he had become convinced that he owed it to Sam to make this gesture. Perhaps as a punishment for his own effeminate inadequacy, perhaps to make atonement for his sister's lethal cruelty. He went back inside, chose another part of the bar to squeeze into, and presented his glass for a refill, which was given by a plump woman, without comment. Despite the fastidious grimace and slight feeling of nausea at the potent smell as he lifted the glass, he forced down another generous amount before stepping outside again.

In the yard, the group of soldiers still occupied the benches. They were noisy, laughing uproariously at almost every remark. Davy stood close by, listening, without comprehending much of what they were saying. It was only when one of them glanced up sharply that Davy realized he was smiling at them. The soldier frowned, looked as though he was about to make a belligerent comment, and Davy blushed. 'Would you mind if I joined you gentlemen?' he stammered awkwardly, the words tumbling out. 'My brother – I — he's in the army. Over in France. I'd – like to buy you a drink, if I may?'

The frown disappeared, there were winks and guffaws. Room was made for him in the middle of the narrow bench. Someone's hand fell resoundingly across his shoulder. 'Very decent of you, Mister! Right lads! Young gent here's offering a round. Who's having what? You sit still, son. Ten bob should cover it. And a scotch for yourself, is it?'

The talk flowed on about him, while he grinned vacuously, shook hands, nodded at the casual greetings. 'What mob's your brother in?' his neighbour asked. Davy gave the details of Sam's regiment. 'Shit! They copped a packet the other week, didn't they? Fuckin' Wipers again! Is he all right? Have you heard?'

'Yes, yes!' Davy nodded vigorously. The motion felt funny, as though something inside his head was loose, like the clapper of a bell. He laughed. 'He's fine. Had a letter this morning. That's why I wanted to – you know. Celebrate.'

'Quite right too, mate! Shall I get another round in? Same again, is it?'

Davy had no idea how long he sat buying and drinking. He suddenly found himself alone, a fine drizzle clinging to his clothes and his face. He was leaning forward, his brow resting against the rough, whitewashed brick of the urinal, which was nothing more than a low-walled enclosure, roofless, with a wooden trough that drained away through the wall somewhere. The stink of the place caught at his throat, he felt the bile rise urgently, clogging his throat. He turned away, fumbling his penis back inside his clothes before he doubled up and spewed violently onto the cobbles in a corner, spattering the front of his boots and his trousers.

A hand clutched at his shoulder, digging into his jacket, holding him upright. Tears mixed with the rain on his cheeks. Over him the evening sky whirled. He saw himself as a minute and worthless speck on the face of the vast, revolving planet.

'Here! It's Master Davy, innit? Mr Herbert's lad?'

Davy blinked into the face of a young soldier. A sharp, runtish, worldly wise face, of dark, coarse features. The figure was slight, scarcely larger than Davy, the uniform looked ill fitting, hung in loose folds. The peaked cap was battered, rested askew on the dark head, showing wiry, greasy curls. 'I'm sorry?' Davy answered politely.

'You don't remember me, do yer? Harold. Harold Walls. I worked up there, in the stables. Remember?' He laughed, leaned in close, breathing beer in Davy's face. 'I had to get up behind you one day. On old Monty. Hold you onto him. You were shittin' yourself! Then your pa whipped your backside for you. You must remember that?'

David did, vividly. All at once, he recalled the feel of the stable lad fitting his body to his, from behind, the press of it, the intimate melding of their flesh, and Davy's surrender to it.

'Ha! That's funny! Cos *I* remember you, too! You was blubbin' your eyes out. You was only a little mite. Down by the stream back o' your grounds. We come along with Tovey's lass. Nelly. Remember?'

Davy saw the taller figure, also in uniform, leering over Harold's shoulder. 'All old pals together, eh?' Harold chuckled. 'Looks like you've had a skinful, Master Davy. Saw you drinking with those bastard engineers. No good they aren't. They'll rob you blind. You stick with Wally an' me. We'll look after you. Let's get out of here.

Spotted Cow's much better, nicer class of folk altogether. They've got a nice little snug. Young gentleman like you shouldn't be pissin' up in here.'

Davy felt a kind of helplessness as he lurched rubber legged between his two guides. Part of his reeling brain was crying out a warning, another part telling it fiercely to shut up. This is what I want, he argued silently. Danger. Excitement. What I deserve.

Time, sensibility, flew, disregarded. He drank, listened to tales of unspeakable horror, of limbs and guts and rats chewing spilt organs of death, none of which he could imagine, none of which could touch him. The burbled accounts were like fairy tales. They meant nothing, had nothing to do with him and Sam. But then they were up, and moving, they were leading, half carrying him, it was pitch black. He was in the cramped back of a car – his father's car – Harold sprawled next to him, the other chap – Walter – driving. 'Where are we going?'

Harold's hands were at him, rubbing with shocking intimacy between his legs. 'You a poufter, Davy?' The face was close to his, the beer breath hot on him.

Davy shuddered, began to weep. 'No,' he answered. 'Let me go.'

'We know what you're after, Davy. Chattin' up soldier boys! You didn't oughter do that. Soldiers can be very nasty. Not like us, eh, Wally?'

The car stopped in a gateway. High trees soughed about them, the spiky grass was wet. Davy felt it soaking his trousers. A push sent him sprawling on his back, then came a vivid flash of agony as a boot drove into his side, then another, and he whimpered, tried to crawl away. He felt the world spinning, receding from him, as a great weight pressed on his chest, and he felt hands seizing the lapels of his jacket, riving at it, dragging it from him. 'Where's that fuckin' wallet of yours, eh? You pouf!' An open palm slapped him hard across the side of his face. He tasted blood as the inside of his mouth was cut by his teeth. The hands were tearing at his clothing still, stripping him there in the wet dark, and he felt his strength draining in that weak, insidious surrender as they plucked him back and forth.

He was back on the floor of the train, among the buffeting legs, and the hands hauling him aloft in shaming triumph 'Sam!' he cried silently, dreaming of the rescue, but there was no Sam to save him from this black nightmare of a new violation and shame.

CHAPTER FIFTEEN

'**I** want her out of this house now! Do you hear me, Father? I've never known such insolence! I thought at one point she was actually going to attack me!' Gerty's voice quivered with outrage. 'She really must be taught a lesson. It just shows what difficulties we're going to face with these people once the war's over. You must get rid of the whole family. Turf her father out of his cottage. Send the lot of them packing.'

She felt her bosom heaving against the constriction of its tight confines. The tears started to her flashing eyes again. She shivered with private revulsion at those few moments of genuine panic, when the red faced, vengeful creature had hovered menacingly over her, forcing Gerty to shrink back involuntarily, lying across her bed, staring up with dread at that great, red, clenched fist she thought was about to be launched at her.

'You selfish little bitch! You don't know what misery you've caused your poor brother with your wickedness! I'm worried sick for him. I don't know what's the matter. He's ill, really ill, and all 'cause of you! I believe he's right. I think it *was* you killed that young gentleman with your cruel ways. I reckon this latest one you've got in tow oughter be told and all!'

Gerty had squealed with impotent fury, lying there pinned by the anger of the towering maid, golden curls fiercely escaping from her twisted white cap. It was only after Nelly had left her, with a thick gurgle of disgust from her throat, that Gerty had been capable of moving from her undignified sprawl. 'How dare you – you – speak to me like that?' she gasped, standing in her doorway, and making sure that Nelly had passed safely out of sight.

Though she hated to admit it, a deep sense of guilt added to her feeling of wretchedness over Sam's death. Perhaps Davy had been right after all. She should have waited, kept the news of her sudden falling for Gordon a secret from poor Sam. She felt terrible enough about it as it was, without her brother's hysterical reaction to the news, and his awful accusations. To say nothing of that clod-hopping Nelly Tovey's wild attack. Did they think she was utterly bereft of feelings or what? Of course she had shed tears, many of them, over Sam's death. But surely it wasn't wicked of her to want to tell the truth, to be honest with him of all people? She had even hoped he might be happy for her, in that she had found what true love really meant. And besides, she had her own powerful anxieties to occupy her.

Her wounded sense of injustice flared again at her father's apparent indifference to her humiliation. Once more, she wondered what on earth was wrong with him. Such an important time for her, too. Surely he realized that? She had brought Gordon down here to stay for the weekend, to meet daddy properly. Their previous meeting had been over dinner at a London hotel. She had been looking forward so much to showing Gordon her home, to having him get to know daddy properly, to have that vital talk she was certain must take place over the short stay.

Must indeed, she reminded herself agitatedly. Her monthly show was now more than a week late. Yet again, she protested her innocence to herself She had not meant to become . . . compromised. It was not a girl's responsibility to look out for such delicate matters. It was up to the man, surely, to protect her? Just mischance, the fortunes of love, for she was too deeply in love to worry about precautions and all that kind of messy thing. Not that Gordon wouldn't do the honourable thing, of course. And not that she couldn't wait to be his bride. In fact, waiting was quite out of the question now. They were partners, in flesh as well as spirit, and the sooner it was recognized officially the better.

Which was why it was so infuriating that her father was suddenly an irascible near stranger. He had scarcely spoken, positively avoided their company. Now, of all times! Davy she might have known would behave badly. Going off the rails completely, throwing some sort of nervous fit, hiding himself away God knows where. And now this final straw. To be attacked, in the privacy of her own bedroom, and by that upstart of a peasant, shrieking and threatening like a fishwife, all apropos of nothing. Gerty could not even recall the innocent remark which had been the tinder flash for the maid's abominable display.

His daughter's shrill buzzing was like that of a half noticed insect to John Herbert's disordered mind. His thoughts were still torturously full of his own looming trouble. He went over yet again every hideous detail of yesterday's meeting with Dr Rivers in his Marylebone office. The heaped indignities which had beset John recently culminated in the doctor's grave affirmation. 'Yes, I'm afraid it's a rather virulent strain of a sexual disease, as I'm sure you must be aware. The painful irritation, the discharge. The swelling. Syphilis is the most likely diagnosis. And I'm afraid there's more discomfort. We must begin treatment right away if we are to be successful in a cure. If you wouldn't mind, strip from the waist down, behind the screen there.'

Agony was a fitting description of what John had had to endure. His penis lay on a bed of white lint. The wicked instrument of torture lay in a kidney dish. Seconds later, his urethra was open, subjected to a fierce, burning penetration as the slender instrument was inserted, and slowly, oh so excruciatingly slowly, drawn back again, relentlessly scouring his most tender flesh, until he gasped, bit at his lips, then whimpered softly like a beaten dog at the pain which brought the sweat out on his brow.

And there would be more, much more of that, as well as the ointments, and the pills, which already were beginning to wreak havoc with his insides, making all but the consumption of the blandest foods a nauseating experience that would send him rushing for the WC within half an hour of eating them.

Rest, and fresh air. Limited exercise, no undue stress. Hah! It made him laugh savagely at the very idea. 'How long have I had it?' he asked Dr Rivers directly.

The consultant shrugged. 'Well, it's possible of course for a disease like this to lie dormant for months, even years. It can even be a congenital thing. Any history of it at all?' John shook his head grimly. He was sure of where he had picked it up, sure that it was of recent origin. He was doubly glad he had not gone to the family physician. 'Your wife must be examined. You must take great care to use your own things. Crockery and so on, bathroom items. You can tell your staff you have some sort of infection. I mean of course—'

'There's no need to trouble my wife,' John observed harshly. 'It's been several years since we had any physical relations. I have – a mistress. She will need to be checked.'

Dr Rivers shrugged. 'If you're certain . . .' he paused slightly. 'However, we're not sure of how exactly the disease can be transmitted – other than sexual intercourse. It's possible any contact – kissing, an accidental mingling of the blood, from a small cut, for example . . .'

But John knew just where and how he had caught it. He remembered a while ago how even he had been shocked secretly at Saffy's wild passion, her abandonment; how her desire seemed to be constantly rekindled, no matter how violently they had made love. How she had kept him in her bed, begging him to spend the night with her, instead of leaving her after he had satisfied himself, as had become his custom at this stage in their long association. And her urgency had excited him, awakened a degree of fervour in him he had thought gone from his possession of her after all these years.

She had known, known the corruption she carried within her! And his careful, secret enquiries had confirmed it. He marvelled now, almost with a reluctant admiration, at her cunning, the depth of her patience for revenge. Well, he would have his, too. And it would be a lot more comprehensive. She would never be allowed the luxury of the last laugh of triumph.

He brought his mind back to his daughter's vehement complaints. 'Do what you think is necessary,' he told Gerty shortly, anxious only to shut her up. 'Tell Mavis the girl must be out by tonight. I'll tell Bolton to give Tovey notice. I'll have to give the fellow a reference. He's been a good worker. Been with us upwards of twenty years, and his father before him.' John suppressed his twinge of conscience. The family was suffering enough insults at the hands of their inferiors. In any case, the fellow would probably find employment easily enough not too far away. There was a shortage of labour everywhere with the war. Even women worked the land now, with this new women's land force or whatever it was called. He dismissed the Toveys easily from his mind. He had other fish to fry.

'What's the matter, David? Please tell me what's happened to you?'

Davy faced Sophie Marshall with that intensely suffering expression. The shadows were smudged under his eyes, the pale, translucent skin seemed stretched tightly over his facial structure, giving the sensitive features a haggard, almost half starved look. The tears shone in his eyes, which were fixed on her with helpless desperation. 'Please!' he said again. 'I have to know — if I am capable of — of behaving like a man — a normal man! I have to know if I can have — have relations with a woman!'

'David, I can't tell you that. You must know—'

'I don't want you to tell me! I want you to show me! Prove it to me!'

She shook her head. The colour rose slowly to the surface, suffusing her with a deepening blush. 'I can't do that either. It isn't possible . . .'

'You mean you won't!' he cried. His emotion made him uncharacteristically cruel. 'I'll pay you! Whatever you want!' Even in his distraction, he could see how deeply he had wounded her. All at once the feverish energy drained from him. He wilted visibly, began to weep softly, and sank down on the hard chair by the table. His fair head drooped, and he stared at his hands folded before him. His voice was laboured, and Sophie had to strain to hear his words. 'I don't know if you heard. My friend – you remember, we talked of him? Sam. He was killed.' He hesitated, looked as though he were about to give some further details, then shook his head wearily. 'When I heard, I went out and got drunk. I was crazy. I met – some soldiers. Bought them drinks.' He shuddered, paused again, while Sophie waited. 'One of them I knew — or rather he knew me. He used to work for us, when I was a child. In the stables . . .' he sounded to Sophie like some one under hypnosis, forced to reveal some terrible inner truths.

'Two of them took me away somewhere — I had my father's car. They attacked me. I couldn't stop them. They beat me . . . then . . . they did things. I couldn't stop them.' He was crying openly, and he lifted his tragic face to her, with that expression of pleading for help.

With a low cry, Sophie moved to him, took him in her arms, held him tightly against the outpouring of his grief. Her hands and mouth were gentle, soothing him, until the violence of his sobbing had died away. He stirred, lifting his wet face from her bosom, and smiled ashamedly. 'I'm sorry. For coming to you like this – for what I said just now. I don't know what made me do it. Will you forgive me?'

She stood, releasing him from her embrace but holding on to his hands. She smiled tenderly down at him. 'Davy, I would be honoured to take you to my bed,' she said bravely. 'It would be wonderful – and it would be the first time for me, too. The first time I would lie with someone I love, to make love. It will happen like that for you, one day.' She paused, drew a deep breath and went on resolutely, 'But it cannot be with me, Davy. There is a physical reason, a medical reason.' She saw his bewilderment, and her heart ached for his unworldliness. 'I have a disease,' she said quietly, 'that comes from the debased life I lead. That is prevalent among women who live as I do . . . and the men who use us.'

A curt note arrived a few evenings later from John Herbert, informing Sophie that he would not come for his prearranged visit. *Something urgent has come up. Business.* Very matter-of-factly, he mentioned an appointment he had made for her to attend a clinic at a nearby hospital. *Just for a general check-up. To make sure you are in good health.*

'He knows,' she said to Clemmy. 'It's obvious, isn't it?'

Clemmy tried to hide her anxiety. She had discovered from one of the girls that someone had been making persistent enquiries about Saffy's habits. She gave a wry smile. 'Well, it's what you wanted, girl, ennit? It can only mean one thing. He's got a dose himself and serve him jolly well right, eh?' But Sophie found little comfort in Clemmy's supposition. Her original courage and the will to strike back at the man who had ruined her life were draining quickly from her.

She decided not to keep the hospital appointment. She waited with growing anxiety while the endless days of a whole week drifted by, without seeing him or hearing any word from him. At the end of it, her nerves felt shredded. She was morbidly alarmed. No one, apart from Clemmy, came near her. Even the normally garrulous Mrs Evans avoided her whenever she could, and Sophie began to suspect all kinds of sinister things. She had the feeling of a net being drawn ever closer about her.

Two more tortured days, then she heard a commotion, heavy treads on the stairs, the landing outside her door. A stern, loud knocking. 'Miss Marshall?' The use of her correct surname set her heart thudding, then it raced into panic at the sight of a policeman behind the speaker, a bowler hated individual in long gabardine. Bringing up the rear was a female, of impressive bulk, and wearing a dark uniform, with a kind of close fitting bonnet to match, like a parish nurse.

'I have here an authority to take you into residence, at the North Ebury Institution, Miss. Would you please pack a bag, just a few necessities, and any valuables, and come with us, please? The nurse here will give you a hand.'

Sophie gazed at him blankly. She could feel her limbs trembling, had an almost overwhelming urge simply to let them give way. She tried and failed to form a coherent sentence.

'You've been certified as medically unsound,' the speaker went on impassively. He held out a sheaf of papers to her. 'Here's the authorization, signed by two doctors. And the consenting signature of the next of kin. Your father. Everything legal and binding. The constable is here just as a precaution, Miss Marshall. Sophie, isn't it? But I'm sure you'll be a good girl. Won't give us any trouble, eh?'

She watched numbly as the nurse began to rummage through her few possessions, dragging her valise from the top of the wardrobe.

An hour later, she was staring fearfully about her at a bleak, white tiled room with an open shower at one end, and a row of ugly, claw footed bathtubs lined up side by side nearby. The nurse who had

accompanied her in the cab to the soot stained brick edifice that was
the North Ebury Work House and Asylum had changed from her
outdoor things into a striped overall. A thinner but equally grim looking woman, similarly dressed, stood by to assist her. 'Right, love,' the
bulkier one said, with a broad smile. 'Everything off. Put it all on that
chair, then get under the shower. We like to start off clean in here.
You don't need to worry about a thing, my dear. We provide everything, right down to your drawers, so come on. You don't want to
miss supper, do you? Chance to meet your new mates. Be delighted
with you, they will.'

The harsh overhead lighting bounced back painfully from the tiles.
It gave a dead looking pallor to her skin, a faint, yellow old ivory
tinge. She could feel the eyes of the two nurses on her as she stripped.
She forced herself not to shrink from the plump one's tight grip on
the soft flesh of her upper arm as she led her to the shower stall.

There were long but narrow arched windows, divided into tiny
square panes of thick glass separated by thick white wooden frames,
too far above the heads of the occupants of the bath house for them
to be able to see what lay behind. They might have caught a vague
glimpse of the cheap, blue and white checked curtains pulled across
them. Behind one of these, peering through the chink between two
of them, John Herbert gazed down on Sophie's pale body, shining
with the water spattering onto it.

'She's still undergoing treatment for venereal disease,' he told the
man at his shoulder. His eyes never left her. 'I've passed on the details
to the office. The notes from her doctor. He was very cooperative.'
John smiled thinly. He watched the fat nurse, who insisted on wrap-
ping Sophie in the coarse white towel and drying her, while Sophie
stood like a submissive child, and who then passed her the ugly items
of clothing in which she dressed.

'She'll be given something. She'll be treated by our doctor here.
We're very thorough, especially about things like that. We don't take
no chances.' The supervisor paused, thought of the bank notes
stowed safely in his pocket, and smiled knowingly. 'There's quite a
number of gentlemen avail themselves of this chance to observe our
patients. I mean the females, of course.' His smile became more

openly lecherous. 'She's a fine looking girl, sir.' He nodded down at the small figure, who was encased in the shapeless striped dress which was the institution's uniform. 'Any time you want to come and have a look, you just see me. I can fix it for you. Nice and discreet.'

'As long as I know she'll remain here,' John said, turning away after a last look at Sophie's retreating form, flanked by her two keepers.

'No worries on that score. Everything's above board and legal like. Her case'll be reviewed in two years, normally. But the board follow the recommendations of the doctor. And yours, of course, if you want one. And next of kin. As long as they sign the papers, she'll be here. The rest of her life, if need be.'

John thought of the bug-eyed horror of the parson, as John revealed the full nature of their daughter's dissolute ways. 'I've tried to protect you all these years. I've sent the payments you've received. I felt responsible. After all, I dismissed her – after the unnatural vices she revealed to my poor wife. It was that that aggravated Mrs Herbert's illness, I'm sure. But now I discover that she has tried to corrupt my son. She has contracted a sexual disease – I fear she has infected the foolish boy . . .' he shook his head, as though the subject was too painful for him to continue, then added finally, 'Incarceration and expert care are her only hope now.'

The devastated priest's overriding concern was for his wife and the rest of the family. 'They must never know!' he said as he signed the paper John proffered him.

CHAPTER SIXTEEN

'**N**ELLY!'

She looked up at the anguished cry. She was kneeling in the middle of the stone floor, surrounded by open boxes. Straw and sheets of newspaper were scattered all round her. The dresser and the walls were stripped of their few pictures and ornaments. Even the large framed photograph of her brother had gone from its pride of place spot. She coloured up, rose, wiping her hands on the piece of sacking she had tied round her middle. 'Master Davy! You're back home at last! That's good. I was that worried for you—'

'Nelly! I heard. I'm so sorry—' Davy choked, swallowed the rising lump in his throat. They stared at each other for several seconds in mute misery. 'It's all my fault!' he blurted distractedly. 'If only I hadn't let on . . .'

She gave a crackling sniff, fighting back the tears which were so close for both of them, managed a brave smile as she wiped at her nose with the back of a wrist. 'No, it weren't you. I'd been dying to let her have a piece of my mind for ages. I shouldn't have spoke out like that. No right—'

'I've tried,' he said desolately. 'I telephoned father. Begged him. I've even tried speaking to Gerty.' Ile shook his head hopelessly.

Nelly's father came in, stopped when he saw their visitor. 'You shouldn't be here, Master David,' he said bluntly. 'We've nothing more to do with you and your folk now.'

'Pa!' Nelly objected passionately. 'Davy just came to see how we were. To offer his sympathy. Come on,' she said truculently. She took Davy by the arm to lead him out of the dim little room. 'We'll talk outside. Just goin' out for a bit of a walk,' she muttered ungraciously over her shoulder.

The autumnal wind tugged at them, flattening Nelly's skirts against her, whipping their hair about. The trees tossed, the dry grass rattled and bent, leaves scurried about the track leading from the cottages. But the sun shone, the rolling white billows of the clouds looked incongruously cheerful and lively. 'We'll be all right, Master Davy,' she said generously, once they were out of sight of the row of dwellings. 'Your pa gave dad a decent reference. He's already had an offer, over at Tynedale. Mam and the rest of us'll stay at my aunty's for a while. Over at Bellington. Just till we sort something out.'

He looked at her wretchedly. 'I feel so bad, Nelly. Everything lately.' He shook his head so forlornly that she reached out, with that familiar little cry, half groan, of compassion and tenderness. She held tightly to his arm, pressed it into her side. He could feel the round of her breast against him.

'Oh, I know, Master Davy. But you'll come through, don't you worry. Just wait. When you get up to college next year, you'll show 'em all, I know you will. You're such a clever chap, with all that writing and reading and that. You were always the bright one. Remember? When Miss Marshall taught you — she always said you were way above your sisters, even though they were so much older.'

But her mention of Sophie smote like a further blade into the grief Davy carried within him. Only two days ago, he had gone to that awful house where she had lived for so long, to seek her out yet again. He was driven by a compulsion he could not deny to talk to the one person in the world he felt might be capable of understanding him, of helping him sort out the riot of conflicting feelings which ran through his fevered brain, might help him come to terms with the terrible events which were weighing him down. There was no one else he could be absolutely honest with about the doubts that assailed him. Not even this splendid girl holding onto his arm; lovely golden Nelly, whose friendship he cherished so much, and who had been his special friend since they were children.

He had not been able to confide to Nelly Miss Marshall's whereabouts, or her sordid way of life as his father's mistress. Shame, maybe even a twisted familial loyalty, prevented him from disclosing the truth. He had given his word, shameful as that was, to keep his father's secret from everyone. Besides, he was reluctant to sully the clear and pure bond that existed between him and the maid. Theirs was a relationship so uniquely free of any murky, ignoble encumbrances he had no wish to cloud its sterling simplicity.

But when he had reached the shabby house in north London he had been met at the foot of the stairs by that fat harridan, Mrs Evans. Accosted by her would be a better term. She had smiled hideously, her painted lips gashing her bloated features. 'Why, I'm amazed! Didn't your pa tell you? She's gone, has our Saffy. Yes! Done a bunk, a moonlight flit. Sneaky little baggage! No one knows what's happened to her, just up and off, and no forwarding address, as yer might say! There's one or two more than disappointed with her, as you can imagine!'

She took his arm, holding it so tightly he felt she was making a prisoner of him. The smile stretched even more fearsomely. 'But there's plenty more fish in the sea, they say, don't they?'

At that moment a girl with falsely bright yellow hair appeared. She was wearing a long skirt, but she had no blouse on. Davy could see her breasts filling a provocatively lace bedecked undergarment, with buttons down its front, following the striking contours of her bosom. Her arms were bare to the shoulder. They looked doughty and plump. He could see the tendrils of dark hair escaping from her armpits. She smiled saucily, came forward and gave a mock little bow, causing her breasts to quiver, and affording him a fine view of their fullness where they peeped swellingly from their casing.

'Clemmy here's a good girl. Great friend of our Saffy, ain't you, Clemmy? She'll take care of you fine, won't you, my dear? And not a word to the old man, if that's the way you want it.' She laid a finger along her fleshy nose to indicate their pact of discretion.

It had already occurred to Davy that he should question the inhabitants of the dubious house about Sophie's disappearance, but at this blatant approach he panicked, struggled free and backed away. He fled, burbling excuses, their contemptuous gaze boring into his back. Later, when he had put some distance between himself and that unsavoury district, he berated himself for his helpless inadequacy, which had rendered him incapable of any positive action.

Now, at the distressing notion that he was about to lose the only true friend he could now lay claim to, he had a powerful urge to tell her the truth, to have no secrets between them. He began to talk, pouring out his confession unsteadily. He told her of his father's secret, of Miss Marshall's wretched life over the past years as his kept woman. Davy drew a deep breath, and plunged on. 'He tried – he made me – he took me to her. He wanted her to – to make a man of me.' He flung the soiled, trite phrase out, shook his head furiously. 'I didn't — we didn't—' his voice died.

His confession was enough to move Nelly's tender heart, to outweigh her disgust and shock at his revelations. She hugged him to her, and he clung in turn. The vast gulf in their rank meant nothing for those precious minutes. When at last they had to face the parting, the evidence of their sadness was reflected in their eyes. 'Please, Nelly. Can I write to you – please? I don't want to lose you. Write to me at home when you're settled. Promise!'

'Oh, Davy! I will! Course I will. My love!' She was a good four inches taller. Her head dipped, then he was enveloped in her crushing embrace. She plastered her mouth to his, he felt her lips, wet, open, pressing on his, and his mouth opened, too. He was dizzy with shock and incomprehension, then his blood surged at the novel passion, its naked strength. He reeled, gasping, when she released him.

'Bye!' She turned, ran. He saw her tall frame, the dark skirt flapping, her black boots, the yellow hair escaping, and streaming like the tasselled fringes of her shawl. He was incapable of movement. He stood there for a long time, the wind stinging on his face. He could feel the imprint of her kiss still, taste her, feel the hardness of her teeth, the incredible wetness of her tongue moving against his. The feeling it had transmitted was spread throughout his body, he was still tingling with it. He shivered, turned away, dazed, and wondering what had happened between them.

The house became even more insulated, an almost silent place. Clara was away now, undergoing training, and hoped to follow Gerty into the Ambulance Corps. Though her older sister was not destined to remain much longer in military garb. The marriage with Gordon Pearce had been arranged, and would take place next month, in October. It seemed uncommonly rushed, but John Herbert had agreed readily enough. 'We don't want a big fuss,' Gerty said nobly. 'What with the war, and this rationing and everything. Besides, Gordon's got so much to think about with his job. We just want to be together, don't we, darling?'

Davy had an idea that Gordon's acquiescent smile, and the nod of his pomaded head, were a lot less rapturous than his fiancée's eager tone, but Davy kept his observations to himself, as he did most things. But, close as he was to physical sickness with nerves, soon after Nelly's abrupt departure, he screwed his courage tightly to the sticking point and actually faced his father with questions concerning Sophie's disappearance.

'So! You've been going back there, have you?' John smiled triumphantly. 'Should I be encouraged by this? Does this mean that you're finally growing into manhood after all?' David's face flamed, but he said nothing. 'Before you get too euphoric,' his father went on cruelly, 'you ought to know that your precious Miss Marshall has been comforting our gallant troops so enthusiastically that she picked up a dose of clap. I learnt that before she vanished, God alone knows where, incidentally. *I* don't, and I don't intend to find out. I'm well shot of the filthy baggage!'

So that was it! Davy felt a pang of compassion. He remembered the acute embarrassment he had caused her when he had made his improvident request that she should have sex, or attempt to, with him. He hadn't properly understood her explanation of why that was not possible. But his father's next words filled him with new alarm.

'I'll make an appointment for you to see Dr Doubleday. We'd better get you checked out. Pox can be a terrible thing if it isn't treated properly. He can come up to the house tomorrow. Make sure you're available.'

'There's no need. I . . .' he stopped, recognized the familiar scorn slide over his father's features. 'We never did it,' he muttered, unable to keep his head from lowering.

'But she said – she was lying! The false little bitch!'

Davy smarted at the insult as though John had struck him. He wanted to cry out, to defend her. A hatred of the imperious figure confronting him swept hotly up into his throat. Well, Sophie had finally taken herself beyond his wicked reach. At least Davy could be happy for that. He cleared his throat. 'She lied for me. To protect me. It was no good.'

'But you've seen her since. You've been back. Several times.'

Davy wondered briefly who had betrayed him. And her. That blonde whore? The revolting Mrs Evans? It didn't matter now. 'Just to see her. To talk. She was – we were friends.'

'Hah!' The full weight of John's contempt lay in that explosion of sound. 'Friends?' His voice rose, rich with sarcasm. 'With a whore? It could only happen to you. Did you even try? Or is it really true? You're a pervert after all! Can't get it up for a woman. I think I've known it all along. Get out of my sight!'

The loneliness and the desolation hit him in full later, for Nelly's absence was like a ghost about the glooming house. Gradually, he became used to the solitude. In childhood, he had always had his sisters, whose autocratic rule ranged from condescending petting to viciously expressed disapproval. Unpredictable as this relationship might be, it meant that there were few hours when he could really consider himself alone. Then had come the rough and tumble ordeal of Riponcourt, when privacy was violated so comprehensively that even bath time became a humiliation to be endured in the company of twenty or more other adolescents. Now, the shock of losing Sam, followed so closely by the loss of Sophie and of his dearest Nelly, drove him in upon himself even more. And yet, in some perverse way, he welcomed his loneliness, wrapped it like a cloak about him.

Gerty's wedding took place in the thick October murk of the capital, so that he was able to attend only for a few hours and then slip away thankfully to catch the evening train back to the country. His mother did not even go. Enid Herbert had become more reclusive than ever. She took all her meals in her room, sometimes neglected even to take her short evening stroll in the seclusion of the rose terrace. Davy made a point of visiting her room for several awkward minutes, generally in the early evening. Conversation would limp along, falter, die. There were few traces of her former beauty now in her pallid features. Her skin was paper thin, even her lips seemed palely bloodless. The brown hair, mostly hidden under a close fitting white cap of old fashioned design, was thin and lifeless, too, while her wasted frame was almost skeletal. One or other of them would soon be compelled to end the painful interlude. 'I must go, mama. I have to get some studying done.'

Or frequently it was Enid who brought it to an end, more directly, with her dry, rustling whisper. 'Leave me, David. I'm tired.'

The year ended, the new began, in a bitter, clamping frost which made the views from the lacy windows a picture postcard scene. No word came from Nelly. Davy eventually got off a stilted note to the aunt Nelly had mentioned, with a request that she pass on his letter, but there was still no reply. Someone said that Bill Tovey was working over at Tynedale, and that Nelly was running a smallholding, with the help of some of her younger brothers and sisters. Davy kept telling himself he would ride over there one day and look for her. Vivid memories of that kiss kept returning to him, often catching him unawares, and confusing him again as to its meaning and what he had felt. His body stirringly reminded him, he would feel that tingling heat spreading all over him, as though he were blushing over his entire skin. Riotous, tumbling thoughts and sensations raced through his mind at such intimate times, jumbled images of Nelly, her strong, lithe frame, her untidy yellow hair, her seeking mouth, the roundness of her soft breasts.

The severe winter suited him. It was in keeping with what he saw as his icy, blasted soul. He deserved his solitary existence, wanted nothing more. He pushed his half-hearted wishes to get in touch with Nelly once more further from the forefront of his mind. He wasn't worthy of her friendship, he had no place in this mad world, where the killing went on and on, into its fourth year, with no sign of an ending. Besides, what was he doing to be longing for a housemaid as his cherished companion? Just another example of his weirdness, people would say, his total incapacity for fitting in, for doing the decent thing.

In the early spring of 1918, Enid Herbert was put into a nursing home on the south coast, where she would spend the remaining short span of her life. She went with the minimum of fuss, a willing enough partner in her banishment. There were times when Davy wondered whether she really knew what was being done to her, so quietly did she accept her removal from her home. On the other hand, he also wondered if she was not perhaps happier to get away, to have the break with her husband made final.

'Your mother's decreasing health makes it difficult to have her looked after properly here,' John told his son, when he came to supervise the move. 'She has to be nursed. It's not a job a maid can undertake. She'll be happier there. We'll visit her whenever we can. Though she seems to have little affection left for the family,' he added, with heavy emphasis, laying Davy's proportion of guilt squarely at his feet.

John Herbert was away two days, settling Enid into her new abode. The evening he returned, after an almost wordless dinner shared with Davy, he retired to his study on the first floor. He sent for Mavis Cockeridge. No longer dressed in maid's uniform, but wearing a dark gown, and with a black ribbon in her neatly tied back hair, she was still an attractive woman, with a pleasing if somewhat slight figure. Her fiancé, the ex-footman from Tynedale, had been posted missing after the Third Battle of Ypres — not long after John had discovered he had the pox and had exacted his revenge upon Sophie.

Seven painful, abstinent months had passed since then. He had been pronounced cured some time ago. 'Well, Mavis,' he said, treating her to a melancholy smile. He rose from his desk, took her by the elbow and led her to the chair by the fire. 'It's done with.' He shook his head, sighed very faintly. 'She'll be better off there. You know how difficult it's been.'

'Oh, I do know, sir. I know how hard it's been for you. With all the work and everything.' Her voice trembled just a little. 'This terrible war. We've all had to pay such a price. And there seems no end to it. Master Davy will have to go soon – to register, I mean. Let's hope they don't take him.'

John made an impatient gesture with his hand, as though to wave the thought of his son from his mind. 'You've remained faithful throughout, Mavis. You don't know how much it's meant to me. I'm not a demonstrative man . . .' he paused, let his voice drop, until it resonated with suppressed feeling. 'As you know, things haven't been too easy. Enid – we haven't truly lived as man and wife — for a long time now. Years, in fact. I want you to know how much I appreciate your loyalty, the way you've stuck by us. Such a young, fine looking woman—'

She blushed, stared up at him, let the tears she could feel well up in her brown eyes. 'I've always been happy here, sir,' she almost whispered. 'I've never wanted to leave. Not even when — after I met Will. My fiancé,' she added needlessly. She felt a tear fall, thought how well it would look. She blinked, to shake free another, lowered her gaze modestly. 'Now, more than ever, I want to stay. To serve you. In any way I can.'

Her last sentence hung on the air. The charged atmosphere was clear to both of them. He came close, put his hand on her shoulder, his fingers pressing heavily through the material of her clothing, to the delicate hard bones beneath.

'A fine looking woman,' he said thickly, then he dropped suddenly onto his knees, buried his face in the dark dress, resting on the thigh he could feel quivering beneath him. Her hands were light, but eloquent, on the back of his neck, and his purged flesh leapt at the thought of its restoration to a pleasure so long denied.

CHAPTER SEVENTEEN

T WO weeks after Enid Herbert moved out of the family home
and Mavis Cockeridge assumed certain duties and rights above
and beyond the usual demands of her position as housekeeper, Gerty
gave birth to a baby girl. The confinement took place at a clinic in
London. Bravely, Gerty had insisted on being as close to her husband
as possible, in spite of the dangers posed by air raids. She was not so
brave during the birth itself, and gasped out imprecations against the
staff, Gordon, and the whole process of God's scheme for procre-
ation, couched in language so shocking that the sister on duty
stepped forward and delivered a ringing slap on a bare, gaping thigh,
which shocked its owner into a breathless squeak of outrage, then
into the altogether more acceptable floods of tears at the cruelties of
the world and the agonizing indignity of her situation.

Gordon had been both appalled and reluctantly admiring at his
wife's command of profane idiom, which he could hear quite clearly
from the corridor where he paced and smoked, until he could stand
it no longer and sought refuge in the nearest bar. The war had a lot
to answer for, he felt, not least the way it had changed the attitudes
and behaviour of young women like Gerty. His life had become
increasingly fraught the further she advanced into the term of her
pregnancy, so that his smoke filled bunker at the War Office took on
more and more the appearance of a haven, and even the dangers of
the Western Front, so frequently and volubly longed for in his conversations with those around him, seemed less of the private nightmare
he had always envisaged.

By the time Davy saw his new and only niece, several days later, both mother and infant were suitably refreshed and groomed. The room was full of flowers, seasonal daffodils sprouting all over the place, while Gerty bloomed exotically, coppery hair aglow and make-up perfectly applied, her fecund, satin covered bosom swelling from between the parted folds of her beribboned angora bed jacket. Davy had seen little of his sister during the past months, much to his relief, for what little contact he did have had swiftly convinced him that being with child did not make her any easier to cope with.

His innocence of the ways of the world was no longer as great as it had previously been. He knew enough to know that an April baby following an October wedding suggested that the law of nature had preceded by some time the law of man. His own quiet, introspective life at home changed, too, about the time that Mary was born. His father began, astonishingly, coming home almost every weekend. Afterwards Davy felt stupid not to have grasped the meaning behind Mavis's assumption of high handedness with the staff, and even at times, though slightly less glaringly, with him. After all, she was still only the housekeeper. Then he caught the looks which sparked furtively between her and her employer, the suppressed atmosphere which crackled all about them, and he scathingly mocked himself for his naïvety. He was surprised at his enduring capacity to be shocked, given all that had happened in his life during the past year or so.

His intention to study had not gone the way he had planned. Apathy settled on him like a close fitting garment after Sam's death, and the loss of Nelly and Miss Marshall. Days drifted greyly by, until, suddenly, it was time to begin applying to colleges. He felt ill prepared, was almost of a mind to postpone things, except that he was certain papa would not allow him to languish at home for a further, idle year. Not that his father was particularly anxious for him to reap the benefit of a varsity education. John Herbert had gone down from Trinity after only one year, and showed little regard for the graduates of that or any other seat of higher learning. Besides, there was another milestone looming more formidably on Davy's near horizon, and that was conscription.

As with so many aspects of his life lately, Davy's thoughts on military service were a tumble of conflicting ideas and emotions. His deep-seated revulsion of violence was unmistakable. The idea of wanting to kill, or even harm, another human being, whatever his nationality or beliefs, was repugnant to him. He supposed then that in his heart he could not deny his pacifism. Yet behind all the jingoistic flag waving and bugle blowing there was the lurking notion that maybe, after all, it *was* right and proper to die for one's country, if that country represented good opposing the forces of evil. But were things so clearly black and white? Were the Germans such bestial marauders that they deserved the title of Hun? Was it the rape of helpless Belgium that had really inspired us to take up arms against the rapist?

Scores of thousands of men had died, were dying, would yet die, in that belief. Including Sam. Sam had held no doubt, had heroically marched forward into battle – a Christian soldier if ever there was one. That was one of the most powerful arguments tugging at Davy. He could somehow atone for Sam's death, and the strangely private circumstances that lay at the root of it, by taking up arms in the gigantic struggle. It was a very personal thing. It haunted him that his one gesture on Sam's death had been to sully the very essence of his manhood, of his own and by extension his beloved Sam's, in the shame of that drunken episode and its terrible conclusion. Did he not owe it to anything that was decent within him to make amends by playing his part in the great conflict, whatever the outcome might be?

Yet the sheer thought of his dressing up as a soldier, of fighting with bullet and bayonet in the hell that he could vividly imagine, was enough to raise shrieks of demoniacal laughter in his troubled mind. How could he, soft handed, soft hearted, turn himself into a killer, sleep cheek by jowl with other brutal killers, in that mud infested, rat infested, corpse infested nightmare? The only answer to such a ludicrous question were those savagely mocking screams of laughter he heard over and over inside his head. And if his thoughts *could* be turned on vengeance against Sam's murderers, he was only too well aware that in his heart he believed that the most guilty lay much nearer home than the battlefield, was presently luxuriating in her pampered role of new motherhood.

In this ambivalent mode, he attended for interview at Trinity and at King's. He strove to adopt a fatalistic attitude towards the medical examination, which was to follow hard upon his eighteenth birthday. Both his frame and constitution were far from robust. The doctors would see that for themselves. They would decide the issue. He was never sure whether he hoped or dreaded that it would be rejection or acceptance.

On the appointed day, he turned up at the offices in Willerby, clutching his yellow National Registration card, along with a dozen fellow conscripts. There was one gangling chap, with round framed spectacles and a prominent Adam's apple, who was dressed in dark suit, clean white winged collar and sober tie. He was a clerk in an insurance firm, his manner polite, his accent cultured. The others were clearly of inferior social status, as voice and clothing indicated. They viewed Davy and the clerk in silence, some suspicious, some with ill concealed hostility, others with deference, though they were soon chatting easily among themselves.

The embarrassment began when they were all ordered by a conspicuously limping corporal to undress. Davy glanced round the long room in the vain hope of finding a cubicle, or some sort of screen behind which he could retire. 'Come on, son. Everything off!' the corporal admonished, at his reticence. 'No need to be shy. There's none of you have got anything we haven't seen before.' There were several dutiful guffaws. Blushing, Davy pushed down his last garment, stepped out of it and hung it on the peg with the rest of his clothing. There were plenty of whispers and muffled sniggers, and one or two obscenities, but Davy was far from being the only one who was overcome with shyness. He was reminded vividly and painfully of his first days at Riponcourt as his cupped hands automatically tried to preserve the last shreds of privacy.

The extended ordeal dragged on, for they were not examined in private, but had to wait in a single line, stepping up to the sole medical officer as their names were called. The examination was brief but thorough and Davy's face was crimson by the time it was completed, with the stethoscope placed against his chest and then his upper back. The racing of his heart must surely give the doctor cause for doubt if not alarm, he thought distractedly.

'Good strong pulse.' The doctor stared at his body, letting his gaze travel over the slender frame, right down to the toes, flexing deep with embarrassment against the wooden floor. David held his breath, aware of his smooth, pale slimness, the boyishness of his body compared with the more robust frames around him. 'Do you want to fight the Hun?' The doctor was staring hard now into his eyes.

Davy's mind raced. Tell him! Say no! You don't want any part of that mad killing! He stammered, tried to meet the steady gaze. 'I want – to do my bit, sir,' he murmured, full of self-loathing at the trite phrase and his cowed tone.

He was still trembling when at last he was allowed to climb back into his clothes. The others were chatting loudly, calling out in their new bonhomie, striving perhaps to hide their own fears of what lay ahead. But already there was a sense of community, a community from which Davy was alienated. Even the clerk had found someone to talk with.

Before they were given their official medical status, the limping corporal came over to him, leaned in close and grinned confidentially. 'Never mind, lad. You don't need a big dick to fight the Jerries. You're in, my son!'

Davy saw the girdered ceiling rush towards him. Instinctively, he spread out his arms and legs to stop himself from turning head over heels as he crashed down on his back into the drum like tautness of the blanket, then was flung up high into the air again. This time the hardness of the barrack room floor smacked the air from his lungs as his persecutors let the blanket down. He lay there, arms at his sides, sobbing breathlessly, staring up at the ring of grinning, mocking faces staring down at him. Despite his familiarity with humiliations such as this during the weeks of his basic training, the shame was as acute as ever. He struggled to ease his mental anguish by dragging out the old adage that it might have been worse, far worse, than these public degradations. There had been nothing to equal the worst of his private nightmares, only the constant, wearing drip of the others' contempt, and these public shamings. Not that they weren't agonizing enough.

'There you go, Bertha! Not the first time you've been tossed in a blanket, I bet!'

Bertha. Another pseudonym to emphasize his lack of masculinity. Not as ingenious, perhaps, as Thumbs. There was nothing they could think of to do with his Christian name. Besides, no one ever used it. But from his surname Bertha was an easy enough derivative, even for these limited intellects.

The gale of laughter was interrupted by a bark, and the recruits parted. The corporal of the hut stood impassively while Davy rose and stood snivelling quietly before him. 'Get dressed, Herbert!' the corporal said, the contempt almost as wounding as the horseplay which had gone before.

Next morning, Davy was ordered to report to his platoon commander. 'You're a sorry specimen of a soldier, Herbert,' the junior officer, probably no older than Davy, informed him. 'You'll never make a fighting man, no matter how desperate we may be.'

'No, sir.' Davy waited apprehensively.

'Captain Lee thinks you're trying to work your ticket. Get out of the army.' Still Davy waited, standing to attention in front of the desk. Through the rain sodden October morning, he could hear the shrill screeches of the various drill sergeants, made faint by the distance from the square. They sounded like demented souls. 'It won't work, if that's your game. You're being transferred. You won't even complete your basic training. You're attached to the officers' mess, as of now. You'll begin work as officers' servant. Get out!'

And so a new, less hazardous phase of his military career began. There were still persecutions, but they were far fewer, because he spent much less time with the other members of his squad. And now that he had been removed as a fighting man from their company, the edge was taken off their tormenting. It was as if they could accept him more easily now that he had been delineated as no longer one of their brotherhood but something far less. In fact several, reluctant enough warriors themselves, privately envied him, and some even evinced a begrudging admiration at his having worked himself such a 'cushy billet'. Davy recognized the contemptuous familiarity, the boisterous displays of mock affection, the pursing of lips and the suggestive noises across the barrack room. It was how he had survived at Riponcourt.

He was little if any better at his new duties: the cleaning of the officers' mess, and their accommodation, the washing up, and the waiting on in the forbidding dining room. But at least his incompetence here was taken as a way of life, tolerated to a far greater degree. The only thing that worried him was that the mincing shows of affection from his fellow servants, and from the NCOs who oversaw them, did not always carry that blatant, recognized falsity they had from his fellow recruits – 'the real soldiers' as his new comrades archly dubbed them.

There was one in particular, Sergeant Robinson, whose slick, greased and artificially blacked hair belied his advancing years, and whose attentions soon gave Davy cause for some disquieting moments. At first, he was pathetically grateful for the friendliness and patience shown by the sergeant. Never, in his limited experience of army life, had Davy come across such tolerance from anything with three stripes on its arm. But late one night, when Davy had been kept back to help lay the long table for next morning's breakfast, Sergeant Robinson padded up behind him so silently on his slippered feet that Davy jumped with alarm to feel a sinewy arm snake round his waist, and long, nicotine stained fingers brush lightly across his narrow chest. The warm, peppermint breath on the back of his neck made his flesh crawl. 'Bertha, lovey. Why don't you come into the pantry when you've finished here? Got a nice drop of wine I've been saving for the right occasion.'

Davy knew the sergeant could feel him trembling. He managed to control his urge to break violently free. He stumbled over his words in his panic. 'No, Sarge. Thanks awfully – but – er, I must – I promised someone back in the hut . . .' the words spilled out, he was hardly aware of them.

Robinson chuckled, gave a last pinch, and released him. 'Got someone else, have you, Ducks? Faithful to the end, are you? You want to be careful who you give your favours to. You know what happens if they catch you? Court martial offence. You could even be shot for it. Mind you, if you ended up in the glasshouse at Aldershot, you'd wish you *had* been shot! Pretty boy like you.' He laughed again and walked away. The trembling did not cease for long minutes afterwards.

One afternoon, Davy was on duty at the coffee machine when he heard Second Lieutenant Reardon's nasal drawl. 'And this is the delightful Bertha. Say hello to Lt Proctor, Bertha. He's just joined us for infantry training.'

'Good God! Thumbs!' The newcomer stared, at a loss for further words. Alfred Proctor had been in the year above Davy at Riponcourt. They gazed in mutual dismay and deep embarrassment, before Proctor made an effort at recovery. 'Well well! Fancy seeing you here, Thumbs! Found your true vocation in life, I see! Ha-ha!'

And that was the tone he adopted for their future meetings in such public circumstances. Davy conceded that the junior officer had little choice. There could be no friendship, only the familiarity of master with servant. Not that Proctor had ever shown any sign of friendship at school. But then, who had? And he had certainly not loomed large among those who enjoyed making Davy's life a misery. Then, a week later, Davy was assigned as Proctor's personal servant. His batman, though he had another junior officer to take care of as well.

Davy wondered later whether someone with a capricious sense of humour had arranged it. Proctor seemed as embarrassed about it as he was. The first time Davy took in the early morning tea, tapping deferentially before entering the tiny cabin, putting down the tray and moving to the window to admit the murky light of late October, Proctor emerged from the blankets and blinked sheepishly. 'Hang on a second, Herbert. Look here. I hope you don't think I had anything to do with this. Fact is, I feel dashed bad about it. Jolly awkward all round, isn't it?'

He rubbed at the top of his head, making his hair stand up in unconsciously comic fashion. 'It's not that I don't — I mean, I haven't been able to — show much friendship, have I? But it's difficult, you see . . .'

Davy smiled sympathetically. 'Of course, I understand. And don't worry. I don't mind. In fact, I'm rather glad I've got the job – sir.' His engaging smile widened. 'It's not that much different from school.

Just think of me as your fag.' Proctor gazed at him with such an expression of relief and gratitude that Davy felt moved by a sudden glow of real affection.

CHAPTER EIGHTEEN

DAVY stood outside the mess in the cold darkness. From inside came the drunken, raucous voices calling, cursing, cheering, some singing the familiar songs over the crashing chords of the piano. Light poured unrestricted through the windows. More distant cheering came from the direction of the playing fields, where the dull flicker of the bonfire showed. Every few minutes flares would go up, and light up the low clouds with their eerie brilliance. That's what it must have been like at the Front, Davy thought, and felt a great welling of relief that it was over. All the years of terrifying slaughter, so suddenly, miraculously, at an end.

He had tried during his brief spell of service so far to ignore as much as he could all the news and endless speculations about the war's progress, in spite of the endless conversations about it that went on all around him. It was not easy, when he had been finally drawn in to the great killing machine itself, and might one day soon be over there, facing its horrors. Now, he could scarcely believe that the prospect, which had clenched his guts at times with fear, was no longer a threat, its vast shadow lifted, literally at the eleventh hour. He tried to convince himself that a small part of him felt disappointment at being denied the test, of losing that chance for atonement, which had hovered in his mind since Sam's death. But he could not sustain that lie to himself. He was fervently relieved.

He had volunteered to be on duty on this great celebration. And its magic had manifested itself even here, for the drunken officers, young and old, had hailed him with familiar affection, like some lucky mascot, or favoured family pet. 'Bertha! Have a drink, darling

157

boy! Go on, something decently alcoholic, for God's sake! Can't have you the only one sober when we're all pissed!'

And now he was, too, he supposed, feeling the smile tugging at the corners of his mouth. But not like that other time. His mind shied away from the nightmare, its violent, puking conclusion, hanging there, spewing, unmanned and crying, while they emptied his wallet, and then . . .

He tore his mind away from the image, looked up at the lights, the gently swaying sky. He had drunk wine, glasses of it, but he felt good. Light and airy, floating, detached, and lonely as always. But pleasantly so. No, no! He would not remember, tried to push away the vision of Sam's smiling face. He turned swiftly and went back inside, to the lighted, raucous drunkenness, the vacuous friendships.

In the early hours, when only the real die-hards were carrying on, and the sofas and arm chairs were littered with passed out revellers, Alfred Proctor came to him, face like chalk, uniform askew, his shirt gaping, showing his singlet and slim throat. 'God! Get me to bed, Thumbs!' he moaned. 'I've just heaved my insides out. Feel terrible!'

With an arm draped over his shoulder, Davy moved at a crouch, guiding the stumbling figure up the staircase and along to his room. He toppled him onto the bed, which squeaked its protest, then began to pull him about, tugging off his upper clothing, while Proctor muttered and groaned, and flopped his limbs like an ill controlled puppet. 'Prop me up, there's a good chap.' He giggled when Davy rolled him over on his side while he placed the two thin pillows at the metal head rail, then eased Proctor back onto them.

He bent, began to pick at the laces of the smart dress shoes, slid them off. 'Don't you mind? Doing all this?' Proctor waved his stockinged foot in the air, and Davy glanced up, smiling at him.

'Not really. Why should I? It's my job. Anyway, for a fellow Ripper,' he joked. Carefully he peeled off a sock. The foot was narrow, delicate looking, and smelt pleasantly of perfumed talcum and expensive soap. Though there was a tiny clump of fine black hairs on the knuckle of the big toe, the overall effect was one of daintiness.

'Are you glad it's over, Thumbs?' The voice sounded suddenly sober, the tone wistful. His thin arms and body in the white singlet looked boyish. It was almost as if they were back at school, Davy thought. Only he had never shared this feeling of insulated intimacy with anyone at Ripponcourt. 'I suppose *I* am,' the reflective voice continued. 'Of course I am. A great victory. And at such cost. But . . .' his voice tailed off, then continued slowly, with that same note of wistfulness. 'I'll never know now, will I? How I would have shaped up over there. I feel – we've been cheated somehow.'

'Come on, sir, let's get you into bed, eh? Lift up a bit. That's it.' Proctor was transformed once more to the helpless, giggling schoolboy as Davy's fingers nimbly unbuckled the belt, unbuttoned the trousers, slipped them off the raised hips, then drew them down the limbs and off. He turned away, folded them carefully and laid them with the other clothing on the chair. He would hang them up later, when he had got his charge under the sheets.

'Some of the boys in the mess were saying – they were going to take me into town. Fix me up with a tart. Before I was posted. You know.' He gazed up in bleary, youthful confidentiality. 'I've never . . . have you, Thumbs? Had a girl – you know?'

Davy blushed deeply, thought of Sophie Marshall. He shook his head, suddenly wanting this confessional intimacy to end.

'Aren't you interested? Don't you want to know?' The voice had that naked, childish curiosity which affected Davy deeply. Again he shook his head swiftly, his face still hot. Clumsy in his embarrassment, he reached out, plucked at the waistband of the wide underpants, tugged them down, and Proctor suddenly giggled disconcertingly. It reminded Davy strongly of the dirty, behind-the-hand sniggers he had heard so often at school. Anxious for Proctor's vulnerable nakedness to be hidden from his sight, he moved, to search for pyjamas to cover the pale and slender body. But a hand shot out, seized on Davy's wrist with compelling grip, held him captive. The voice thickened, with a new kind of intensity, the whisper unnerving him, like an unexpected caress. 'At school. What they used to say about you – all those jokes. Was it true? I – sometimes – you remember Gibson? Little Ralph? He and I – we were chums. You know.'

A wild urge rose within Davy to laugh hysterically. The long, sniggering arm of school days, reaching out to him: one huge, writhing, adolescent hot pot of frustrated sexual urges, cut off from any normal influence; from girls, from sisters, and mothers, so that soon poor Mrs Rowe, the thick bodied, whale boned, plain middle aged matron, was the subject of endless obscene speculation and fantasy.

And now here was Proctor, a minute ago bewailing the fact that he was denied the chance to kill fellow human beings, lying sprawled and naked like some virgin sacrifice, clinging to his hand. The laughter rang again in Davy's wine fevered brain. Sam, Sophie, his father, Gerty, Nelly, the brute force of the two soldiers, Harold and Walter – all swirled round in a kaleidoscope of almost unbearable emotion: savagery, mockery, tenderness, sadness.

Suddenly Proctor began to weep, softly but unrestrained, his gaping chest lifting and falling in his grief. He cried with the abandonment of childhood, a desolation as naked as his helpless body. Davy felt an overwhelming compassion and identification with his distress. He was no longer embarrassed by their intimate proximity. He fitted himself to the pale form, lay down beside him on the bed, cradled him in his arms, felt the tragic face turn in towards him, breathed in the freshness of the sweet, damp skin. His lips were close to the dark, cropped hair, as he whispered, 'We ought to get you into bed.'

'Come on, you young bastard! Who gave you permission to sneak off? We're all going—'

Davy struggled up, his face a wide-eyed, gaping caricature of his guilt. Three grinning, swaying, drunken officers stood there, blinking idiotically. The figure on the bed didn't move, did not open the tightly closed eyes.

'You filthy little – you disgusting little queer!'

Hands tore at him, flung him headlong against the wall, plucked him up and hurled him through the door. Blows rained down, he sank to the floor, curled up, hands over his head, as cruel boots thudded into him, crashing the breath from him, bursting in flashing cascades of violence which his swimming senses told him spelt his end. He moved towards the roaring darkness of oblivion with surrendered gratitude.

*

Davy's mind was so deeply occupied with the task of keeping his body upright, and controlling the tremors which attacked him like an ague, that the lieutenant colonel's words rolled over him as part of the physical discomfort he was enduring. His ribs were still tightly strapped, which added to the difficulties of breathing brought on by the stress of his situation. It took some time for him to register that fortune was at last being kind to him, and that the terrors he had dreamed were not to be.

He had slowly drifted back to comprehensible agony to find himself slumped on the stone floor of the guardroom, choking on his own bile and lying in a puddle of his own urine. The white haze had turned to redness, but he still could not see properly, heard only the thunder of his own sobbing breath, until the sergeant's thick whisper tickled his ear like a lover's caress. 'What those gentlemen gave you is nothing compared to what you'll go through when they get you in detention quarters, you little pouf! Now clean up your stinking piss and shut that row!'

The two days and nights which followed, spent in drug hazed lethargy in the Sick Bay, had seemed like a sanctuary, from which he had been dragged, still in agony and with the livid bruises on his swollen face, the others covering his body hidden beneath the thick serge of the uniform, to spend a further three days in the guard house. It seemed an eternity of pain and mental anguish.

Now, pale and teetering, he tried to stand like a soldier in front of his escort, facing the senior officer, alone behind the wide desk. Davy followed the provost sergeant's advice, and said nothing.

'You could have faced a summary court martial, a long prison sentence. You've brought disgrace to the regiment, and deep, deep disgrace upon yourself, not to mention the young officer of whom you took such foul advantage. There is no excuse, none whatever, for your despicable act. And at the very time of victory. You have sullied the glory of all those thousands who have sacrificed their lives.'

The lieutenant colonel paused, the revulsion etched on his sallow features, while he reined in his emotion. 'If you had been an officer –

God forbid — I would have expected you to show some idea of honour, even in your wretched condition. Your own revolver might have drawn the curtain on your unnatural conduct. Your own background . . . you come from a decent home, I understand . . .' he raised his hands in baffled incomprehension. 'Second Lt Proctor has privately entered a mitigating word on your behalf.' His nose and mouth pinched in distaste, a clear enough comment on Proctor's somewhat dubious role as victim of the assault. 'He is resigning his commission, in case you didn't know, and will leave the service at once. You will not be charged with sexual inversion. We have no wish to parade our shame, to cast any stain on our proud record at this sensitive time. You will be given a dishonourable discharge, with immediate effect. The reason on your papers is LMF. Lack of moral fibre. As of twelve hundred hours, you are no longer one of us. We are done with you. If I were an officer in the field, and you were on active service, I would have you taken out and shot. Now get out. Out of the army, and out of my sight! God help you, wherever you go.'

'Prisoner! 'Bout turn! Quick march!'

Once more, Davy stood before a desk, this time in surroundings familiar to him since his conscious memory had begun. And once more, despite his sternest efforts, his body shook and his stomach churned nauseously. His father's voice, rich in detestation, cut into him, at a time when Davy thought he must surely be inured to mental and spiritual pain. Scorn and humiliation had been heaped on him, from everyone who had known of his shame: his sisters; his brother-in-law's tight-lipped, expressive silence; even Mavis's curl of lip and withering stare. Like a shadowy pariah, he had wandered miserably around the fringes of the house, which was decorated with the trappings of Christmas, bustling with preparations for the festivities, complete with the crib and little Mary's wide-eyed innocence.

His father had returned the previous evening. Davy had not joined the family gathering before the fire in the drawing room. The summons had come next morning, after he had sat like an unseen ghost through the ordeal of breakfast. Now was the time for another sentencing.

162

'I have never held out any hope of you. You've been an unfailing source of disappointment to me, from your earliest infancy. I don't know whether we can blame your mother for your deplorable character, your lack of manliness. And it will not change. I can see that now. Just how deep your effeteness goes I hesitate to guess, but I fear the worst. And now this. At the very time we are celebrating the greatest victory in our nation's history, I find you bring a disgrace to this family I thought even you incapable of. A dishonourable discharge. Lack of moral fibre.'

A great sense of the injustice of all of this welled up regurgitat-ingly in Davy. He choked on the hypocrisy of his father's florid outrage at his son's 'dishonour' and lack of morals. When all those years ago he had betrayed the sanctity of his marriage, had ruined the life of an innocent girl, and still continued in his adulterous ways, and under this very roof. Though his heart hammered at his ribs, Davy found courage – a new courage – to speak out. 'You've never even asked to hear what happened—'

John Herbert held up his hand and let the phrases roll off his tongue like a high court judge. 'I don't even wish to hear the details, or your snivelling excuses. They could hardly add to my sense of shame.'

'You have no sense of shame!' David's cry seemed to echo in the claustrophobic room. For an instant the words rang in the silence that epitomized the shock of their release. David knew he had surprised his father by his reaction, and felt an altogether unfamiliar and savage thrill of pride. He said nothing more, watched the dark colour spread through the stern features.

His father pulled himself up short, as though he was suddenly at a loss for words. He put his hands flat, palms down, on the desk's surface. His voice was harsh still, but implacable, the judge again. 'I am finished with you, David. You're no longer welcome here. I wish I could say you're no longer my son. I want you to leave this house. Pack what you need. I'll arrange to have your things sent on, when you have a place to stay. Let me know.'

He reached into the drawer, took out a sheaf of papers. 'Here is a banker's draft. A sum of money to help you establish yourself. Call it a severance settlement. I do not want it back – not that the thought of repayment would ever enter your mind, I'm sure! You'll also see here there is an allowance, which will be paid each month. A small one, but one you will be able to live on, with limited means, of course. Unless you should ever be in a position to earn a living.' The deep contempt indicated his conviction that such a course would never be possible. 'I do not wish to communicate with you again. You can go now.'

Scenes flashed before Davy's eyes. His father's arm about Sophie, holding her to him, his mouth on hers. The possessive glance cast over Mavis's trim form. His fierce grip on the terrified boy's shoulder as he held him over the stable rail and wielded the riding crop with burning viciousness. Hurt and injustice swelled chokingly again within him, and he strove once more against the storm of emotion to speak out. 'Gladly. This has never been a happy home for me. I'll take as little of your money as I can – and one day you'll get it back – every penny!'

PART III

MASTER AND MAID

CHAPTER NINETEEN

'SO? How is the brave new world of victory in here then?' The sneer of tone and look was transparent on John Herbert's face, and Sophie concentrated hard on hiding any trace of hurt he might inflict. She had learnt in the harsh life of the institution that the one thing she had left was that little nugget of untouchability she kept within herself. It had been a hard nurturing and she guarded it jealously. She willed it to exert its influence now, as she sat on the wooden bench and faced him across the wooden table. The air was redolent with the institution smell: stale, unappetising cooking, Lysol and floor polish, with a faint underlay of public lavatories and incontinent humanity.

She shrugged, did not answer in any other way. She wished she had had the nerve to refuse to see him. But she knew the price of such defiance. In the past two years in here, she had learnt all over again the cruel art of survival.

'You're looking a little pale, my dear,' he said, with mock concern. 'Are they looking after you?'

Her chin lifted a little, she met his taunting gaze. 'I'm well enough. I've got a new job now. Did you know? I'm out of the laundry for good. I help in the office. Records and so on. Very pleasant really.' She knew she had scored. Her heart gave a little fillip of triumph at the tic of annoyance her keen eye detected beneath his smile. She wondered how far she dared go. Her heart beating faster with an almost heady sense of danger, she went on, 'I'm allowed out one afternoon, too. Thursday. We go for walks.'

'My word! Freedom, eh?' he sneered. 'Do you all have to walk in a crocodile, holding one another's sleeve? Do you get to wear anything different for these excursions into the world?'

He nodded at the loose fitting overall she wore, tied round the middle, and under it the coarse striped dress, the ugly grey stockings, and the scuffed clogs. She was all too aware of the unattractive picture she showed, her hair cut short, hanging straight and thick, an uneven fringe across her brow, clipped back behind the ears with the long metal pins. As so often before, she wondered at his implacable cruelty. It was the first time he had visited in more than six months. She had even begun to hope she was free of him at last, even though it was he who had imprisoned her here, who would, she was certain, ensure that she stayed here, probably for the rest of her days, or until she was prematurely old and broken, like a few frightened specimens she had seen turned out after years here.

Or perhaps he had been here more recently. Perhaps he had taken his place among the 'peepers', hidden behind the high windows of the ablutions room, who, Lou and many others claimed, gathered to watch the inmates take their weekly bath or shower. It seemed unlikely, but you never knew. It never troubled her as she undressed, hung her clothes on a peg, and stood in line with the others.

'Your case will be coming up for review soon,' he said, his gaze fixed eagerly on her. The mask of her neutrality stayed firmly in place. Again the slight shrug of the shoulders. 'Do you hope to be released?'

She met his gaze levelly, wondered if he still found her sexually attractive. She knew how her looks had deteriorated: the sallow complexion marred by the tiny cluster of red spots beneath the surface on her cheeks, the result of diet and harsh soap, and lack of good, clean air. But in here she was still regarded as a beauty. She was still desired, by Lou, her protector, and the plump warden, Dunham; and others. Yes, she had learnt the technique of survival, just as she had during her long stay at Mrs Evans'.

'It would be foolish to hope, wouldn't it?' she answered calmly. 'I have no reason to think my father would change his mind . . .' she paused, then went ahead. 'Or you. I'm also sure the doctors will endorse your view on my dementia.' She could not keep her silence, even though she was fully conscious of the danger of antagonizing him. She gave a low laugh. 'Besides, it's not so bad now. After all, my wicked vice is no great drawback. Some even appreciate it.'

She was afraid she had gone too far at the flash of real hate which flickered over his features before he could conceal it. 'My word! Little Saffy lives on, eh? I'm afraid you're luckier than poor Enid then. My wife is put away, too.' He glanced about him expressively. 'In surroundings a little more salubrious than these, I hasten to add. But her mind is clearly unhinged.' She saw the familiar cruelty of his smile as he went on as if in afterthought, 'Oh yes! And my son, of course. He, too, has been removed from my life. Forever. He has proved all the worst fears I have held about him since his childhood. He is something less than a man, for all your sterling efforts, my dear.'

His smile broadened, for, at last, he had seen evidence that he had inflicted pain on her. 'I've thrown him out. He hides away in some dingy pit in London here. In fact, quite close to where our little love nest was situated, which will give you a fair idea of his circumstances. He exists on a meagre allowance. It's from his mother's money anyway. At least, I assume he does. I neither see him nor hear from him. I believe his tender hearted sisters keep in touch, but, as for me, I have no wish to clap eyes on him, or acknowledge him in any way.' He paused. 'One of your few failures, Saffy, my dear. I speak of your talents as a whore, of course.'

Somehow she fought down the welling grief inside. He must not be allowed this triumph. 'No indeed!' she returned, her voice rallying. 'There was no failure there, as I assured you.'

'You needn't bother to go on with your pathetic little lie. He confessed all to me himself. He told me how he failed to rise to the occasion, if you'll pardon the pun.'

'No!' she insisted, still maintaining her calm note of amusement. 'It's he who is lying to you. We made love. More than once. He visited me several times. I thought you—'

'Yes! To *talk*!' He gave the last word a ringing condemnation. 'To take tea with a whore! Like the mincing little fairy he is!'

'Perhaps he didn't want to hurt your feelings,' she said deliberately, in a voice devoid of all emotion. 'But I give you my word–' she smiled – 'the word, as you say, of a whore many times over. Believe me, we made love. We fulfilled each other's fiercest expectations. And you know the depth of my experience. David is by far the most satisfying lover I have ever known. Of course, I speak only of men,' she added, in her own final thrust of cruelty, and, for several precious seconds, stored greedily in her memory, she experienced the thrill of dominating victory in the dark passion of blood which rushed to his face, and the sprouting of the first seed of doubt in those dark eyes.

Nelly stared at the figure clad in old, worn khaki, leaning against the wall of the Beehive public house. 'That's Wally Hindmarch,' her young brother, Bill, declared. 'Remember? How do, Wally!' Bill called out. 'Comin' in for a pint?'

'You treatin'?'

Bill nodded, and the figure pushed itself away from the wall, swung the single crutch under the left arm. Nelly saw the pinned up trouser leg, the left limb ending at the knee. She clicked her tongue in annoyance. They had done well selling all their vegetables for a half way decent price, and now Bill was ready to throw his share of the wages she allowed him down his throat, and worse, down others' throats. Not that she didn't feel sorry for this crippled lad. There were thousands like him, the ones some folk called the lucky ones, who had come back maimed, dependent on charity, from their families or from the public. She guessed he had been lounging outside the pub in the hope that someone would come along as Bill had.

The lad was balancing there, staring up at her, his unshaven face split in a grin, both obsequious and bold at the same time. 'It's Nelly, ain't it? How you doing? Your dad's gone from the Herberts' place, I heard? And you – weren't you working up there an' all?' He hopped around, put his hand on the edge of the small, flat cart. 'Why don't you come in and have a glass, too?' he urged. 'Tie up the old donkey over there. We can have a chat. Just as well you got out of there. Been some goin's on up there lately, from what I hear.'

Nelly was torn with indecision. She was always going on about Bill and the others chucking their money away in pubs. She kept away from such places, though she had popped in for the odd glass of cider on rare occasions – if she was at the market with her father, or her Uncle Dan. And Wally Hindmarch's remark about the Herberts had caught her like a snagging hook. She recalled the unkempt figure staring up at her as a patched-trousered ragamuffin of nine or ten, the day she had found poor Davy blubbering down by the stream after he'd been beaten by his bitch of a sister.

She felt an element of fate in this chance meeting. Beyond coincidence. Davy had occupied such a special, tender place in her heart, through all the long interval of their separation. He was never far from the surface of her thoughts, present so strongly in her turbulent emotions. So many times she had argued hotly with herself, fought the urge to get in touch, to try somehow to discover how he was, what he was doing. But always the secret shock, and shame, at the depth of her feelings came to stay her.

She could not categorize, even to her own satisfaction, her feelings for him. Not love. It couldn't be. She shrank away from the word. How could she love him? What right had she? It was improper for her even to imagine such a thing. He was Master Davy, she far below him, a domestic, a drudge. Not even that now. A labouring girl, grubbing about in the dirt, digging out turnips and potatoes, her nails broken and black with the earth, the skin on her face and neck and her arms coarsened and burned a deep brown by the sun and the wind. Her back ached and her muscles swelled out, with sinewy strength in her arms, bulged on her sturdy thighs and calves, so that when she studied herself on bath nights in the scullery she was both ashamed and guiltily proud of her tall, square shouldered frame. 'Stronger than most lads, our Nelly!' her brothers and sisters joked. Except they were not really joking. She proved it in many a rough and tumble with them, and in the arm wrestling contests she was reluctantly dragged into at their instigation.

But, dismayed as she was at her own perversity, this feeling for Master Davy could not be dislodged. At times, it was almost like a physical thing – a lump lodged somewhere near the centre of her chest, rammed beneath her sternum, constantly reminding her of her sense of loss, of deprivation. There were other sensations, more shaming, and just as powerful, though fortunately they did not manifest themselves as often, for they brought deep tears and hot pangs of conscience at her private depravity.

They assailed her usually in moments of intimate solitude, when she sat, knees drawn up, in the tin bathtub, or when she sat on the smooth boards of the outhouse, staring dreamily at the daylight probing under the bolted door, and over the saw-toothed top of its flaking wooden surface, on the back of which hung the neatly cut squares of newspaper, their corners drilled through and threaded on the string tied to the long, rusty nail. As a child, that had been her job. She enjoyed painstakingly wielding the scissors. 'Be careful, Nel,' her father used to tease. 'You always cut the best stories off in the middle!'

It was that last kiss, the last time they had been together. It was all her wayward fault. She tormented herself imagining what he must have thought of her, kissing so wantonly like that. But she shivered, her body throbbed, each time she remembered, and vivid, sinful pictures tumbled in her mind. She did not even like boys, she told herself. 'You're a fine looking lass,' her father would say. 'You'll be twenty-three next. Time you found yourself a good man. Must be lots of lads broken hearted over you. The right one'll be along shortly.'

'There's no one I'd be wanting!' she'd answer, tossing her head, pretending to a light-heartedness she did not feel. Inside, she felt closer to the prickle of tears when anyone spoke to her like that. She vowed there would never be anyone she would give herself to. Not like that. Not with her body, not as a lover. And still, in spite of all her efforts, she thought and dreamed of Master Davy, and fought sternly against her longing to know of him.

She found herself swinging lithely down from the cart, tethering the donkey, following the lads into the dark inn. In deference to her, they sat in the back room. The 'best room', the regulars called it. There were a few couples sitting at the round tables, and, in one corner, a noisy, laughing group of girls, all on their own. 'That's something you wouldn't have seen afore the war,' Wally commented, staring across at them avidly. He winked at Nelly. 'They'll be giving you the vote next!' he quipped. 'Unless you start them daft suffragette campaigns again!'

'I'd have nowt to do with any of that lot!' Nelly said dismissively. 'What you heard about Brierton House then?' she asked, naming the Herbert home. The question came out more abruptly than she intended, but she couldn't help it. She leaned forward tensely.

'I was talking to the Wells lass. Maggy. Remember? Her brother, Harold, used to work up at the stables. He copped it at Cambrai, November, '17, not long after we got back from leave. Here. You remember the young lad? Herbert's son, David, wasn't it? Right bloody little fairy – pardon my French.' He leered at Nelly, then he continued with a sense of drama, 'Me and Harold saw him in this very pub, just afore we went back off leave. He was chattin' up some army lads. Liked soldiers, he did!' He winked, his stubble face stretched in a lascivious grin. 'The little ponce got his call-up, too late to do any fighting of course! But he got slung out. You can guess what for!' He gave another guffaw, another lecherous roll of his eyes.

'All too much for old man Herbert, apparently. He'd just got his missus carted off to some nursing home on the coast. Batty as they come. Anyway, when he finds out what Davy's been up to, he kicks him out. Just like that. Not a penny to his name. Maggy said she heard he'd gone off to London, living in some tip of a place. No doubt he thought a pretty boy like him could make a living up in the Smoke, eh? But seems he caught this flu, she heard. There's thousands dying of it up there. He might have popped his clogs by now. Serve the little fairy right!' he concluded, with righteous viciousness. 'I didn't lose this lot for the likes of poncing toffs like him!'

During all this Nelly had remained perfectly still. Neither of her companions had noticed her rigid pallor, the intensity with which she stared the whole time at Wally's expressive face. She gave a visible shudder. She could hardly force her words out through the rush of emotion engulfing her. 'It's a pity you didn't lose your vicious, lying, filthy tongue instead! Have this drink on me, eh?' She stood, flung the contents of her glass in his astonished face, and left before she yielded to the urge to follow them with the glass itself.

Hours later, she was waiting by the common at the end of the village when Bill came into sight. His face was red and sweating, with drink and with anger. 'You mad bitch!' he fumed. 'What the hell's wrong with you? I had to walk half way afore I got a lift. And poor Wally—'

'Shut up!' she snapped. 'Listen. Tomorrow first thing you got to drive me over to the Wells'. I have to talk to her. Their Betty still works up at Brierton. Then I'll probably want you to take me into Willerby, to the station.' He gazed at her, his anger forgotten. 'And not a word to nobody, mind! On your life! You understand?' Her large, work hardened hand reached out, seized the front of his shirt, clutched it tightly and drew him into her. She shook him urgently and his head nodded.

Nelly had never been further than Willerby. London was truly terrifying for her. Wearing her best jacket and skirt, of thick tweed despite the lingering warmth of late summer, for best clothes had to be durable enough to last at least half a lifetime and then handed down, and with her golden hair captured and pinned underneath her wide brimmed hat, she stood sweating and overawed in the concourse of Waterloo Station, most of her possessions stowed in the canvas satchel and cloth bag deposited at her feet.

Her striking figure and tanned complexion proclaimed her unfamiliarity with the city. She was approached within minutes by a small man with a heavy moustache. A ribboned straw boater was set at a jaunty angle, his linen jacket was open to reveal a luridly striped waistcoat. Light coloured trousers completed his dandyish appearance. 'Hello, my darling!' he greeted her, with a dazzling grin. 'Newly arrived, are you? Need any help?'

She eyed him suspiciously, showed him the sheet of paper she clutched in her hand. On it was the address it had taken her so much effort and pleading to ascertain from the Wells girl, whom she had to bribe to find out surreptitiously where Davy's belongings had been sent to. 'Ooh, that's north London, darlin',' the moustache grinned. 'You come and have a cuppa with me and I'll take you there meself in a jiff. Fine looking gal like you needs a bloke to look after her. Know what I mean?'

Nelly thought she did. Her grip tightened on the piece of paper. 'I'll manage for myself, thank you!' she said emphatically. She swung the heavy bags onto her shoulders, and headed off towards the streaming entrance and the smoky sunlight. She chose a policeman, who tipped a finger to his helmet and spoke with kind politeness, pointing out the omnibus stop where she could wait. Her only experience of petrol vehicles had been the rare Sunday School charabanc outings. She sat nervously as close to the door as she could, hidden behind the barricade of luggage clutched on her knee, until the conductor told her this was her stop.

Her anxiety grew, as swiftly as her shoulders ached with the burden they bore. She kept stopping, holding out the paper, noting with distress the unsavoury appearance of the streets, bemused by the endless rows of tall buildings, the jostling crowds of total strangers. She thought of the village, the eventfulness of a single stranger's face on the wide, grass lined roadway.

Her parents would have found the note she had laboriously written the night before. A poor enough explanation of her desertion, though she would, as she had promised, write to them again, giving details of where she was staying and when she would be coming home. When she knew when that would be. Maybe today, she thought grimly, if Master Davy could not be found. It was a good six months since he had left his home. He might well have moved on, could be anywhere in this vast, terrifying nightmare of a place.

At last she found the street. She glanced up at the grimy steps, checking the numbers. It seemed to go on forever, but then she was at the building. She leaned briefly against the front railings, catching her breath, breathing a silent prayer. In the dim and fetid hallway of the ground floor, she enquired of a thin child, was directed upward. Gasping now, she climbed, lugging her bags like a beast of burden. Step after climbing step, round corners, pausing on short landings, until she had reached the fourth and topmost storey. His name was printed in pencil, pinned to the scratched and peeling door. She felt the tears of relief start to her eyes as she raised a hand and knocked.

CHAPTER TWENTY

'**M**ASTER Davy!' The words she had run over so many times in her head had gone. He gawped at her, his face flushed, its beauty marred by gauntness, darkness stitched with sickness. And something else: a sadness she could feel almost as a palpable substance cloaking his slim figure. The room was stuffy, airless, its grimy windows closed. He was wearing a striped, dirty looking night-shirt, had clearly just risen from the tumbled, grey-white sheets turned back on a narrow bed. He was shivering, staring at her as though she were a ghost.

'Where – Nelly! Where have you – how did you find me?'

'I've come to look after you. I'm going to take care of you. Oh, Master Davy! My dear! I didn't know – I only heard about you day before yesterday. My darling boy! I've thought of you—'

Then they were hugging, straining together, she could feel his thin-ness through the nightshirt, feel his trembling frame pressing to her, and she wept for love, and pity. He wept, too, with happiness and relief, and a dazed gratitude at the sudden lifting of his loneliness, the miracle of her strong yet soft form, the pure, fresh sweetness of her, and the feeling of a bond as close as the bodies that clung together as though they would never be parted again.

Her face was red when they finally broke the embrace, and she had to fight against the embarrassment which gripped her at the rawness of their combined emotional release. She covered it with her old brisk, bustling manner. 'Good heavens! Just look at you, all skin and bone. And with nothing on but your nightshirt! You'll catch your – just sit there till I straighten out this bed for you. Then you hop straight back in and I'll see about getting this place sorted out.' She looked about with grim intention. 'And there's plenty for me to do an' all, by the looks of it.' Swiftly she remade the bed, noticing the grubby condition of the bed linen, all part of the general squalor. 'There now!' she said when she was done. 'In you get! And no nonsense!' She smiled broadly, to cover the deep ache and worry she felt in her heart for his pitiful condition, the skinniness of his limbs, thin as sticks as he moved to obey her, the ravages of the sickness, the two discs of red like a clown's paint on his haggard face, the feverish brightness of the eyes, and the deep shadows which surrounded them. 'We've got to get you well, Master Davy. Got here in the nick of time, I reckon!'

'Oh, Nelly!' He held out his slender, white hand, which she covered with her strong grip.

'Things are goin' to be different from now on. You'll see. We'll have you better in no time!'

'Where are you staying?'

She felt the blood rising to her face once more at his question, but her blue eyes met his and she didn't look away. 'Why, right here, Master Davy. At least for the minute. Till we got you back on your feet again. So you'll just have to put up with me. I'll be as bad as old bossy-boots Miss Gerty, so the sooner you get better the sooner you'll be rid of me!' The look he gave was worth much more than the words he could not speak.

Davy stared at the blue and white cotton counterpane hanging on its string, which formed the screen Nelly had rigged up to hide them from each other. He lay back, stretched under the crumpled sheets, with that warm, newly wakened feeling, of weakened, luxurious decadence. He listened to the soft sounds of her rising, the whisper of clothing being pulled on, snapped into place. The blanket she had hung up swayed as she folded up her own sheets and the arrangement of cushions that was her makeshift bed on the floor. He heard her move, heard the trickle of water from the jug into the enamel bowl, then the noise of her washing.

'Good morning, Nelly. Did you manage to sleep?'

177

'Oh, Master Davy. Mornin'.' Her head and shoulders appeared. The golden hair was all awry, hanging in its long strands about her shoulders, her face glowing, freshly washed, and pink, too, in that characteristic mix of shyness and pleasure he so loved to see. She was still in her underthings. He could see the wide white straps of her under-bodice bisecting her fine shoulders. He was ashamed of his wayward thoughts on the rest of her frame, still decently hidden by the cloth. 'Sleep all right, did you?' she enquired. 'Won't be a moment. I'm nearly done.'

She ducked out of sight, and he knew she would be pulling on her stockings, fastening her skirt, lacing up her boots, before she folded away the fragile barrier between them. He lay on in the warm bed, guiltily savouring the teasing, lazy excitement of his own body. He watched her reappear, whisk away the counterpane and fold it competently, before she took down the string stretched across the room. 'There we are. Another day, and not such a nice one, either.' She was already drawing back the thin curtains from the rain-spotted windows.

'You know, Nelly, you really should let me sleep on the cushions for a while. It's not fair. You've been down on the floor for so many nights. You must have your turn in here. And now you're working as well . . .' his voice tailed off, and the expected vehement refutal of his suggestion came forth, as he knew it would. 'You're not my servant, Nelly,' he resumed, knowing he was wasting his breath with such argument. For that was exactly how she saw herself, however unusual or even improper it might seem. His personal servant – maid, valet, cook – she saw to everything. Since she had arrived, he had almost literally done nothing for himself. 'You're my dearest, my only friend,' he added quietly.

'Give over! I'm just goin' to get you a bit of breakfast. And there'll be some hot water in the pan for your wash later on. But don't you hurry yourself. Take your time. You're still not strong, don't forget.' She had coloured up at his words, moved quickly, looking flustered, caught up in embarrassment, but also in pleasure.

She went out along the landing to the tiny kitchenette, and he lay back once more, and enjoyed the sensation of well being that made him stretch like a cat beneath the blankets. It was true what he had told her. His throat tightened with tenderness and gratitude. She had saved him, he was convinced. Sheer apathy would have finished him off before another winter came on, he was sure, if he had been left to fend for himself. Nelly did everything for him, including the most intimate and private ministrations at the height of his sickness, bathing his sweat soaked body on the bed when he had been too weak to rise, and helping his poor, wasted frame onto the chamber pot.

She had even braved the formidable landlady, Mrs Chapman, who had come upstairs breathing through her flared nostrils with grim anticipation when she had discovered that Nelly was spending her nights as well days in his room. 'Not right, is it, Mr Herbert?' she said, revelling in her role of outraged respectability. 'I know you're a young gentleman, even if your means are small enough, but that don't make it any better, does it? I mean to say, what are folk to think, with this young woman staying here—'

Nelly had given more than she got. She faced the older woman squarely. 'Madam. I worked for Mr Herbert's family, as did my father. I've known him since we were both children. And I'm a respectable girl, I've never done any wrong, and never will.' Though her face burned, she ploughed on bravely. 'I sleep down here on a shake-me-down and we have a blanket hung up as a screen between us that stays there all night till we're decent again in the morning. And if you don't believe us, ma'am, you're welcome to come up and check for yourself, any time. Tonight, if you like.'

Mrs Chapman was clearly taken aback, for Nelly's innocence was eloquently proclaimed, in her looks as well as her forthright tone. 'As for that, I'm not a narrow minded person myself,' the landlady answered, 'and I'm sure what you've told me is the truth.' Her manner had changed to clear conciliation. 'Only there is the fact that it is the two of you sharing the room, that's meant for one. And that's paid for for one,' she added significantly.

Nelly had already learnt just how straitened Davy's means were. She had been genuinely outraged when he had diffidently told her he could not afford to pay her. 'I didn't come here for wages, Master

Davy!' she protested, so hotly he blushed for shame. 'I came cos you need some help. You're not well, and I want to see you better.'

It was Nelly who had suggested a way out of the landlady's difficulty. 'How about if I help you out here, with the cleaning, and maybe a bit of laundry? I'm strong enough, and I know how to scrub and dust.' She grinned across at Davy. 'I been doing it since I was little, 'ent I, Master Davy?'

Which was why now, after bringing him his breakfast of porridge and bread and jam on a tray, she prepared to go off downstairs and begin the duties which would keep her busy until two o' clock or later.

'I feel terrible,' he said, not for the first time, as he obediently leaned forward while she plumped up the pillows and rearranged them behind him. 'You do so much, Nelly. You're even working like a slave for Mrs Chapman as well as looking after me. I really must start trying to find a job. Anything—'

She put the tin tray down across his knee. 'Shush now. You're just starting to get on the mend. We can't have you going out early morn in this terrible weather. Coming home God knows when, in all this fog. I'll not have it, all right?' She gave a mock punch to the side of his face, leaning in close. Their faces were only inches apart, their eyes met, and she saw the tenderness in his, and he in hers. It held them, so that for a long second they could not look away, and when they did they were both deeply moved. 'You just stay there for a while. Get up later. We can take our walk later on if it's stopped raining. I'll pop back up and see you presently, all right?'

'All right.' He caught her hand, held it to his cheek, and kissed her reddened knuckles before she could withdraw it.

But when he was alone, he felt again that restless sense of impatience with his own weakness – a weakness of will as much as body, and he castigated himself for it. He could not go on letting Nelly wear herself out like this, looking after him, and skivvying for Mrs Chapman, who was he was sure taking full advantage of his saviour's complaisance. He heard again the contemptuous tone of his father in that last speech of dismissal, when he had referred to Davy's incapacity to maintain himself – and his own rash promise that he would pay back the modest sum John Herbert had advanced, and the even more meagre allowance forwarded each month to keep him in this sorry state.

There must be something he could do to earn his own living. But what? He thought of Nelly's cheerful strength, her toiling so unstint-ingly at the menial tasks which she had known and which had sustained her all her young life, and all at once he discovered that he envied her such simplicity. His own privileged upbringing had fitted him for nothing. Even his father, brutal and unfeeling as he was, had proved adept at adding to the already considerable wealth of the family, in the hard world of business. A world thoroughly alien to Davy, and one he felt entirely unfitted for. Not that he need trouble himself about such concerns. His father had disowned him, cast him out as totally unworthy of any inheritance. Perhaps rightly so, David brooded. But there must be *something* he could do, something to earn enough to get them out of these dreary city streets, and the drudgery Nelly so selflessly accepted as her lot. It came on him as a revelation that his thoughts for the future had automatically included Nelly. It both shocked and thrilled him, and he rose from the bed to face the grey day with a new fire of resolution within him.

A few days later, Nelly was down on the ground floor, working in Mrs Chapman's kitchen at the end of the long passage, when she heard a minor commotion at the front door. Mrs Chapman's flus-tered tones were superseded by a refined drawl, which caught Nelly's attention. She peeped cautiously along the dim passageway in time to catch a glimpse of an elegantly fur coated figure, with fair, crimped curls showing beneath one of the modern, close fitting cloche hats. A flash of silk stockinged leg over fashionably patent short boots was revealed as the figure swept to the foot of the stairs. 'Don't bother showing me up, thank you. It's on the top floor, isn't it? I should just about make it.'

Nelly's heart was pounding. She had thought the voice was Gertrude's, belatedly realized it was the younger sister, Clara, who was on her way to Davy's room. Her urgent protective desire moved her along the passage before she pulled herself up short. Mrs Chapman's eyes were alive with excitement. She spoke to Nelly almost as if they were sharing some lightly scandalous secret. 'Mr

Herbert's sister! Paying him a call, she said. They've been before, you know. Not that one, though.'

She turned away, and yelled from the top of the front steps to the crowd of street children who had rapidly gathered around the motorcar. Nelly stood there with one hand resting indecisively on the globe which crested the newel post. She had no right to interfere, she scolded herself. No right at all to go barging in on Master Davy and his own sister. Yet her belly churned with uneasiness, she had a deep urge to go rushing up there, to shield him from their cruel contempt. Maybe she could wait a decent bit, give them the chance to have their own say, then go up and see if they wanted tea. At least Davy was up and dressed, that much she did know, for she had taken a cup of tea to him less than half an hour ago. She felt a seizure of dismay as she recalled his untidy appearance. His collarless shirt, his braces. She really ought not to let him sit about like that, like any common working chap. Bitterly, she thought how it would confirm Clara's ideas of his shiftlessness, the way he had let himself slide.

Upstairs, Davy's thoughts were remarkably similar as he opened the door and was astonished to see the glamorous figure standing there. His fingers flew automatically to his neck, fumbled with his shirtfront as though hoping to find collar and tie magically in place. 'Clara! What a surprise! I didn't – you should've warned me. It's not—' he gestured helplessly behind him at the cluttered, shabby room, the still unmade bed.

Clara's nose wrinkled expressively. She made no effort to hide her disgust as, on his delayed invitation, she entered, pointedly drawing her coat tighter about her. 'My God, Davy! How on earth can you live like this?' She glanced around in exaggerated revulsion.

Quickly, he tugged the topmost quilt over the disordered sheets, grabbed at some newspapers on the worn armchair. 'There. Have a seat. It's quite comfortable.'

She did so, crossed her elegant limbs, the folds of the fur coat falling away to show a thick tweed skirt, and the silk clad calf with its shiny boot swinging back and forth. 'We had the do for my twenty-first at home last week. Thanks for your card, by the way. A nice surprise.'

He coloured, imagining the sneers which must have greeted its obvious cheapness, the comments, or more eloquent lack of them, at the fact that he did not send any present. 'It wasn't much,' he murmured feebly. 'Sorry I couldn't manage a gift.'

She shrugged dismissively. No doubt she had done well enough without his contribution. She certainly looked exotic in these surrounds, he reflected. For him, Clara would never be quite the dazzling beauty he had always considered Gerty, though she was probably more in line with the type becoming more fashionable now, as the new century moved to the close of its second decade. Slim, petite, with less emphasis on womanly curves, there was almost an androgynous quality about the young society nymphs now, with the slighter, less rigidly supported bosom, narrower hips, their shorter dresses and freer movements. And bolder manner, undoubtedly.

In answer to his polite enquiry after her latest beau, the Honourable Victor Cornell, she gave a wicked laugh. 'Poor Vic. He thought we were going to announce our engagement at the party. So did papa. He was mightily put out when I told him no. He'd like to think we'd hooked a son of an earl in the family, however low down on the list of heirs Vic might be! He was never impressed with Gerty's Gordon. You've heard, have you? He's probably going to have to leave the army, after all. Seems there's not much chance of promotion now that the killing's all stopped. They'll be cutting back on all the Forces, they reckon.' She lowered her voice to a sensual thickness. 'Gerty's up the spout again. She's not showing yet, of course, but she'll be like a house end this time. She and Gordon are at it like knives apparently, night after night. Not that he'll be getting much more, poor soul!'

She giggled, delighted at the rising blush she discerned, and Davy's glance of discomfort. 'Vic can't wait to get started. Thinks we should try each other out, he says. See if we're suited. No chance, though! I'll keep him hanging on a while. What say you, little brother?'

He gave an uncomfortable start, tried to think of something to say, and failed.

'Are *you* still as pure as the driven snow?' she mocked, batting her made-up eyes at him. She looked round expressively. 'You won't meet many nice girls round here, I expect. Mind you, if it's experience you're after you're in the right spot. Driving here, the place seemed full of tarts, lurking on every doorstep. Every other house looks like it's a brothel.' Her laugh gurgled again, then the familiar look of contempt settled on her pretty features. 'Surely you can find somewhere a bit more decent to live? Haven't you any contacts from school who can help? You could try begging a bit more out of papa, if it comes to that. I know he won't have you back at Brierton, but if you're craven enough, he might take pity – give you a bit more cash.'

There was a soft tapping at the door. 'Master Davy? You all right? Can I get you anything?' Nelly's untidy head came round the door, then her body emerged into view. She was in her old thick jumper and working skirt, with her homemade pinny tied round her waist. Her sleeves were pushed up above her elbows, her tanned arms and red hands on display.

For an almost comic moment Clara's elegant poise was shattered. Her jaw dropped, she gaped at the apparition. 'Nelly? Nelly Tovey! What are you . . .' she glanced back at Davy, who stared in crimsoning guilt. She waited for an explanation.

It was Nelly who broke the awkward silence. 'I heard Master Davy was livin' here on his own. That he was sick. I came to see him. I'm staying to look after him.'

'But surely . . . you're staying here? In the house?'

Nelly was twisting her hands in her apron. 'Yes, Miss. I sleep on a shake-me-down.' Her yellow head nodded vaguely into the interior of the room. 'He needed someone. He was really ill. He's a lot better now.'

Her open face took on a sullen, defensive look. Davy conquered his nervousness, forced himself to speak up for her. 'She's been an absolute brick. Treats me like a king. Won't let me do a thing.' He strove to inject a light-hearted note into the tense atmosphere, and failed abysmally. 'Now, what about some tea?'

'Yes, I'll go and make some. It—'

'Don't bother on my account!' Clara said cuttingly, once more looking about her pointedly, to emphasize her refusal. 'I just popped in for a quick visit. I see I can leave you in capable hands. The reason I came was to invite you to a little dinner. Gerty and Gordon. Vic, of course. Perhaps just one or two others. At the Eldon Grill. Just an addendum to my coming of age. Do you have any clothes?' she asked brutally, fixing him with a steely look. 'Dress, I mean.' His face even redder, he nodded. It's next Wednesday, eight o' clock. Do try and make it. And don't forget to clean your nails and wash behind your ears.'

She stood, and Davy rose, too, advanced towards her for a brotherly peck on the cheek. She held up both hands, backed away a little, with a laugh. 'Good heavens, no! I don't want to catch anything! And don't come down. It's like climbing the Eiger getting here. Your . . . er . . . Nelly can show me out.'

At the foot of the stairs, Clara said grandly, 'Thank you.' She turned for one last shot. 'Try to see that he looks presentable. God knows what his dress suit looks like – if he hasn't already pawned it.'

'He won't let you down. He never has.'

Clara raised her curved eyebrows. 'Well now! That's a matter of opinion, isn't it? But that's what I like about you country girls. Feisty as ever.' She gave her trilling laugh and walked carefully down the steps, where a relieved looking chauffeur was holding the passenger door.

Nelly felt the tears stinging at the back of her eyes. All at once she saw her behaviour through the eyes of Clara and her ilk. Saw herself as the great, galumphing country lass she was, clumsy and graceless. And acting utterly foolishly and immorally, living with Master Davy like this. Surely everybody would be gossiping and sniggering about them? She felt again the hot fury she had known when she had flung the drink in Wally Hindmarch's leering face. She turned, and fled back up the stairs, towards the room which had become such a haven to her, where she wished she and Davy could live forever, cut off from the whole unfeeling world that lay in wait for them.

CHAPTER TWENTY-ONE

'**W**ELL, I suppose we ought to congratulate you. It's all a bit sordid, though, isn't it? Sharing a bed with the maid! I know we've all heard of *droit de seigneur* and *noblesse oblige* and all that, but really!' Gerty appealed to the others, her pencilled eyebrows raised, and there was a ripple of laughter.

Davy felt the heat coursing through his features. He knew his refusal to respond only made her worse. The attack had started almost as soon as the waitresses brought the first course. He had been enduring it for several minutes now, with Gerty as Chief Inquisitor, the others as her appreciative audience.

'We don't share a bed!' His shame and nervousness caused him to stammer slightly over his reply, and he was angry with himself for not keeping his own vow of silence. But it was not only his own image and character being assaulted, but that of the person who he had come to realize meant more to him than anyone else in his lonely world. 'We never – she never—'

'Oh, my God! Don't tell me, please! It gets more depraved every minute. You're cohabiting but not doing it! Is that what you're saying?'

'She looks after me.'

'I'll bet she does!' Gerty pursued. 'Big strapping girl like that!' She glanced around for her cheap laugh, which was delivered on cue.

He let her carry on without any further response on his part, and she tired soon enough of his non-resistance. The conversation was diverted to her own affairs. The Honourable Victor said, 'I understand congratulations are in order.' Gerty had discreetly made it

186

known to Clara that her pregnancy could be announced. He raised his glass to her, and then, his smile broadening, to an embarrassed Gordon. 'Still,' the young man went on daringly, 'one has to pay for one's pleasures, eh?'

'The pleasure's all his, I assure you,' Gerty answered sourly, and Davy, relieved as he was to be out of the limelight, felt sorry for his brother-in-law in the muted sniggers that followed her remark.

But later, in the plush lounge where they lingered over coffee and brandies, Gerty returned more seriously to Davy's situation. 'Listen. We're going to get you out of that slum,' she declared, in that manner of hers that brooked no argument. 'You can come and stay at our place. Gordon's about to be posted over to Ireland. All hell going on over there, as you can imagine. The government's going to let everyone down and back out of the whole thing. But at least it'll mean he can stay in the army a while longer. Of course, it would be quite impossible for me to go over there with him, so you can move in with us. Keep me company while he's away.' She beamed a triumphant smile at him. 'We've only a small apartment, as you know. And we'll still have Mary's nanny living in, but I dare say we'll manage. You haven't any stuff of your own, have you? The car should do it all right.' She laughed again, leaned closer and put her hand on his arm. 'I'll take care of you properly, little brother. Put some meat on those bones. Anything to save you from that big-footed bumpkin. Far too uppity, that madam. Doesn't know her place. And a lot of that was your fault, Davy, you know it was. You've no idea how to treat servants.'

'Thank you.' He was stammering again, his heart thudding painfully. 'It's very kind of you, but – I can't stay with you. I know you mean well—'

'What do you mean, can't stay? Don't be ridiculous!' Her pretty, well-groomed features took on a look of astonishment as she realized he meant what he was saying. 'You can't go on – living with that – that creature! It's disgusting. For God's sake! She's a servant! It's perverse! It's not as though she's your mistress! Is she?' She made her question sound like an accusation.

'Of course not! I've told you. It's not like that—'

'Then what on earth is there to stop you moving in? Surely you can't be happy in that slum? And you don't have to feel any responsibility for her. She came of her own free will, didn't she? Sought you out — took advantage of you, when you were ill—'

'Saved my life, you mean!' The force of his words stopped her in her tracks. She stared in surprise. Her husband cleared his throat in rumbling embarrassment.

'Perhaps we should leave this for the moment. We don't want to spoil the party . . .' he glanced uncomfortably towards Clara, whose animated features indicated that she was relishing the interchange.

Gerty raised her left hand, waving aside Gordon's interruption as though it were a bothersome insect. Though her face still retained the stamp of its beauty, her features had filled out a little with her pregnancy, and her colour was high. A faint frown creased her brow, and she stared at Davy with narrowed eyes, as though she were studying him carefully. 'My God! That's a bit melodramatic, isn't it? You sound almost as though you're besotted with the girl!'

'I think maybe I am!'

The quiet words had a stunning effect on the whole table. 'Don't be ridiculous, David!' Her voice was breathless with her shock and indignation. 'You can't possibly—'

All at once, Davy felt as though a great weight were being lifted from his shoulders. He experienced a wild recklessness beyond anything he had known. 'She's only a servant! That's what you're going to say. She's a common maidservant!' He flung the words at all the startled, well bred faces about him. He realized that he had risen, stood gazing down at all of them. They were staring back, transfixed. 'Well, all that means absolutely nothing to me. I've never fitted in, with any of this.' He glanced around the exclusive dining room of the hotel, gestured fiercely with his raised arm. 'Never! I've learnt, over the last year, just how meaningless it all is! I don't care about any of it. All I care about is Nelly! Nelly Tovey – *my* Nelly!'

Gerty's mouth was open. Now her eyes were wide, her expression of amazement almost comical. For once she seemed utterly at a loss for words, and her behaviour was representative of the others at the table. Davy was trembling, but he strove to hold himself in check. 'As you can all so clearly see, I don't belong here at all. So I'll say good night. Thank you for the splendid meal.' Somehow he managed to avoid hurrying as he gave a slight bow in Clara's direction, then turned and left his gaping, still silent audience. The reaction set in when he was safely outside in the cold, lamp lit dark, and he leaned, gasping and shuddering against a wall, his head spinning before he could collect himself and move on.

He wandered through the busy West End thoroughfares, in a daze, and was scarcely aware of the crowds, the bright shop windows around him. At last he noticed that his steps had been taking him instinctively north, away from the fashionable centre, the lights growing dimmer, the traffic quietening. He saw the wooden frame and canvas of a tea stall. He dug for change in his pocket and made his way across the road. A sizeable group of young people, the men cloth capped and mufflered, the women with heads wrapped in scarves, stared at his evening dress beneath his mackintosh. He took the scalding mug of tea, cupping his palms around it, and stood to one side.

'Wotcher, dearie! Slummin' it tonight, are we?' The girl stared boldly, her dark, crimped head tilted back appraisingly. She was bareheaded, in spite of the chill, and a glinting tortoise shell comb shone in her black curls. Her coat was well cut, with a high astrakhan collar turned up at the back of her neck. The face was young, and pretty enough, but her brassy stare and the heavily applied make-up pronounced her a tart. He saw silk stockings and flimsy heeled shoes, more suitable for the dance floor than winter pavements. 'Fancy takin' a girl for a drink, do yer?'

'Would you like a cup of tea?' he asked, fumbling in his pocket. 'I think . . .'

'Blimey! You know how to give a girl a good time, doncha?' She turned to the people nearby, who were smiling in anticipation. 'Mr Rockefeller here! You tryin' to lead me astray, with your offers of cups of char?'

'No – I just meant—' in total confusion, face aflame, he thrust his still almost full mug on the counter and turned and fled once more.

'Don't run away, pretty boy! We won't eat yer!'

189

The voices receded. He strode down the long street. He felt lonely and helpless, adrift in a harsh, alien world. Then he thought of the warmth of his room, the lamplight, the curtains drawn to keep out the darkness and the cold unfriendliness. And Nelly, waiting there for him.

When Davy had gone, Nelly felt strange, unusually jittery and ill at ease. She was afraid for him, worried what those smart, wicked sisters of his would do to him, how they would hurt him with their cruel mockery. She wished she could be there to protect him, at the same time all too aware that she had no place there, in that society. Unless it was as a uniformed servant, standing silently by to wait on them.

She felt a queasiness, a low, nagging pain in her belly, and she folded her hands over it. She did some rapid calculating. Her monthly wasn't due for another week, but she wasn't always regular. Usually it was bad, dragging on for days: the sickness, then the back ache, and finally that awful, low, clenching pain right down inside her. She hated it, for she couldn't always hide the discomfort it caused her.

Davy, bless him, was getting to know her. Getting to recognize the symptoms, her withdrawn quietness. She never snapped at him the way she used to back home with her brothers and sisters, but she was not her normal, chattering, outgoing self. All she had to say was, 'I got a bad gut,' and he would nod, like as not colour up a bit, too – she smiled fondly at this thought – and he would be extra gentle and tender. 'You sit down, Nelly. You have a rest. Let me do something.'

She smiled again. Not that he was much good at anything round the house. As if to corroborate her, she saw the scummy, grey water still in the tub when she went down to the bathroom. He would never think to empty it himself, poor lamb. He wasn't brought up that way. On impulse, she bolted the door, quickly peeled off her clothes. The water was lukewarm, but she crouched and fumbled with a match, braving the exploding roar of the tall geyser, to get a thin trickle of hot water from it.

She lowered herself, stretched out her legs, felt the caressing flow of the water all about her lower body. She lifted the flannel he had used, let the water flow onto her breasts. She thought of his body in here, touching the surfaces her flesh was touching, felt a deep, stirring shiver of sexuality shake her, and she lay back, moaning softly. They said – the sniggering girls back home – that a woman's period pains eased once she'd done it with a man. 'They'll ease it all right!' Betty Lowry had spluttered with her coarse laugh. 'Stop it altogether, more like! Then you're really in trouble!' She thought of Master Davy. He wasn't like that, like the rest of those dirty, sniggering youths at home. And she didn't care, she assured herself hotly. She wasn't, either. Not like Betty and the rest, always talking, giggling, thinking about it. Quickly, she dried herself with his damp towel and climbed back into her clothes.

The counterpane was in place, draped over the string. She arranged her cushion-bed on the floor, sat restlessly for a while, tried to sew. She kept getting up and going to the window, though all she could see was darkness and the dim shapes of the rooftops and chimney pots, all smoking thickly away to burden the air with their soot. One thing you had to say for the country, at least the air was cleaner there. She was more worried than she let on for Davy, with the onset of another winter and his chest still weak. Of course he's going to be late! she told herself at ten-thirty. You know well enough what the toffs are like with their dining and wining. They'll bring him home in their motor when they're ready. Best thing you can do is get to bed, my girl.

She undressed again, savouring the feel of her cleanliness, the scent of the soap on her body. She pulled on the old shift she wore as nightdress. It didn't even reach her knees any more, but so what? There was no one likely to see her, was there? She moved round to Davy's bed, turned back the covers as she usually did, picked up his striped nightshirt to lay it out on the pillow for him. It was soft, smelt stirringly of him, and she held it to her cheek. Suddenly she buried her face in it, felt the hot rush of that shameful excitement return in full measure. Just for a minute she surrendered to it, stretched herself out on the bed, holding the nightshirt still to her burning face.

'What? Oh, Master Davy! What—' she rolled over, blinked foolishly about her, the shift riding up across her thighs. He was standing gazing at her, his thin face drawn, working with emotion. He had pulled off his coat and jacket, and the black tie. His white shirt gaped where he had plucked free the studded starched front.

'Please, Nelly! Don't move! Stay with me. Please!' He threw himself beside her, clutched at her, burrowing his head into her breast, and she turned, both shocked and unable to deny him. She hugged him tightly to her, encircling his thin frame with her arms.

They lay clasping each other, their bodies touching, their hearts beating hard. 'I love you, Nelly. I mean it, I swear to God. I don't ever want to lose you. I don't care what people think, what they might say about us. I never want to be away from you, do you understand?'

She was crying, and she pressed his face deeper into her softness to show him she did. He moved, struggled to lift his face, and lay his cheek against her neck. 'I love you, as men love women. I need you.'

She slept in his arms. Some time in the night, she didn't know when, he had undressed, and they were under the blankets together, still clinging, legs and arms wrapped about each other, belly to belly in warm contact.

He woke in the morning in a dream of bursting sexuality, only to find it was true, that the glory of feeling spilled over into the reality of waking, that Nelly's fingers, at first timid, grew bolder, enflaming, the way his own hand moved to her beating, hungry flesh. 'Lie still, Master Davy!' she panted, and he felt her thigh moving over him, enfolding him. 'I promise I'll learn for you, and you for me. We'll learn together. Keep still now.'

They were no longer troubled by visits from his sisters. Nelly made one trip back to her home, refusing to countenance Davy's accompanying her, in spite of his pleas to do so. She told him nothing of the unpleasant reality of the scathing condemnations, which even her father joined in. 'I'm not his woman,' she bravely insisted. 'I just look after him. Take care of him.'

'Why? Does he still fancy the soldier boys then?' Billy sneered brutally, and she flung herself at him, clawing, spitting, until she was dragged off, and left the cottage for the last time.

192

Days turned to weeks, then to months, and they were content and happy with each other. Apart from their loving, she continued to behave as she had done always. She washed and cooked and cleaned for him, and nursed him devotedly through the bouts of bronchitis which were a recurring threat in times of damp and cold. She continued to work for Mrs Chapman, who had become a good friend to them. She had swiftly seen the change in them, guessed that they were partners in the true sense. 'When is he going to make an honest woman of you?' she asked regularly, and Nelly would blush, and shake her head with that shy smile.

'Come off it, Mrs C. Master Davy's a proper gent. I told you. I'm just happy to be with him. To do for him.'

'You do for him all right!' Mrs Chapman would snigger, and Nelly blushed even more prettily, to the landlady's chuckling delight.

The news came suddenly one morning, in a brief note from Gerty, the first communication he had had from his family since the night of the dinner at the Eldon Grill, that Enid Herbert had died in the nursing home on the south coast. 'A heart attack. Quite sudden.' Nelly held Davy while they cried quietly together. It was over two years since he had seen her. Apart from the fact that his father had forbidden him to visit, Enid herself had shown virtually no interest in him the last time they had met. It grieved him now to think what a distant, unknown quantity his mother had been.

He attended the funeral, and suffered the mortification of having the entire family ignore him, both before and after the service. He was glad that, just as Nelly had faced the ordeal of returning to her home alone, he too persuaded her not to accompany him on this sad occasion. He had hoped that the sadness of losing their mother might at least lead to a temporary reconciliation with his sisters – his father was a different matter altogether. Indeed, Davy was not at all sure how he himself would react on such a poignant occasion should his father make any overtures of peace towards him. He was not surprised when no such overtures were forthcoming, but he could not help the sadness which gripped him at the way Gerty and Clara, their faces hidden beneath the black veils, resolutely turned away from him. He left the graveyard to go straight to the station, and back to the one person he was sure of.

More weeks passed, and they were back in the grip of another dankly foggy November when a buff coloured envelope came for Davy. It was from a firm of London solicitors, with whom he had never had dealings. It was in their drab office a gloomy day or two later that Davy learnt he was a beneficiary in his mother's will – a will made years before, and one which his father clearly had had no knowledge of.

'I'm quite rich,' he told Nelly. He was still bemused as he sat there, his face portraying conflicting emotions. 'Quite a big sum. It was money from her side of the family, apparently. Money I don't think papa ever knew about. She's left it all to us. Gerty and Clara and me. We'll be able to move out of here. Find a decent place to live. Oh, Nelly! Aren't you pleased?'

'Of course I am!' Only she didn't look it. She looked almost regretful, and uncertain. 'P'raps you won't need me any more. You only have to say, Davy. I won't mind. You'll be able to live decent now, like you ought to have done all this time.' She was startled, and even a little alarmed at the sudden determination she saw in his face.

'Shut up, Nelly. We've got some very serious planning to do.'

CHAPTER TWENTY-TWO

T HE daffodils made a brave show of colour, sprouting between the blackened gravestones of the soot-grimed London church. Overhead, the cold sky was a new, bright blue, the clouds high, white fluff balls. A day of hope.

Davy's body, shivering against the spring wind in spite of his thick clothing, ached with love and compassion. Nelly's face was still marked with her tears. Her complexion was smooth, restored already by the weeks they had spent at their new country home. He longed to be back there, alone with her, insulated as they could always be against the harshness of this world outside. He vowed he would take away from her lovely face that look of uncertainty, of fear and apprehension. He thanked God, humbly, that at last, after weeks of frantic pleading, he had got her to overcome her doubts, her entrenched belief that what he proposed was foolishness at best, at worst madness.

He felt some hard little grains spatter on the back of his neck and jerked round. Nelly let out a cry of mock distress, and ducked at the volley of rice flung at her. Some caught in the veil of her dark blue hat, caught in the collar of her fashionable winter coat. That was one thing she had been adamant about. She would not marry in white, no matter how hard he pleaded, or how many eyebrows it had raised, not to mention the eloquently compressed lips of the vicar when they had arranged for the ceremony. Davy had given in. He was too overwhelmed with relief at having won her consent to marry at all to dig his heels in any further. 'I'm not entitled,' she had argued bluntly. 'I'm yours. You know I am. I share your bed. Body and soul I'm yours.'

'I want to make an honest woman of you.' But his attempt at flippancy had done nothing to alleviate the troubled expression he saw. 'It's not enough for *me*,' he went on quietly. 'I want to share my life with you. Give you my name. Give you all that I can. You deserve so much more.'

She was still troubled, deeply so, but with acknowledgement of his love Davy had discovered a hitherto unknown determination within himself. Nelly's resistance crumbled against its strength, and against the love they both felt. They had come the closest they had ever done to a serious quarrel when they began the discussion of their future. It was a battle Davy had been deeply afraid he would lose. 'I just want us to go on as we are,' Nelly stated, her colour rising. 'We're perfectly happy as we are, aren't we? And I don't care what folk say. Let 'em gossip.' She tried desperately to convert him to her way of thinking with her typical touch of humour. 'Why spoil the story for them? The handsome young gent who's brought a blonde floozy as his housekeeper! Bit of scandal! They love it!'

'Kiss the bride!' Mrs Chapman screeched, flinging more rice. Her son, and son-in-law, jostled forward, scuffling for the privilege, and Nelly laughingly surrendered, offered her cheek.

'I just want to get back home,' she whispered to Davy, at the modest wedding feast in the hotel not far from the church.

He nodded. It would have been nice to marry at St John's, the church in the village, near Loxton Cottage, which they had bought soon after Christmas, and moved into in January. It was more or less as they had dreamed, though the rose bushes were pruned almost to the ground, and the garden, which would be a riot of colour in distant summer, hidden under three inches of snow. Out the back, there was a reasonable orchard, and plenty of land for the smallholding Nelly swore she would establish.

She had cried in earnest when he convinced her his proposal of marriage was something he wanted more than anything. 'I'm not fit. Tisn't right, Davy. Not for the likes of me an' you.'

'You're more than fit. There's no one else I'd want to share my life with. I love you, Nelly. I want God at least to know it. I want to make my vows before Him.'

He had protested when, after finally giving in and accepting his proposal, she had insisted they should marry in distant London, and keep it secret, even after the wedding. 'But – but – I want everyone to know. I want them all to see – you've done me the greatest honour any woman could.'

She shook her head, smiled at him tenderly. 'And have them all sniggering and laughing behind our backs? The gentleman who married his maidservant? No, my love. I'll marry you, if that's what you want, but I won't have 'em all mocking us for it. Better to let them go on thinking how wicked we are. We'll have the laugh on all of them.'

On their wedding night, safely back in Loxton Cottage, the bedroom was lit with the cosy glow of the oil lamps. The crisp white sheets were turned back, two huge bunches of daffodils stood in vases either side of the small fireplace. He had bought her a trousseau. He lay on top of the bed, watching as she undressed, slowly, fully conscious of his eyes on her, and roused deeply by the knowledge. The lace frilled silks slipped off, one by one, the silk stockings from her long legs. The silk of the nightdress flowing down her lithe body gleamed in the caressing light. It was so fine he could see the dim shadow of her at her loins as she moved towards him.

'There's something I want to do,' she murmured. She slipped the silk up again, over her thighs, baring herself to the waist, straddling him as she knelt on the bed. She reached down, fought his own nightshirt up, to free his belly. Her fingers reached between them as she let her weight slowly descend upon his upper thighs, and he felt the brush of her against his most sensitive skin. He swelled mightily, gave a soft whimper. Her weight was ever more urgent, thrusting him down into the yielding softness of the bed, and he surrendered gladly, to her dominating thrust, his own spearing into her tightness.

He gazed up in a daze of wonder at her jouncing breasts, encased in the shimmering silk, saw her golden hair tumbling, flying about her as she rode him and they both cried out in the fierce, lost ecstasy of the new joining of their bodies in their love.

The garden was in the fullness of its summer richness, foxgloves rear-ing, the delphinium drooping with rich royal blue, the tumbling bright orange of the nasturtiums spilling onto the narrow, flagged paths. The bees droned in the lavender, and Davy sagged peacefully in the garishly striped deckchair, the newspaper forgotten at his feet. Nelly was, as always, about her business somewhere at the back. Earlier he had watched her leaning out of an upper window, vigorously shaking one of the rugs before rubbing at the insides of the square panes of glass.

He had long since given up trying to persuade her to engage more help with the housework, especially as she was working so hard with the smallholding they had created. At least she had accepted the necessity of his joining her in her endeavour, and of hiring two young lads to assist in getting the land into shape. He had worked hard under her benign tutelage, and had found the unaccustomed physical labour, though fatiguing at first, rewarding both to body and mind. Of course, she still tried to cosset him, to shield him from the most exhausting of the manual work, but she could see the beneficial effects of so much time and effort spent in the clean country air. It showed in his complexion, and in the new robustness of his lean frame. His face and neck, the deep V to his breastbone, and his arms to way above the elbows were deeply tanned, as the year advanced into more clement weather. 'Why, Davy! You look like any strapping farmhand!' she laughed, when he undressed. He took a keen interest, too, in the commercial aspect of their newborn venture, and it was here that she gladly acknowledged the essential role he played. 'I'm not learned enough to be doing with all this,' she admitted willingly, as he enthusiastically set about finding markets for their produce.

'We need to start with the poultry. And pigs. Maybe a few milk cows.'

'Yes, Master!' She pretended to tug at a forelock. 'We shall have to call you Farmer Herbert next!' And her blue eyes shone with her love and admiration.

He no longer worried about the village gossips, or the ambiguous smiles as folk commented on what a treasure his handsome housekeeper must be. Nor even at Nelly's insisting on keeping up the part when their rare visitors called, putting on her dark dress, and bringing in the tea things, or the drinks, with her respectfully familiar, 'There we are, Master Davy,' as she served them, then retired until they were gone.

And she was, indeed, still his housekeeper, as well as his beloved wife. She still did everything for him, still polished his shoes, brought them to him, crouched lovingly as she fitted them to his feet. A smile played involuntarily about his lips at the thought that sprang to his mind. Only in the encapsuled wonder of the bedroom did she become the all-loving tyrant, the splendid valkyrie who rode him to the apocalypse of consummation. He sighed blissfully, stretched back, happy with his surrender to his mood of idle contentment.

The last days had made him appreciate to the full the refuge and the happiness he had found here. A telegram had arrived from Gertrude some time ago, informing him that his father was gravely ill, and that it was doubtful if he would survive. Davy had not seen or heard from any of his family since long before his wedding. In fact, the last time he had met up with his sisters had been on that fateful night in the London hotel, to celebrate Clara's coming of age. His father had had a stroke. For several days survival had been unsure, but he had lived. If anything, it was perhaps less merciful than death, for his father was helplessly crippled, unable even to feed himself, his face a contorted mask, from which one fearsome livid eye blazed his impotent fury: a fury that could not be expressed in any other way than the jerk of the lopsided head, and the baying unintelligible snarl that came from the twisted, drooling mouth.

Davy wept for him. How could anyone not feel pity for this tormented wreck of a human being, however sadistic he might have been? Davy knew he himself would have no part to play in what would take place at Brierton, nor did he wish to. Gerty was there, with her two children and their nanny. Mary was four now, and Johnny just over a year. A grandson. Named after his grandfather, but never to bear the family name. He wondered what his father felt about that. No one could tell any more. The two infants were terrified of the drooling, glaring figure and shunned him whenever possible. As did the rest of his family. John Herbert's only familiar now was the muscular nurse, Miss Lithgow, who did the most

199

personal and intimate things for him with all her impersonal efficiency and answered his incoherent growlings as if they were the prattle of a merry child.

Gerty was already established in the house, and was making arrangements for Gordon to quit his job in the city and take over the running of the estate. It seemed to be in accordance with John Herbert's wishes, or so the family solicitors claimed. Clara still had not married her son of an earl, but was using the entrée into high society Victor had provided, and she was manipulating a string of suitors, or beaux before narrowing her choice and selecting her spouse. She came home to see her father when he was sufficiently recovered to sit in a wheel chair, though she found more than a minute or two of his actual gargling, glaring presence too much for her fastidious sensibility. 'He'd be far better off in a home,' she advised succinctly. 'They can care for him properly there.'

'He's being nursed here perfectly adequately,' Gerty insisted. Davy wondered uncharitably how much her filial duty owed to the fact that she and Gordon were set to take over the management of Brierton House and all that pertained to it.

'Better than a captain in a foot regiment, eh, Gordon?' Clara observed cynically, before taking herself off into Willerby for a meeting with the family solicitors, to make certain that her rights and dues would be safeguarded and were well documented. After that she was heading off to the south of France, in company with a host of bright and titled young things, where the season was about to get under way.

'Father *is* still alive!' Gerty said, nostrils flaring, but her dominance over her younger sister had long since waned.

'But for how long? And with you and your brood ensconced here, it's as well to know what's what,' Clara declared bluntly. 'At least you needn't worry about it, Davy,' she smiled maliciously. 'Papa cut you out years ago. Just keep popping up in front of that glaring eye of his and you'll finish off the job in no time, I should think!'

She might well be right, Davy thought, and had no intention to put her theory to the test, but kept out of his father's presence as much as possible.

One who did suffer badly from John Herbert's misfortune was

Mavis Cockeridge, whose downfall was well merited, even if Gerty did take an undoubted measure of satisfaction in delivering the killing blow herself. 'You might have been my father's kept woman, but *we* won't keep you any longer, Mavis. I hope you've packed already? I want you out of the house by tomorrow at the latest. You'll receive your month's wages in lieu.'

Mavis was tearful but not surprised. However, she would not yield in total abjection. 'I'll need a reference,' she said resentfully. 'I've fulfilled my duties—'

'And what might they have been – exactly?' Gerty fired back acidly. 'I'm hardly the one to say whether you fulfilled them satisfactorily or not, am I?' But she did give the departing Mavis a brief testimonial. After all, the scandal of Mavis's role in the household was local, and Gerty was well aware of the foolishness of making the ex-housekeeper/mistress seek wider and more sensational redress.

Davy was anxious to get back to his home. His sisters knew nothing of his marriage, and he did not feel that now would be an appropriate time to deliver such a bombshell. The night before he was due to leave, he received a summons from Gerty, and went along the lighted corridor to his father's study, where he found Gerty sitting at the formidable desk, whose drawers were open. There was also a filing cabinet, gaping wide, and papers scattered over the desktop and the floor. Her grey eyes were round with astonishment. 'Look at this! Remember Miss Marshall? Your beloved governess! Look!' She held out an impressively official sheaf of documents, and he glanced at the upper one. It was the pronouncement of her incarceration in the workhouse.

He glanced quickly through the other papers, the doctors' affirmation, her father's signature, as well as John's. He felt the rising horror like a stirring at the back of his neck. Four years! And there was the latest, less than two years ago, confirming her captivity.

'Well well!' Gerty gave a deep, throaty laugh. 'Your little Miss Goody-Goody was not all she seemed, the little slut! Dementia indeed! Carrying the pox and God knows what besides!'

The sickened feeling which had kept him silent as he had swiftly scanned the awful truth of Sophie's disappearance gave way to his fury at Gerty's callousness. 'My God! How can you be so cruel? She's been locked up for four years! Imprisoned – all through father's wickedness!'

He might have expected her blistering attack on him for his challenge, but she was staring at him through narrowed, speculative eyes.

'You're not surprised by this, are you? Did you know about this?' Her fingers rapped on the open file before her.

He nodded at the papers. 'I didn't know about *this*. About him having her shut away.' His gaze lifted to meet hers, and she was startled again, at the new strength and resolution she saw there. 'But I knew she was his mistress. I knew he kept her hidden away in a shabby room in London after he sent her away from here. He took me to her, before I was called up to the army. He wanted her to make a man of me!' He hurled the soiled, trite phrase at her with the full force of his bitterness.

The colour swept up into Gerty's throat and face. 'Oh, Davy! It must have been—'

His sense of the injustice of it all overrode his natural compassion. 'I'm sure you would have had a good laugh if you'd known about it. You and Clara, and your smart friends! After all, you played your part in getting Miss Marshall dismissed, didn't you? The poisonous lies you told—'

'Davy! That's not true! I had no idea—'

'It didn't stop you spreading your wickedness, did it?' His voice cracked and quavered. 'I thought she'd run away from him. When she disappeared. I thought she'd finally found the courage to escape.'

'Davy, listen. I didn't know what daddy would do. How could I? I was just a child! We all were—'

'You weren't a child when you had Nelly dismissed! When you had the family thrown out! When Sam . . . you wrote and told Sam . . .' he was breathing hard. The anger and the sadness choked him into silence.

Her face was even more flushed, her grey eyes shone with tears, as she tried to swallow back both her hurt at the shocking power of his accusations, and the guilt they stirred within her. It was her bad conscience that made her hit back at him. 'That girl again! Nelly

Tovey! You're besotted with her! You're no better than father, after all! Living in shame and squalor, with a maid for your mistress. I wouldn't—'

'You should come and visit us at Loxton Cottage. You'd be surprised. But then, you couldn't do that, could you, Gerty? Not someone as high and mighty as you believe yourself to be! You once called me an invert. Do you remember? Well, thanks to Nelly you need have no further fears on *that* score!' As she opened her mouth, he swept on before she could speak. 'And you're wrong on another count, too. She's not my mistress — she's my wife!'

Her jaw dropped further, and she sat for long seconds staring after him when he had quit the room.

CHAPTER TWENTY-THREE

SOPHIE Marshall sat opposite him, behind a neat desk. There was little resemblance to the lovely young figure he had known in the schoolroom of Brierton, or even the fallen but still beautiful girl he had rediscovered at Mrs Evans'. She was still slim and erect, but she wore an old-fashioned white bonnet gathered about her face, and the wisps of hair which escaped at her brow looked thin and lifeless. Grey and white – her clothes, her complexion, everything about her seemed contained in that drab combination. Her face was gaunt and lined, and her eyes old with the hostile experience of a savage world. Until she smiled: a sad smile, and he saw the ruin of the beauty he remembered suddenly revealed.

'We can do something, surely?' he pleaded. 'Get you out of here! If only we'd known—'

'You're kind, David. Just as you always were. But I could leave now of my own free will. Any time I chose.' Another smile as she gestured around her at the plain, dark bareness of the office. 'You see I have a senior position now. Supervisor. I can do useful work here. I am content. There are those who need me—'

'But your family! Your parents—'

'There are others taking care of them. I can see that their material needs are provided for. It would only cause pain for me to go back there. I've done wrong, David. Oh yes.' She held up her hand as his protest formed on his lips. 'I have. I was responsible for my own downfall. I know that now. Maybe I knew it even then, at Brierton. There was a flaw in my . . . nature.' He could see how difficult it was for her to speak. He wanted to stop her, but she was forcing herself on. 'Even then, I think I knew deep down that what I tried to think of as love was something far less . . . far more base. Your father . . .' she struggled once more to go on. 'I sought my revenge. And he is punished for his wickedness. Isn't he?' She gazed at him, and he nodded.

'Will you keep in touch?' he asked when he took her hand on leaving. He hesitated, then said shyly, 'I'm married now.' He could not help blushing. 'Nelly Tovey. I don't know if you remember her? She was the gardener's girl, lived in the village.' He paused again. 'She didn't – she was reluctant . . . I'm a very lucky man,' he ended simply.

He saw again, even more strongly, the beauty he remembered as the dark eyes filled with shining tears. 'And she's lucky, too, my dear. I'm so glad for you.' She leaned forward, and her lips were soft as they brushed against his cheek.

He was sitting once more on the lawn of the humming, fragrant garden, the bird song and the heavy warmth of the sun striking through his clothing, and his contentment was like a prayer of thanksgiving. What more could he possibly wish for? he asked himself, confident of his answer.

He was dozing when Nelly's shadow fell across him. She was holding a tray of tea things, which she placed carefully on the grass by his feet. He blinked at her, yawned. 'What? Is it tea time already? I'm sorry, love. And you've been beavering away as usual. What a lazy chump I am!'

There was something about her, an air of suppressed excitement that added to her beauty. The top buttons of her blouse were undone, he could see the beginnings of the dividing line of her breasts. She lowered herself, spreading her summer skirt to sit at his feet. She put her forearm over his knee. 'I was going to wait another day or two,' she said. Her yellow hair was loosely, carelessly tied in a bun, and thick tendrils had come loose, about her face and neck. He admired the turn of her neck, the long tendons standing out as she lowered her gaze, with uncharacteristic hesitancy.

'What is it?' he asked, the first flutters of alarm rising. 'What's the matter?'

'No point in waiting any longer, though. It's right enough, I reckon.'
He sat forward, clutched at her hand. 'What's wrong?' he cried
tensely.

She smiled up at him wryly, squinting slightly against the afternoon sun. 'Not so observant after all, are you, Davy? Maybe you
don't know me so well as you think.'

He stared at her, impatient and anxious at her mystery, her enig-
matic expression. 'You haven't noticed,' she went on, with fond
accusation. 'I haven't had my monthly this month. Missed it by more
than a fortnight now. Reckon I'll have to be going to pay the doctor
a visit soon.'

He came onto his knees in front of her, caught at both her hands.
'My God!' His face was a picture of worried concern. 'Of course you
must! You should have said – we'll make an appointment. It's probably nothing. You mustn't alarm yourself—'

He was stammering in his anxiety, until he saw that she was laughing quietly, and he gaped at her, at a loss. 'Don't say that. Don't call
it nothing, Davy. I know fine well what it is. It's all very well for you
to tell me it's nothing, but it 'ent every day a woman finds she's going
to have a baby.'

She laughed again, much louder, at the expressions which flew one
after the other across his face: incredulity, shock, wonder, joy. And,
most important of all to her, love.

He was speechless, clasped her hands to his chest, then hugged her
fiercely to him. She could see the tears shining in his eyes, and she
leaned forward until their brows were touching as they knelt. She
smiled again, and murmured softly, exaggerating the country burr of
her voice. 'So them old girls was right after all, my duck! Married life
do ease the gripes after all, Master Davy, sir!'

The sultry September weather had broken. The bruise-dark clouds
had been gathering throughout the day, the humidity pressing down.
Distant thunder rumbled, like somebody moving heavy furniture in
an upper room, then came closer, and lightning flickered down in
vivid streaks. The detonating cracks which followed on made folks
wince, and the ex-soldiers among them tremble. At tea time the rain

came in a solid grey deluge, a curtain sweeping forward across the fields to pound the village, drum on the roofs and turn the thatch dark and sodden. The wide roadway ran like a stream of milky tea. But the harvest, all except for a few laggards' fields, was gathered, and folks braved the downpour with coats and shawls thrown over their heads and best clothes to head for the lamp lit cheer of the village hall.

It was Davy's idea to host a traditional harvest supper, and there were plenty of willing helpers, to see to the food and drink and to decorate the long room, with the trestle tables lining two of the walls, and the bar set up by the entrance, at the opposite end to the makeshift stage. The pianist, violinist, and accordionist were already vigorously at play, and some of the younger element had insisted on rigging up a gramophone for what they believed would provide more up-to-date entertainment later in the evening.

Davy covertly watched Nelly, who he thought had never looked lovelier, as she bustled about with the other women and young girls to bring the food to the tables. Her face was pink, with excitement, folks would think, though he knew it was from her embarrassment and apprehension. He was penitent at having to inflict this ordeal upon her, yet he could think of no better way to do what he wanted more than anything else, and that was to end the sham obscurity of their relationship and present her to the world, this admittedly small enough world, as his consort.

He watched her every night now, with deep and grateful pride in her ripening body, her blooming figure. Dressed, there was only that indefinable glow about her, visible to none but him, which bore evidence of the new life she was carrying. 'We don't need to tell nobody yet,' she said pleadingly. 'I won't start to show for ages yet. Baby won't be born till spring. March, April.' They had travelled to Hertford for her first medical examination, to learn that everything was proceeding normally – 'as nature intended,' the cheerful, middle-aged doctor had confirmed. Nelly had been adamant that they should make the journey of fifteen miles rather than visit the local doctor. 'I know what village life is like. Nothing's kept confidential, there's no secrets. Not for long. Specially where there's scandal involved!'

'But there is no scandal!' Davy protested. 'We're man and wife.'
He deeply regretted allowing himself to be persuaded that it was
better to keep their marriage as secret as possible. Nelly had been
wrong to prefer the gossip and salacious rumours as to what her exact
role was at Loxton Cottage. She was afraid that the truth, the
marriage of a former serving girl to someone far beyond her social
status, would bring far greater opprobrium. But now the situation
demanded to be resolved. When her belly began to round, as it must
soon, he did not want their happiness to be tainted with evil slander.

Typically, she had donned a long flowered pinafore over her fashionable dark dress, the one she had worn to her wedding, and was
busy with the best of them. He knew how sick she must be feeling
inside, how rapidly her heart was beating, her nerves stretched at
what lay ahead. He was nervous, too, but there was a heady recklessness, and the conviction that whatever happened he was doing the
right thing, that spurred him on.

When the meal was ready, he stood and drew Nelly to his side, felt
the clamminess of her hand as she cast her eyes down, her colour
heightening. He had intended to wait until the meal was over and
they were ready for the dancing before he made his speech, but all at
once he felt he could not bear to have her suffer any longer. As the
vicar was clearing his throat, ready to say grace, Davy raised his
hand. His face was hot, his voice strident with nerves as he spoke up.
'I was going to leave my short speech until after we've all eaten this
splendid meal, but I'm afraid I can't do that. I must speak – before I
lose my courage.'

There was a chorus of laughter, then a spattering of applause,
which grew to a general acclaim. 'Speak up there, Mr Herbert! Say
your piece!' There was an air of anticipation, too, on several faces, a
tension as they noticed his arm clamped about the blonde girl's waist,
holding her to his side as though he would not let her escape. All at
once he was aware of the silence, the staring faces waiting.

'We've not been honest with you.' His voice was loud, and
strained. There was a soft, collective expulsion of breath, bodies stiffened, mouths remained open as they leaned forward, hanging on his
words. 'We were reluctant at first, strangers as we were, but now I

can't keep our secret any longer. And I want to put an end to any talk . . .' Nelly kept her head lowered, staring at her hands clasped about her middle. The tips of her ears showed red, her face flamed. 'I'm proud to tell you that this young lady beside me is my wife.'

He could feel her shaking. He tightened his grip, afraid that she might actually break away from him and flee. 'We were married back in the spring, up in London.' There were several gasps and exclamations of astonishment. 'We didn't want to make it public. We both knew there were many who would not have approved.'

The small audience knew full well his meaning. Already the low buzz of excited whispers reflected the shockingness of his disclosure. They were aware of the 'young gentleman's' background, in spite of the modest homestead and his working of his bit of land like any farmer. And of his housekeeper's background, too. Plenty to talk about here, food to keep the gossip tongues wagging through the long winter. But not right now, at this awkward moment, as the murmurs died down to embarrassed silence, and no one seemed to know what to say or do to break the frozen stillness.

Davy could feel the red glow on his features, but he lifted his head and met all those eyes squarely, cleared his throat and spoke again. 'I just want you all to know that when Nelly consented to be my wife that day she made me the happiest and the proudest man in all the world!'

Of all unlikely heroes, it was the tall, severely spare vicar, with his long scholar's features and grey-fringed, shining bald head, who broke the spell and saved the evening. The representative of the established church, that bastion of tradition in a changing world, was one from whom they would have feared and expected the most rigid opposition. 'Rich man in his castle and poor man at his gate' was an arrangement the Church of England, especially in such rural areas, willingly upheld. But now the vicar rose impressively to his feet, and began to applaud, slowly and theatrically, the claps echoing like gunshots. His deep pulpit voice resonated around the hall. 'Bravo! Bravo! Congratulations — Mr and Mrs Herbert! And thank you for your confidence, and trust.'

The words burst the bubble of tension, and the hall erupted in cries and more applause. 'Three cheers for Mr an' Mrs 'Erbert!'

Nelly, red faced still, was smiling through her tears, surrounded by the women who crowded round to embrace her, while Davy's hand was shaken like a pump, his shoulders sore from the vigorous blows of welcome they received.

Of course, the gossiping tongues still wagged, the sniggers and malicious behind-the-hand ribaldry took place in the village inn and elsewhere, especially when the fact of Nelly's pregnancy became known. 'Now we know why he married her!' those tongues chortled, ignoring the inconvenient evidence of the birth following a year after the wedding. 'You actually seen the date on the marriage paper?' the die-hard cynics queried. But though the young couple were the subject of what would have been hurtful salacious humour had they heard it, comparatively few expressed any real or continuing disapproval, thanks to the vicar and his small band of church stalwarts.

The baby came on the penultimate day of March. By the beginning of that month, Nelly was huge, and Davy stared with awe and great trepidation, which he strove valiantly to hide, at her tight, blue-veined drum of a belly, with its cresting distended sworl of navel, and the heavy, big-nippled breasts which rested on the dome. On the morning of the thirtieth, Nelly woke him, complaining of 'twinges'.

'Right! Lie still! Don't move! I'll go for Mrs Gould – and send to Dr Patterson, eh?' He was up, dragging off his nightshirt, trying not to let her see how frightened he was.

'No, no! Not yet, Davy. We'll wait a bit. He ain't comin' yet a while.' She insisted on using the male pronoun whenever she referred to the baby. 'Mam said she could always tell. With me being so big, I know it's going to be a little boy.'

'But—'

'Listen, I've told you. I was growed up enough for the last two my mam had. I know what's going on, believe me. We'll wait.'

But by mid-morning, there could be no doubt, and the midwife came round, with her assistant, and Davy was banished from the front bedroom. Only Dr Patterson was permitted entry to the mystic female cabal which had taken over the upper storey. 'Things are going perfectly normally,' he assured Davy. 'Be a while yet, though, I should say. Maybe later this afternoon.'

When the doctor had gone, promising that he would look in again 'in a few hours', Davy hovered anxiously at the foot of the narrow stairs. When Mrs Gould, sleeves rolled and white apron spotless, appeared, Davy asked her if he might go up and see Nelly. The woman's eyebrows lifted in horror. 'Certainly not, Mr Herbert! This is no time for a wife to be bothered with her man! The very idea! You've played *your* part in this business, thank you very much! Why don't you go and find something to do? You'll be sent for when required.'

Chastened, Davy pulled on gumboots, wrapped up in scarf and heavy coat against the cold, driving showers and went out to the fields. He had invested in a small tractor, and was learning to handle the intricacies of the temperamental motor. Most of the small tenant farmers round about were still sceptical. They all relied on horses for the ploughing and the heavy work on the land. They looked with scorn on the puttering, smoky, smelly machine, and the amount of time Davy spent crouched over its 'innards'. 'You wanna get vetinary to take a look!' they joked, but Davy much preferred his tinkering to managing the great docile beasts of burden. Today, though, the strip of land not yet sown was too sodden to work over. He pulled the tarpaulin back over the machine, tying the cords securely and went to help Alan, one of their two helpers, to tend the rows of tender shoots recently planted.

But after a short time, he wandered restlessly away, back through the newly dug garden and across the sodden lawn to the back door. As he eased off the muddy boots in the small vestibule, and peeled off his outer coat, his heart jumped at the sharp, clear yelp of pain he heard from above. Socks flapping, he raced through to the passageway and the bottom of the stairs. There was a deep, rending groan, and a sob, then cries of encouragement. He called up. 'Nelly! What is it? Are you all right?'

Dr Patterson's assistant, a young, pretty woman, came racing downstairs, a large pan in her hands. She looked hot and flustered, her black hair escaping in corkscrew curls from the scarf she had tied

round it. 'What d'you think's the matter with her?' she fired at him
as she brushed past. 'Keep out the way and let us get on with it!'

Suddenly he wanted to run away again, as he heard the cries, the
shouts of agony, coming from up above. He went into the parlour
and stood staring out at the rain slanting down across the grass and
the flowerbeds, where the first slender daffodils were beginning to
show. He remembered the wedding night, the huge yellow bunches
at either side of the fireplace. The fierce joy of singing blood and
flesh as they rode together . . . he started to pray, his fear making his
whole body shake as he clasped his hands convulsively before him.

CHAPTER TWENTY-FOUR

'**I** don't mind too much if he's shortened to Bill, but one thing I won't have and that's Willy!' Nelly was vehement in her refusal to countenance the diminution of their baby's name, and Davy agreed with her.

'He'll always be William to us, love, and to everyone else if I have a say in it.'

There had been considerable discussion over the choosing of a name. Nelly had tenderly suggested Samuel, and Davy had been deeply touched. Tempted for a moment, too, but then he had leaned forward and kissed her brow. 'No, my love. Dear as Sam was, I don't want our child to be associated with anything that touches sadness.' He stared at the bulk of Nelly lying beside him, and rested his palm on the mound of her belly. 'But we're proud of such good stock, aren't we? We've already got a grandson John in the family. What about William? I just know your parents are going to be so proud when they see him.'

So convincing was Nelly's assurance that she was carrying a boy, the discussion of girls' names was far briefer. Besides, Davy was quite firm in his decision. 'Helen she's to be, and no argument!'

'Oh no! Not another Nell!'

'No, there could never be!' Davy asserted. 'Helen she'll be, and a little beauty.'

'We'll see,' Nelly answered complacently, and on March 30, they did.

'Right as usual,' Davy managed, against the lump in his throat, when he was finally allowed into the bedroom, where his newly washed and tidied wife lay, tired but radiant, with their son already at her breast.

'All that fuss about such a tiny mite!' Dr Patterson teased. 'Less than half a stone by the kitchen scales!'

'A tiny, *perfect* mite!' Nelly amended, and Davy wholeheartedly agreed, as he saw the delicate shade of the skin, the exquisiteness of the cheeks, and the perfection of the tiny, pink, suckling mouth. An unbidden picture of Baby Olwyn flashed into his mind, and he felt a clutch of fear in the midst of his happiness. He made a vow to God that he would do anything to protect and preserve this fragile, beautiful gift of life which had been brought to them.

They wrote to their respective families. A short, stiff note of congratulations came from Brierton, signed 'Gerty and Gordon', and soon afterwards a parcel, containing the family christening shawl, and many exquisite and expensive baby things, a whole layette from a fashionable London store. Some time later a telegram arrived from Clara: CONGRATULATIONS LITTLE BRO STOP DIDN'T KNOW YOU HAD IT IN YOU STOP.

The letter which came from Nelly's parents was as stilted, if somewhat less eloquently phrased, as Gerty's. But it ended far more positively, with a request that they might come to visit. William was two months old when the visit took place. A girl had been hired well before the baby's birth to help with cleaning and cooking, and in the days before Nelly's folks were due to arrive, under Nelly's eagle-eyed supervision and participation, the cottage was 'bottomed', in spite of all Davy's pleas for her not to overtax herself.

'Let me go to meet them on my own,' Davy pleaded. 'I can take the trap over to Snelton to pick them up from the station. Give me a chance to talk to them. You can wait here. Get everything ready for them.'

Nelly looked as worried as he felt, but she nodded. She clung to him before he left. 'Don't mind 'em, Davy. We know what's right for us.'

It was deeply awkward at first, but Davy was determined to meet head on the difficulties they were all caught up in. 'I know you don't approve of our marriage.' His nervousness made him abrupt. 'But I love her – so much. I know how lucky I am – and I won't let her down, I swear.'

Mrs Tovey's ready tears and her mothering embrace melted the crippling embarrassment. 'You done the right thing by her, Master Davy,' her husband conceded stiffly, before Davy cut him short.

'Please! None of that. Your daughter is my wife. I'm proud of her – and of her family. I'd be honoured if you'd look on me as part of it. Forget what's past. And forgive it, if you can.'

'Well said and amen to that!' Bill Tovey flung his strong arms about his son-in-law and pulled him close. 'I'm glad to see you ain't got a motor yet. Here, come on, climb up, mother. And let's go and see this grandson of ours, eh?'

The visit was a great success, in spite of all the fears Davy and Nelly had suffered prior to her parents' arrival. Sitting collarless and in his braces before the range in the small kitchen, on the evening before their departure, Bill Tovey took the chance while the women-folk were upstairs with the baby to speak his mind. 'I never seen her so happy, Davy,' he confided. He jabbed the stem of his pipe towards the ceiling. 'I don't care what folks'll say. Long as you stick by one another, you'll be all right. We was wrong to take agin you, I own that. You'll always be welcome at ours.'

'Thank you . . .' Davy did not know how to address him now. 'Mr Tovey' was far too distant and formal, yet somehow he could not bring himself to use Nelly's usual address of 'Pa'. But he felt a wave of gratitude for the older couple's generous acceptance of him, espe-cially in view of the unfortunate history between the families. He had tried to express his regret, but his father-in-law had gruffly cut him short.

'Don't you worry on that score, Davy boy! We're happy as laddy over at Tynedale. End our days there, we will, I reckon.' He, too, was caught in embarrassment as he was compelled to pursue his thought. 'What about your family? I heard what happened to your dad — and I'm sorry for it, I really am. But what about your sisters? Miss Gertrude and that feller of hers? Have they come round?'

Davy's face was flushed as he gave a quick shake of his head. 'They sent those gifts – the things for William. And wrote congratulating us. But . . . I haven't seen them, not for a year or more. I told them about our marriage.'

Mr Tovey stretched his stockinged feet towards the red glow from the small stove and puffed on his pipe, sending the aromatic wreath of blue smoke up to the rafters. 'Well, it's their loss, ain't it, son?' he said fiercely, with a nod. 'Reckon you got all the family you need right here under this roof, ain't that right?'

William had celebrated his first birthday, and was taking his first tottering steps before Davy met up with his family again. He had heard from them. Gerty had written another stiff letter, to accompany the generously large parcel of gifts for Christmas. And a letter came from Clara, too, bearing the exotic stamp of the British East African Territories, where she was wintering, and where, she hinted with her usual flippancy, she might well be staying more permanently. Another member of the illustrious Cornell family owned vast tracts of land in the colony of Kenya, and Victor had shown interest in staying on and farming some of it. Clara had gone so far as to accept his proposal and they were now engaged.

It's in the Times, *dear boy. Though you probably never get beyond the Yokels' Gazette these days. I shall be quite sorry to be no longer the subject of scurrilous gossip. Mind you, it's early days. We haven't tied the knot yet! So there we are. I might end up a farmer's wife after all, like your charming Nelly!*

'Bloomin' cheek!' Nelly said complacently, when she read the letter in front of the kitchen stove. 'Can't see her up at dawn in gumboots milking the cows!'

'No. She'll probably have as many of the natives working as servants in the house as Gerty and Gordon employ on the whole estate!'

He was in his stockinged feet, having just come in himself from the smallholding. She suddenly reached out and captured his hand. She felt its work hardened coarseness, and its still slim narrowness. Since her pregnancy, he had taken over more and more the running of the business. She was deeply proud of the way he had thrown himself into it. She was happy to acknowledge that he was doing better at it than she would have done if left to her own efforts. They had

216

expanded, with poultry and pigs, and a small herd of milkers, so that the term 'small' holding hardly applied any more. 'Do you mind?' she asked, her blue eyes suddenly serious. 'I mean not being a part of it. Brierton and all that?'

His answer was immediate, and she could not deny its truth, and the deep, tender gratitude it roused in her. 'No, never! It doesn't matter, any of that. My life wasn't anything till you.' William cried out and came staggering, hands out to clutch at his mother's apron as she clung tight to Davy.

Another letter from Gerty came a few weeks later. *There's been a big and quite remarkable improvement in Father, though Nurse Lithgow and Dr Doubleday both say it can happen quite often. He's recovered some speech, and Lithgow says it will improve more in time. He's been asking to see you. He's very insistent. You and William, of course. Please try and visit. And of course your wife is very welcome, too. I think this is a good time to put the past behind us.*

Davy could guess how hard it must have been for her to write this.

'She couldn't bring herself to use my name!' Nelly said bitterly, and Davy eyed her with some dismay at her tone.

'You don't have to go if you don't want to,' he offered. And even more reluctantly he added, 'And I won't, either, if you don't want me to.'

'Oh, Davy, no! I didn't mean – of course you must go. And William, too!' Her face was pink now, and reflected her uncertainty. 'And me an' all – if you want me along, that is. Or maybe you'd rather go on your own. I mean you and William. Be easier like, eh?'

'Not at all. All or none! Whither I goest . . . or something like that!' He grinned at her, and she nodded, struggling to hide the anxiety she could feel clenching at her.

The closed and weeping left eye was covered now with a black patch, which somehow seemed to tone down the ferocity of its glaring, yellowed companion. Either that or the helpless inner rage of the stricken invalid had been eased with this small enough recovery of some of his faculties. John Herbert had limited use of his lower limbs and his right arm and hand was now sufficiently in control for him to make limited movement, even to print out untidy scrawled words on a pad, like a child's first efforts. Most significant of all was his speech, though at first Davy had thought this was in some way a cruel refinement of his torture, so slurred and difficult to interpret were the guttural sounds that came from his rolling tongue, his twisting lips and spittle-flecked working jaw.

There was an element of the grotesque, almost of bizarre sick humour in the first minutes of Davy's first interview with his father alone. It had been bad enough with the others there. Little William had fallen back, the tears coming, at the horror of the frightening apparition in the wheel chair, towards which mummy and daddy were inexplicably dragging him and whose claws were reaching out to devour him. He fought and twisted in terror, and the monster suddenly gave a wild cry and grimace and flung itself back into its chair, nodding, and he was allowed to flee, burying himself into the comforting arms and skirts of his sweet smelling new aunty with the beautiful red hair that shone. Meanwhile, Nelly had only just stopped herself from dropping a curtsey, and submitted to the clasp of those dry claws on her wrists. She even leaned over and kissed the neatly parted and combed grey hair, smelt its attractive male pomatum, shocked at the sacrilegious thought, which flashed through her mind as she bent over the stricken figure, that had she made such obeisance to the old hale John Herbert at least one hand would have shot round to fondle the swell of her buttocks.

Davy had wheeled him out onto the terrace, where his mother used to take her afternoon walks. Clinging to Davy's arm, his father had taken the few tottering steps to the stone bench, where Davy settled him and tucked the blanket tightly about him. 'Shin!' his father said urgently, reaching out to draw him close. 'Of shinsh!'

Davy's mind raced. Shins? He glanced down at the solidly booted feet. Were his legs hurting? The figure seemed deeply, alarmingly agitated, kept repeating the word, and clutching frantically at David. 'Ba-a-ad! Bad! Me!' He beat his own chest, nodding vigorously. 'Shin!' It dawned on Davy gradually, as much from his father's desperate agony to communicate as from interpreting those strangled sounds, that what he was trying to say was that he had sinned. That

John Herbert was finally acknowledging the awful wickedness of so much of his life. When he saw that Davy had at last understood, and awkwardly tried to reassure him, and to embrace him, he relaxed, and even showed a flash of the former determined pride. 'Show beet! Show beet!' By now, Davy was familiar enough with the unfamiliar sounds to be able to translate them more easily. So be it, his father was saying. He would not bend and grovel, Davy guessed, even when he stood before his Maker.

However, he was trying to make amends on earth, as far as he was able. And it was his wish to atone which brought family relationship to a new crisis point. Davy had felt sorry for Gerty as she had striven to overcome her prejudice concerning his marriage to Nelly. He knew that for his sister it would always remain a mismatch of the grossest offence to both convention and the natural order. To her, the different social classes were different species and should not be mixed. Her effort at punctilious politeness towards her sister-in-law was a great one, and Davy appreciated how much it must cost her. Gordon he found much more easygoing, though ever mindful of Gerty's feelings, and wary of them. But he appeared to be making a reasonable attempt at slipping into the role of 'squire' and guardian of the Herbert fortunes necessitated by John's illness. With of course the essential managerial guidance of Bolton's successor, Mr Sims.

'You know, you'd be welcome to move in any time,' Gordon told Davy awkwardly, out of Gerty's hearing. 'The house is big enough to take us all, without us falling over each other's feet. And there's plenty to do with the estate. I gather you're making quite a go of farming these days.'

It was clear he had a fair idea of which way the wind was blowing. The change of its direction was confirmed a day or two later when a meeting was convened at Brierton by John Herbert with the head of the family's firm of solicitors, to make the announcements confirmed by John's fierce nods of corroboration. Nelly, who had looked as strained and worried as Gerty when the notice of the meeting was given, had taken the chance to escape with William over to her parents' at Tynedale for a few days. 'You should be here,' Davy said. 'You're family.'

'It'll be difficult enough. I don't want to make matters worse. You'll be all right. And you'll tell me what's happened, won't you? You can drive over and pick me up on Tuesday. We'll still have to be going back home Wednesday – at least one of us will,' she declared, in a tone that reflected her general air of uncertainty about the future.

The announcement, made in the morning room as they sat around the long table, did not take long. Davy was reinstated in full as heir to the estate and the house. Gordon blushed brick red, Gerty sat in stunned silence, despite her anticipation of just such an outcome. Her pallor was reinforced by the vivid richness of her piled coppery hair. 'Shri' thing, Gersh!' her father gurgled at her, while Nurse Lithgow stood erect in her dark uniform behind his wheel chair. 'Ure provi'eh for. Children. All oo.'

She felt the bitterness welling, and her knuckles were white on the arms of her seat. The tears stung her grey eyes. She kept silent. Of course, she had known all along that she would be provided for. But she was no longer mistress of this house. Gordon was no longer the master elect of the estate. They would not be turned out. But could she bear to live under this roof with Davy and his ex-maid, to acknowledge Nelly Tovey (she could never think of her as a Herbert) as true chatelaine of Brierton?

Her face looked drawn, almost old when, after Nurse Lithgow had wheeled John out and the solicitor had left, she and her husband faced Davy in the sunny room. Her eyes still shone with tears, but she held her head high. 'Well, bro. All's well that ends well, eh? I knew it would come to this, of course. And I'm sure you feel I've got my just desserts.' Gordon's colour was even higher and he stirred, perhaps in attempt to stem the outburst he was expecting, perhaps in protest at the excluding use of the singular pronoun. But she was struggling hard to rein in her emotion and to put on a dignified front. She cleared her throat, tried to disguise the tremor in her voice. 'We can't just up and off in a day or two. You'll have to give us time – to arrange things. Find accommodation, fix things. Perhaps we could move up to town – an apartment. Gordon will need to look around . . .'

'What?' Davy gazed at her, his surprise genuine. 'Why on earth . . . ? Surely you don't want to leave here? Take the children away? And Gordon's happy here, aren't you?' He turned to his brother-in-law, who was staring at him in bemusement.

All at once, twin spots of red appeared on Gerty's pallid cheeks. Those splendid eyelashes flickered as she lowered her gaze. She said softly, 'I don't really think we can stay. It would be difficult – you and Nelly, and the children . . .'

'Good God! You don't think *I* want to move back here?' He sounded shocked. 'I'm going to have to tell Father. I can't up and off and leave our place. Not after all we've done. It's just beginning to succeed! And it's our home.'

Gerty's stiff expression was cracking, her mouth quivered, and the tears clung like gems to those rich lashes. 'But . . . but I thought—'

'Oh, Gerty! I couldn't dream of giving up what we've got, what Nelly and I have worked so hard for!' He turned to include Gordon. 'You're doing so well here, you know the business much better than I do. And as far as the house is concerned.' He gave a small, almost sad smile. 'I can't say it ever meant much to me. I was never happy here.' The look he directed towards Gerty was almost apologetic. 'Not once we'd grown up a bit.' He leaned earnestly towards her. 'Listen. It's *your* home. Papa's happy enough – he would hate it if you took the children away. You belong here. We'll come up and visit. See papa.' There was a pause, then he put out his hand, laid it gently over Gerty's cool fist. 'And we'd be delighted if you'd come and see us in *our* home. We really would!'

It was perhaps only the second or third time in her life that Gerty had felt unadulterated love for her brother, as she flung her arms around him and wet his cheek with her grateful tears.

He had taken the small Ford to go and collect Nelly from her parents'. The big estate of Tynedale was almost twenty miles away. To get there he had to pass through the village on the road to Willerby where many of the Brierton estate workers dwelt, and where Bill Tovey had lived with his family before John Herbert had turned him out. The familiar countryside aroused a number of painful memories as Davy drove along the quiet roadway, whose surface was still not tar macadamed. You were still more likely to meet a horse drawn vehicle than another car on this stretch. He noticed a solitary figure walking by the grass verge, heading towards the junction with the Willerby road. It was clad in a worn old khaki blouse, and limping along on crutches. A war veteran, with one leg missing below the knee. There were still many such, far too many, trying to get by on an inadequate pension and whatever work they could pick up, or begging for charity on any busy street. He pulled up and saw the grateful smile on the dirty and stubbled features.

'Ah! God bless yer, guv'nor! Long walk when you're peg-leggin' it like me. Thanks a million. Bit down on me luck just now, as yer can see!'

Davy felt his gorge rising, the skin crawling. He knew at once that it was his attacker, the one called Wally. The unkempt, ragged figure had already laid the crutches together and thrust them into the back of the car before nimbly hauling and swinging himself into the passenger seat beside Davy.

'Just as far as the junction with Willerby'll do me fine, mister.' Davy realized with a shock that the man had utterly failed to recognize him. Wally wasn't even looking at him, staring ahead through the windscreen, sighing with the relief and luxury of sitting at ease. There was an unpleasant smell of stale sweat and a faint underlay of alcohol coming from him. Davy was shaking violently. He felt dreamlike as he clumsily fumbled into gear, got the car moving once more.

'Copped this lot at the Somme. Thought I was done for, all right. Lost most of me mates that day.' He paused, said with theatrical bitterness, 'Sometimes I wish I 'ad snuffed it. Bin bloody hard for me ever since, I tell yer!'

Davy felt disgust and anger choking him, so that he could hardly force his words out. He jammed down his feet, hauled at the handbrake and the tyres slithered and bounced over the dry dust, enveloping the car in a swirling brown cloud. Wally Hindmarsh gave a frightened squeal as he hurtled forward, his hands held out to prevent his face smashing into the windscreen. Davy's voice was thick in the sudden silence. 'And what about your *mate*, Harold? Was he one of the ones who snuffed it? Eh?'

'Yeah, that's right. He did!' The unshaven jaw had dropped. ' 'Ow the 'ell . . . ? Oh, Christ!' He was staring at Davy, and his face reflected the shock he experienced at his belated recognition of the lean, tanned figure. 'Jesus! It's Davy Herbert! I'd no idea, honest to God!'

'So! You're a war hero now, then? One of our gallant boys, fighting for a better world!'

'Listen! That was a long time ago, mate! We was all pissed, weren't we? Waitin' to go back to that hell. We didn't—'

Davy dug his hands into the ragged army jacket, twisting and lifting, dragging the figure up from the seat, flinging him back through the low doorway. Wally fell backwards, smashing down onto the dusty lane in another miniature cloud of dust, the breath whooshing audibly from the thin body. Davy scrabbled across from behind the wheel, grabbed the crutches from the back seat. He jumped down into the roadway, where Wally still lay winded and fearful, on his back, staring up at him. Davy raised the crutches high, and saw the figure hunch up, awaiting the savage blows, with a shrill whimper of fear. He flung the sticks viciously at the body, standing over him. Davy felt an elemental thrill of rage, a pounding excitement, thick and dangerously attractive. He wanted to kick the body sprawled in the dirt, rip and pound it to shreds.

'I done my bit!' Wally was sobbing, his hands still held over his head, the crutches lying unnoticed across him. 'I didn't hang back! I fought!'

'I know. A land fit for heroes. I know what a hero you are.' Davy was breathing heavily as he turned away, walked around and climbed back in the driving seat. The engine sputtered, shook into life, and he rolled away. Wally was still lying there, only his head raised, watching the car drive off.

'What is it? What happened?' Nelly had come out as soon as she heard the engine. William came hurtling out behind her.

'Daddy!'

Davy scooped him up, hugged him tightly, laid his face along the

223

smooth cheek. He put him down.

Nelly's blue eyes were troubled. She was still watching him, waiting for him to speak. He knew what she was expecting to hear. Still she waited, silent, tense. 'We'd best not be too long,' he said. 'We've got some packing to do. We've got a long trip ahead of us tomorrow.' He slipped an arm round her shoulder. 'I can't wait to get back home to Loxton. Can you, Nelly?'

It was like seeing the sun coming in full radiance from behind a cloud as her blue eyes cleared and gazed on him. 'No, I can't, my love.'